"Tyler, when you look at me, what do you see?"

Once the question was out, Melissa held her breath, not quite sure she wanted a response.

"I see pain. I see courage. I see strength."

Emptiness, yearning, whistled through her, making her sway. "Do you see a woman?"

"Yes." He placed his hand over her heart. Something in her sighed.

"I want to know..." Brashly she stepped forward and pressed her lips to his, lingering, absorbing the long slow shiver that went through her. She felt her blood heat. "I want to know..." she murmured against his lips. "I need—"

"Melissa..."

"I need—" Hot tears squeezed between her closed eyelids.

He kissed the line of tears, making them gush faster.

"Please, Tyler..." She wasn't sure if she was asking him to stop or to continue.

"I promise not to hurt you," he said between drugging kisses that made her weak.

"It's already too late for that," she whispered as she pressed herself closer to him....

Dear Harlequin Intrigue Reader,

Spring is in the air...and so is mystery. And just as always, Harlequin Intrigue has a spectacular lineup of breathtaking romantic suspense for you to enjoy.

Continuing her oh-so-sexy HEROES INC. trilogy, Susan Kearney brings us *Defending the Heiress*—which should say it all. As if anyone *wouldn't* want to be personally protected by a hunk!

Veteran Harlequin Intrigue author Caroline Burnes has crafted a super Southern gothic miniseries. THE LEGEND OF BLACKTHORN has everything—skeletons in the closet, a cast of unique characters and even a handsome masked phantom who rides a black stallion. And can he kiss! *Rider in the Mist* is the first of two classic tales.

The Cradle Mission by Rita Herron is another installment in her NIGHTHAWK ISLAND series. This time a cop has to protect his dead brother's baby and the beautiful woman left to care for the child. But why is someone dead set on rocking the cradle...?

Finally, Sylvie Kurtz leads us down into one woman's horror—so deep, she's all but unreachable...until she meets and trusts one man to lead her out of the darkness in *Under Lock and Key*.

We hope you savor all four titles and return again next month for more exciting stories.

Sincerely,

Denise O'Sullivan
Senior Editor
Harlequin Intrigue

UNDER LOCK AND KEY

SYLVIE KURTZ

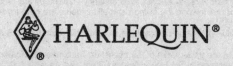

HARLEQUIN®

TORONTO • NEW YORK • LONDON
AMSTERDAM • PARIS • SYDNEY • HAMBURG
STOCKHOLM • ATHENS • TOKYO • MILAN • MADRID
PRAGUE • WARSAW • BUDAPEST • AUCKLAND

For Chuck, who loves me—ugly side and all
A Special Thanks to:
Susan Amann at the Wadleigh Memorial Library and
Kelly at Dr. Chatson's office (Nashua Plastic Surgery)
for their help with research.
Mary Jernigan for sharing her experience.

ISBN 0-373-22712-4

UNDER LOCK AND KEY

Copyright © 2003 by Sylvie Kurtz

ABOUT THE AUTHOR

Flying an eight-hour solo cross-country in a Piper Arrow with only the airplane's crackling radio and a large bag of M&M's for company, Sylvie Kurtz realized a pilot's life wasn't for her. The stories zooming in and out of her mind proved more entertaining than the flight itself. Not a quitter, she finished her pilot's course and earned her commercial license and instrument rating.

Since then, she has traded in her wings for a keyboard, where she lets her imagination soar to create fictional adventures that explore the power of love and the thrill of suspense. When not writing, she enjoys the outdoors with her husband and two children, quilt making, photography and reading whatever catches her interest.

You can write to Sylvie at
P.O. Box 702, Milford, NH 03055.
And visit her Web site at www.sylviekurtz.com.

Books by Sylvie Kurtz

HARLEQUIN INTRIGUE
527—ONE TEXAS NIGHT
575—BLACKMAILED BRIDE
600—ALYSSA AGAIN
653—REMEMBERING RED THUNDER*
657—RED THUNDER RECKONING*
712—UNDER LOCK AND KEY

*Flesh and Blood

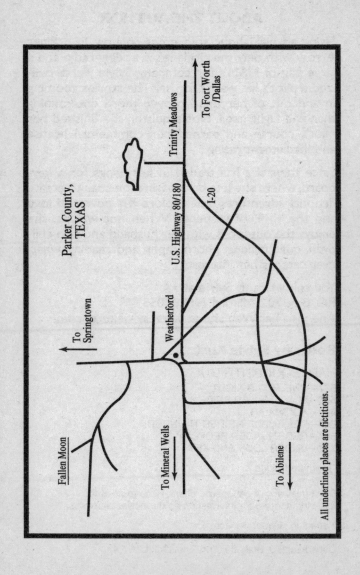

Parker County, TEXAS

To Fort Worth /Dallas

Trinity Meadows

I-20

U.S. Highway 80/180

Weatherford

To Springtown

Fallen Moon

To Mineral Wells

To Abilene

All underlined places are fictitious.

CAST OF CHARACTERS

Melissa Carnes—Someone is stirring the pot of her "witch" reputation in order to scare her off her land.

Tyler Blackwell—He has a debt to pay and will honor his promise to keep Melissa safe.

Lindsey Blackwell—Did Tyler's wife have to die?

Freddy Gold—Melissa's uncle has a hunch that something evil is afoot at Thornwylde.

Ray Lundy—The stable manager is looking for a job promotion.

William Carnes—Melissa's father may have started his rich career with a lie.

Sable Lorel Carnes—She married Melissa's father for his money and isn't pleased she wasn't given control over his billions when he died.

Tia Carnes—How badly does Melissa's half sister want to catch her man?

Sheriff Tate—Believes the "witch" stories only too gladly.

J. R. Randall—The philanthropic businessman wants something that isn't his.

GRACE'S CHOCOLATE CHUNK PECAN BROWNIES

4 oz unsweetened dark baking chocolate
3/4 cup butter
2 cups sugar
3 eggs
1 tsp vanilla
1 cup flour
1 cup coarsely chopped pecans, toasted to bring
  out flavor
1 cup semisweet chocolate chunks

Heat oven to 350°F. Line a 13" x 9" baking pan with foil, extending over the edges to form handles. Grease foil.

Microwave the unsweetened chocolate and butter in large microwavable bowl on High for 2 minutes—or until the butter is melted. Stir until the chocolate is melted.

Stir sugar into chocolate mixture until well blended. Mix in eggs and vanilla. Stir in flour, nuts and chocolate chunks until well blended. Spread in prepared pan.

Bake 30 to 35 minutes or until toothpick inserted in center comes out with fudgy crumbs. Do not overbake.

Cool in pan. Lift out of pan by foil handles. Place onto a cutting board. Cut into squares. Makes 24.

Can be stored in a cool, dry place. Do not refrigerate.

Chapter One

"I thought you were my friend." Tyler Blackwell loomed above the seated Freddy Gold, owner and editor-in-chief of *Texas Gold*. How could Freddy ask something like this from him knowing where he was coming from? Wasn't it hard enough for him to start again? But to start like this? Tyler blasted his friend with every expletive he knew.

Freddy calmly leaned back in his cordovan-leather chair and stared at him.

"Tyler, it's precisely because you're my friend that I'm giving you this assignment." Freddy turned away from him in his swivel chair and went back to work. "I owe her, Tyler. It's the least I can do. And you owe me. So I'm calling in my chip. Make sure nothing happens to Melissa Carnes."

What did Freddy have to do with her? She was nothing but a crazy artist who never came out of her self-imposed isolation. And Freddy had a dozen journalists on staff who'd kill for an opportunity to ingratiate themselves to the boss. "Why me?"

"I trust you. I don't dare trust anyone else when it comes to my niece."

"Your niece? Freddy—"

"She needs a champion. For once, she needs someone on her side."

Tyler sneered. The last time he'd tried to be a champion, his wife had died. "If it's a champion you're looking for, you're looking in the wrong place."

"I know that if you give me your word, you won't bail out on me until the job's done. You'll keep her safe."

"After Lindsey, you can still say that?"

"Because of Lindsey, yes."

That vote of confidence silenced him for a while. Since Lindsey's death, even *he* didn't trust himself.

"I know you," Freddy said. "I've taught you everything you know."

Tyler had come a long way since he and Freddy had been beat journalists together ten years ago. Tyler was just starting then, and Freddy was getting ready to move on to bigger and better things. Freddy had indeed taught him everything he knew. But some things you couldn't prepare for, and no amount of training could get you ready for some blows. Still, Freddy was always there for him—even when everyone else had given up—and that loyalty had to count for something.

"So who's this big bad wolf who's after your little lamb?" Tyler asked, sinking into one of Freddy's well-appointed leather chairs. He'd hear what Freddy had to say. Then he'd lay out a rational argument as to why he couldn't take on the responsibility of looking out for someone else. Freddy would have to listen to logic.

"I'm not sure."

"You're not sure?"

"It's a feeling…" He shrugged.

Tyler stared incredulously at his friend. "Freddy Gold's calling in a chip on a feeling?"

"Yeah."

Seeing Freddy so unsure of himself was strange. Tyler contemplated the man in front of him, noticed through his haze of frustration that Freddy had aged seemingly overnight. His jowls, usually so easy to jiggle with laughter, sagged. Puffed smudges made purple half-moons beneath his eyes. Lines spidered from the corners of his mouth.

"So what exactly is it you want me to do?" Tyler asked.

"I want you to protect her. Keep her safe."

"From what?"

Freddy marched his pen across his knuckles. The muffled noise of telephones and voices on the other side of the office wall filled the uncomfortable silence. Slowly he pulled open the middle drawer of the desk and drew out an envelope. "This came two days ago."

He pushed the envelope across the desk.

Tyler started to reach for it, then sprang up from the chair, backing away, hands held palms out in front of him. "I can't."

"It's an article about Thornwylde Castle where Melissa lives," Freddy said as he unfolded the newsprint. "And a bishop." From his hand, a black chess piece rolled out onto the desk. "It's a warning, Tyler. Someone's playing a game, and I don't like it. I need you there."

"It's just an article." Tyler ran a hand over his face, not liking the sinking feeling weighing him down. "How do you get a warning out of a chess piece?"

"Chess is a game of war. Bishops can move in any direction, but must keep on a diagonal. They're valuable because they can make long, narrow moves."

In spite of his best intentions, Tyler couldn't quite bite off the questions that sprang up. "Who sent the package?"

"I'm working on that." Freddy hid the bishop in the

envelope and returned the whole to the drawer. "Melissa's had a hard life, but in some ways, she's very innocent. She won't know how to defend herself."

Who? What? Where? When? How? Instinct kicked in. It felt like old times when the merest hint of a question had sent him sniffing for answers. His limbs became jittery. He tried not to think of all the Tennessee bourbon and oblivion he'd only recently given up, but it was like trying not to think of a blue elephant. The bottle with the black label was all he could see. The fire of the dark liquid was all he could taste. The sweet blackness of nothing was all he desired. He shook his head. *Stay here. Stay focused.* "You already suspect someone."

"She's a rich woman who'll be even richer in a month. Money makes people do unspeakable things." Freddy frowned, his pen etching deep grooves into the pad on his desk.

Tyler licked his dry lips, tried not to taste the phantom whiskey and rested his backside against the edge of the credenza. "Why don't you just tell her to be careful and be done with it? Why do I need to go there?"

"Because...we're estranged. She would dismiss anything I told her." The admission seemed painful to swallow. But then, mistakes always were. Tyler should know. He had a Texas-size one stuck in his craw. "She can't know I sent you. She'll just send you away."

Tyler leaned forward. He couldn't do this. Not even for Freddy. "Just how do you propose I accomplish this feat?"

"Find the story. Like you've done a hundred times."

But this time it would be different. "There are ways for her to protect her money from poachers. What story is there?"

"Start with the money, work up to her family. Her stepmother has big social ambitions and that doesn't come cheap. Her half sister lives for pleasure—also an expensive hobby.''

Tyler sprang from his chair, leaned his fists on the desk's top and glared at his friend. ''Are you insane? You want to send me into the middle of a family feud?''

''No, I'm dead serious.'' Freddy kept scribbling, as if the action could keep him anchored while Tyler blustered. ''Twenty-two years ago, my sister told me she didn't feel safe at the castle. A week later she was dead. I dismissed her fears. I don't want to make the same mistake again.''

Mistakes, Tyler had made so many already. And here was Freddy, desperate to send him right into the middle of another. ''I can't. Not after—''

''When you fall off a horse, you have to climb back on the sucker before he can kick you while you're down.''

Too late. He's already kicked. Tyler dropped to the chair like a stone. This wouldn't work. It just wouldn't work. ''How am I supposed to get in there to talk to her? You think a recluse is going to open her home to a stranger? Let him peek at her books and play knight to her damsel?''

''You'll pretend to be writing an article on her stallion. Eclipse is a champion. She won't turn down press for him.''

That made sense. An article in the most respected news magazine in the state was publicity no one could afford to turn down. ''That'll work for an hour, maybe two. After that, what?''

''You'll think of something.''

Tyler knew himself well enough after the ravages of the past year to understand that his decisiveness had become rusted, his vision blurred, his drive stalled. But most of all, he knew he didn't want to be the Tyler Blackwell of a year ago. And that was what Freddy was asking him to do. He'd spent his life becoming Tyler Blackwell, ace reporter, the dog who wouldn't let go of the bone until he could drop it, meat and all, into the reader's lap on the morning paper's front page. Truth had once been all-important. But his drive for truth—and his ego—had also cost him the woman he loved, and in less than a year, his career. If he was to start over, he wanted something different.

"I'll have my secretary call Deanna and let her know you're coming," Freddy said, jotting a note to himself.

"Who's Deanna?"

"Deanna Ziegler is Melissa's friend. To get to Melissa you have to go through Dee."

"Have this Deanna person warn her."

"It's not that simple."

Nothing about this situation was simple. "You said you weren't on speaking terms. Why would this Deanna allow a reporter you send to write about the stallion?"

"An article in *Texas Gold* with horses show season in full bloom is good business, and Melissa is a good businesswoman. She doesn't trust me, but she trusts what I've done with the magazine."

A headache was starting to drum at Tyler's temples. "Why are you doing this?"

Freddy put his pen down, wove the fingers of his hands together and closed his eyes. A moment later he lifted his gaze. In Freddy's dark eyes Tyler saw a despair close to his own and knew he had no choice. Freddy needed to protect Melissa from this possible foe as much as Tyler needed to find some logic for Lindsey's death.

"After her mother died," Freddy said, "Melissa needed me, and I let her down because I was too busy building my career. I thought she was safe with her family. She wasn't. I owe her.''

The jangle of the phone interrupted their conversation.

"Rena?" Freddy said, a frown creasing his forehead. Rena was Freddy's stunning wife, fifteen years younger than the old bear and the center of Freddy's universe since he'd met her two years ago. Rena was also seven and a half months into a difficult pregnancy. "I'll be right there, sweetheart."

"Rena all right?" Tyler asked. Freddy didn't need the worry about his wife on top of the worry about his niece.

"The doctors think they might not be able to stop the baby from coming this time. I'm off to the hospital."

Freddy hustled his bulk toward his office door. "I let Melissa down, Tyler. I need some redemption—especially now." Freddy raised his hands in a helpless gesture, and Tyler realized Freddy was trying to make the world right for Rena and their soon-to-be-born child by rectifying past mistakes and maybe even appeasing the gods of fate. For whatever reason, he still didn't feel worthy of Rena's love. Couldn't he tell just by looking into his wife's eyes that she adored him, soft middle, thinning hair and all?

"I can count on you?" Freddy asked, hesitating at the door.

Tyler nodded. Trust Freddy to know exactly what to say to make him feel like a heel. Who else had given him a million and a half chances? Who else had never given up on him—even when he'd given up on himself? Guilt was as good a motivator as any, and Tyler felt guilty enough for letting Freddy down.

He grabbed the file with Melissa Carnes's name off Freddy's desk and strode out of the office behind Freddy. *Just get it over and done with.*

Fast.

TYLER COULDN'T SEE a thing. The furious rhythm of the wipers couldn't keep up with the torrents of rain plastering his windshield. His headlights were useless on the dark country road, and he cursed his stubbornness.

He should have waited until morning. But no, Tyler Blackwell had to do everything his own way. Maybe Freddy was right and he did have a suicidal streak. Why else would he be driving on this godforsaken road in the middle of a deluge? After all, May and mobile home-eating storms were synonymous. Had he unconsciously wanted a spring twister to rip him away from this unpleasant assignment? On the other hand, maybe he wanted to prove that he wasn't a washed-up has-been, that no storm could stop him. Whether he wanted to prove that to himself or to Freddy, he hadn't decided yet. All he knew for sure was that he wanted his debt to Freddy canceled. Get in. Get the answers. Get out. Once he'd made up his mind, he'd seen no reason to put off the inevitable.

Damn, where was all this rain coming from? Spring weather in Texas was temperamental, but this was ridiculous. Slowing to a crawl, he leaned forward over the steering wheel and peered into nothingness. There should be signs of civilization. A light. Anything. The town of Fallen Moon couldn't be more than a few miles ahead. He'd get a room there and find Melissa Carnes in the morning.

He'd just decided to stop and wait for the rain to thin when his Jeep dipped to the left and the road disappeared beneath the wheels. He grappled with the steering wheel, trying to find the road again. Too late. Gravity took over and plunged him into a deep ditch.

The Jeep bounced, slid sideways and came to a grinding halt, sending Tyler crashing into the left side of the vehicle and his head deflecting off the window. Pinpricks of bright light romped before his eyes, then faded like spent firecrackers when he shook his head.

The acrid stench of gasoline filled his nose. A warm trickle of blood ran down his temple. The sting of rain pouring in from the cracked window pelted his face. When he tried to move to get his bearings, dizziness overwhelmed him.

He reached up to touch his forehead and connected with the roll bar, instead. If it hadn't been for the bar, he'd be dead. And against all odds, he was surprised he was glad to be alive.

The engine wheezed spasmodically, but the lights were out. Tyler saw nothing, not even the hand he waved in front of his face. Slowly, deliberately, to keep his head from swinging crazily like one of those bobbing-head dolls in a car window, he fumbled for the ignition switch and turned off the engine. He reached for the door handle. Pain shot through his wrist.

"Okay. Take it easy." Securing his hurt wrist against his bruised ribs, he twisted his body and pulled himself through the window with his good arm. Rain assaulted him with a vengeance.

Another bolt of lightning rent the sky, giving him a chance to reexamine his position. Then he braced himself against the Jeep's frame and jumped. Slipping on the muddy embankment, he lost his balance and landed in the water at the bottom of the ditch. As he sat, water filled his cowboy boots and seeped through his jeans and cotton shirt.

The rain turned into pea-size hail. Numbed instincts prickled back to life. Survival proved stronger than the pessimism of the past year.

Tyler forced himself to stand. Pain throbbed through

his body and ended in his head with the pounding of a hundred hammers.

"Tyler Blackwell is back," he warned the rain. Thunder mocked him.

He clawed his way out of the ditch, pulling up his body with sheer determination until he found the road. Lightning flashed at regular intervals, lighting his way. Wincing with every step, he trudged toward town.

What kind of trouble could a recluse get herself into within the confines of a castle? Melissa Carnes painted pictures, and she rode horses, for crying out loud. Freddy's instincts were wrong this time. It was the baby, the guilt. There was no psychotic stalker, no wicked stepmother, no greedy half sister out to harm his niece.

"I hope you're worth it, lady." He gritted his teeth and concentrated on walking.

"Damn you, Freddy, for cashing in your chip, and damn you, Lindsey, for dying." No, he didn't mean that. It wasn't her fault. He sneered. Yeah, most people would say it was *his* fault. His beautiful wife. If he hadn't been so ambitious. If he'd known when to let go. If he hadn't pushed the wrong person too far. Then Lindsey would still be alive, and he'd still be a hero. He rested for a moment against a sign that read No Outlet. "Great. Just great. I'm heading nowhere."

The road came to a sudden end. Lightning crazed the sky, flickering a mirage before him. The photographs had not done Thornwylde Castle justice.

Before him was a fortress straight out of Camelot—moat, drawbridge, towers and all. Castles belonged in England, not the wilds of North Texas. Took a rich eccentric like William Carnes to import a castle and plop it on land more suited to ranch bungalows. Took a peculiar woman like Melissa Carnes to live there and pass herself off as a witch. But she was Freddy's niece, and Tyler had promised to keep her safe.

Head pounding, he dragged himself over the wooden bridge that spanned a water-filled moat and found himself faced with a barred and closed entrance gate. Three stairs, that to his aching body, seemed as unscalable as Mount Everest, stood to the left and led to a smaller door. With his last ounce of strength he hoisted himself up the steps and knocked on the door.

He leaned against the rain-slicked wood. His body crumpled under his weight and his face buried itself in the prickly doormat. A wave of heaviness surged through him and filled him with the same darkness that surrounded him.

And as the last thread of thought snapped into black, an overwhelming sense of evil engulfed him.

RAY LUNDY sat alone in the cab of his pickup truck in the middle of nowhere, waiting for the prearranged two-short-and-one-long signals of light. He couldn't have asked for a better atmosphere if he'd had a straight line to God. Drenching rain poured from a sky darker than Hades, and the eerie strobelike dance of the wizened oak branches around him added just the right touch.

His contact wanted anonymity. Well, hell, you couldn't get more lost than in this part of Parker County. Ray pressed the button that lit his digital watch. He'd give his contact five more minutes, then he'd leave.

Only fools went out on a night like this. Even the witch wouldn't venture out of her castle tonight. No, anyone with half a brain would stay home, heeding the weatherman's forecast of possible tornadoes in the North-Texas area.

Though the purr of the idling engine offered a measure

of comfort, Ray flipped on the heater button to stave off the chill. He didn't dare turn on the radio. Not that anyone would be out on a night like this, but he'd hate to be caught unawares. Instead, he let the rhythm of the rain on the pickup's roof keep his thoughts company.

Ray knew he was a fool, but if things kept going his way, it wouldn't be for much longer. Soon, very soon, he'd give his job the kiss-off and be his own man. He'd get back what was owed him. Then he'd be the one giving orders, sending whipping boys to do the dirty work and him reaping all the rewards. A smile curled his lips at the headiness of the thought. Yeah, he could handle that.

Through the heavy downpour Ray saw the weak signal. He hit his headlights in answer. Let the contact get wet. *I may be a fool, but I ain't stupid.*

The contact, dressed all in black, yanked the rusty door open and slid into the passenger seat. "Couldn't you have picked a drier spot?"

"Yeah," Ray said, exaggerating his drawl. "Guess I could've. But then I'd have missed a great sight. Tch, tch. Rain and leather and silk just don't mix, do they."

He laughed and drew a cigar from his coat pocket. Once he lit the stogie, he took a slow drag, inhaling deeply before he deliberately blew smoke rings in his contact's face, enjoying the action even more than the poke he'd had earlier with the new stable girl. He was the one pulling strings now. Power. There was nothing to beat sheer power. It was his birthright, and he'd get it back— no matter whose strings he had to yank to get the results he wanted.

"Why all the secrecy?" Ray asked.

The contact shifted to avoid the smoke. "Nobody can know I'm involved. It has to look like it's her idea. I have just over a month to run Melissa Carnes off her land."

Ray stopped blowing smoke rings. Now wasn't that interesting? Melissa Carnes would have been his last guess for this little enterprise. Oh, yeah, this was definitely his lucky day. "It'll take me less than a day to plug a bullet in her brain. Everyone knows the witch likes to ride at night."

"No, you jackass! It has to look like it's her idea to leave."

See if you talk to me in that tone of voice when this is over, you bottomfeeder... Ray took a long pull on the cigar. *I'm in charge here.* "Why?"

"You're paid to follow orders, not to ask questions."

"I like to understand the psychology behind the job." *And see how it fits with my game plan.*

The contact reached over and scrunched Ray's shirt collar in a tangle of fingers. "Understand this—if you don't do things my way, you don't get paid. Got it?"

Ray pushed away the powerless grip. The nerve of this pawn to think he had any say over the direction of play. "All right, don't have a hissy fit."

I'm in charge, Ray reminded himself. He couldn't hide the smile coming from deep inside, and he tasted once more the sweet flavor of power. His power over people like the contact; people who usually considered him scum.

Who was scum now?

"So," Ray said, blowing more smoke straight at the aristocratic nose, "what do you want?"

"I need her running scared." The contact paused.

Lightning cut jagged lines across the black sky. Thunder boomed farther to the south. One of Ray's greatest skills was reading people, and what he saw now was desperation. This desperation would buy him his crown. "I don't come cheap."

"Once Melissa Carnes is off her land, you'll get your slice."

"I like my cake with lots of icing." Ray savored the thought, the power. His, all his.

"There's enough to go around."

Ray blew another string of smoke rings and marveled at their perfection. "Did you read about the mason who broke his leg at the witch's castle?"

"What does that have to do with anything?"

"Ever heard of the telephone game?"

"I don't get it."

Of course not. "How do you get rid of a witch?"

Impatience wrenched the contact's pretty features into their true plug-ugliness, so Ray gave the brainless cockroach its answer. "With a witch-hunt."

Chapter Two

A noise disturbed Melissa's gloomy thoughts. Her ears, tuned by years of living nearly alone in her immense castle, picked up the discordant sound. She listened, wary, then plopped her paintbrush into a jar of water. Someone was at the gatehouse.

The same thing happened every year around this time. The seasonal storms and the threat of tornadoes made a perfect backdrop for the dares and counterdares of local high-school kids. What could be more ghoulish than catching a glimpse of the witch when the heavens roiled with evil?

Why couldn't they leave her alone? What had she ever done to them?

Fists tight at her sides, she marched down the creaky wooden steps. She'd had enough and wasn't going to take the taunts this time. They wanted the witch; they'd get the witch. As she reached the bottom of the stairs, she donned her black poncho, its hood strategically placed for the best effect. She grabbed the flashlight on the small table by the door and strode across the courtyard.

Melissa paused by the gatehouse door, listening for the telltale noise of the thrill seekers' presence, and heard nothing. Flashlight in hand, she readied to illuminate her pale face and set the fear of God into the little hoodlums.

She threw open the heavy door, placed the flashlight in its most effective position for fright and gave them her best cackle. She expected shrieks of terror. Instead, she heard a soft moan like that of a wounded animal. Turning her light on the crumpled body at her feet, she took in the bloody face and muddy clothes.

Stiletto-sharp instincts honed by pain and hatred told her to shut the door and ignore the wounded man on her doorstep. She didn't need a stranger intruding on her privacy. Frenzied lightning, followed by a deep rumble, seemed to second her decision. The wail of tornado sirens from town added urgency.

Melissa stood frozen, grasping the door like a lifeline. If she left him there, he might die. The sky quieted. The hard beating of her heart and the shallowness of her breath replaced the thunder. Pollen-laden rain streamed down her face.

Sighing regretfully, she crouched next to the man. As much as she'd like to, even the witch in her couldn't leave a wounded man out on a night like this.

"Grace!" Her shout competed with a new crash of thunder and the whip of the wind for her housekeeper's attention. "Grace!"

At six feet, Grace Jackson towered above many men. Her checkered past afforded her as much notoriety as Melissa's reclusiveness did. Most townsfolk had learned to fear Grace Jackson's wrath as much as Melissa's alleged hexes.

The door to Grace's apartment opened. "What are you doing down there, child?"

"I need your help. I can't move him by myself."

"Him? What are you talking about?" Grace snapped

on the dim light above the stairs and moved down the creaky wooden steps with a lightness that belied her two-hundred-pound bulk.

"Lordy!" Grace whistled. "What happened to him?"

"Don't know. I found him on the doorstep."

Grace bent down to examine the man draped across the top of the steps. She swiped the mud off his cheek. "This man's gonna bring trouble. I feel it in my bones."

"Trouble or not, we need to get him out of the rain."

With a sigh, Grace hefted the stranger up in her capable arms. "Take his feet."

They moved him inside, then Melissa closed and barred the door behind them.

"Upstairs to my apartment," Grace said, adjusting her grip under the man's arms.

Melissa nodded and helped Grace carry him to her apartment. Once they'd settled him on the bed in the spare room, Melissa was only too glad to let Grace take over. A stranger—a man, at that—was something she'd rather not deal with. Especially not tonight when the longing for normalcy stirred such deep cravings.

She stood, intent on returning to her own tower, when Grace looked up at her and said, "What are you waiting for, girl? I'm gonna need your help."

"Me?" Melissa brushed a hand to her chest. "What for?"

"He's deadweight, honey. I can't strip him out of them wet clothes by myself."

Melissa reluctantly shed her poncho, shaking off the excess water before she hung it on the knob.

"I'll need more light," Grace said.

Melissa nodded, then extracted a black silk shawl from her pocket and carefully arranged it around her face, leaving only her eyes uncovered before Grace turned on the light in her spare room.

Grace sat beside the unconscious man on the twin bed. "Help me hold him up so we can see where he's hurt and get them wet clothes off him."

"Grace?" Melissa's voice wavered with uncertainty.

"Missy, we gotta see how bad he's hurt," Grace answered with a touch of impatience. She ran her hands over the prone figure with the practiced ease of a nurse. Melissa watched, fascinated by the man on the bed.

He was a beautiful creature—the epitome of the tall, dark and handsome hero in those romantic movies her friend Dee insisted on sharing with her once a week.

Even with his brow furrowed in pain, his face had a quality of strength. The impression came from the high cheekbones, the sharp cut of his jaw, she decided, and rated his bone structure as excellent. His long eyelashes lay against smooth skin that was too pale to be healthy. Only the slightly sardonic twist of his mouth and the drying blood on his forehead marred the perfect proportions of his oval face. Drawn to those full lips, she tried to imagine how they would taste. She frowned. Where had that thought come from?

"What do you suppose happened to him?" Melissa asked to distract her wayward thoughts.

"Looks like a car wreck. Weather like this, wouldn't surprise me none." Grace finished her inspection and covered him with the blanket. "I don't think he's too bad off," she continued. "Left wrist sprained, two bruised ribs and probably a concussion, judging by the bump on his head. If he don't wake up soon, I'm gonna have to take him to the hospital." Grace pointed to the side of the bed near the man's middle. "Go sit there." Grace gently held the stranger up. "You do the buttons."

With shaky fingers, Melissa fumbled with the buttons of his denim shirt. Light and shadow played over pectorals whose pleasing definition had her itching for a pencil and paper. Her frown deepened. He was a man. She didn't draw men. The spray of dark hair centered on his torso mesmerized her. She followed its course until it disappeared in the waistband of his jeans. After a moment of hesitation she unbuckled his belt, unsnapped the button of his fly and pulled down the zipper just enough to free the shirttail. With curiosity, she noted how the soft dark line of hair continued down into his navy shorts, automatically cataloging the fascinating lines made by bones and muscles over stomach and hips. She sucked in a breath at the painful purpling bloom of bruises over his left ribs.

With the shirt loosened, Grace leaned the man forward so that his head lay on Melissa's shoulder. He moaned in pain. Instinctively Melissa wrapped her arms protectively around his waist and trembled as his body relaxed against hers. He was heavy on her chest, and she tensed under the weight as Grace proceeded to remove the shirt.

Relax. He can't hurt you; he's unconscious. Watching all those romantic movies hadn't prepared her for the solidness of a man or for the irrational feeling of loss sinking through her like a rock in spring mud.

"Push him back easy," Grace ordered. "I'm gonna go get some bandages for that cut."

With a small sigh of relief, Melissa did as Grace asked. While Grace was gone, her gaze returned once more to the stranger's lips. Artistic analysis, she told herself. Her hand reached for her heart and she knuckled the soft pining ache there. *He's not the one,* she thought. *He can't give you what you want—no one can.*

She started to move away, then found her hand—as if it had a mind of its own—wandering toward that beautiful face. With a fingertip, she traced the edge of the bruise on his forehead, trailed down the sharp definition of his cheekbone and found his mouth. A study of proportion, she told herself, and tried to push away the notions of heat and softness and stark maleness. Would he begrudge her a moment of fantasy?

With uncharacteristic abandon, she loosened her shawl and gave in to temptation. A spark of electricity ran between them when she touched her lips to his. A small gasp escaped her as she jerked back in surprise. When she kissed him a second time, his lips felt cold and lifeless.

Just as well, she thought. He was no Snow White waiting for a wake-up kiss, and she definitely wasn't Princess Charming. Love at first kiss was the invention of moviemakers. Everyone knew that. When he woke up, he'd most likely think he'd landed on the set of a horror movie, not some sort of romance. Still, she couldn't resist one last touch, this time with her finger to his lips.

His eyes fluttered open and he mumbled, "Lindsey, don't leave me, Lindsey."

Spurred by a shot of adrenaline, Melissa scrambled off the bed and rewrapped the shawl around her face. When she turned to face him, he lay still once more, and the momentary speeding of her heart returned to normal.

Armed with scissors and bandages of all kind, Grace reappeared. She positioned herself opposite Melissa. Her hands moved quickly as they cleaned, patched and secured the various wounds.

Prodded by Grace, Melissa once again took up a post by his head. Sympathy for a creature in pain soon edged out her natural wariness of the human male. All the while Grace tended him, Melissa stroked the stranger's straight brown hair, soothed him when he moaned. In his call to the mysterious Lindsey, Melissa had heard a familiar ring of grief. Who was Lindsey? How had she hurt him? Melissa calmed him with the same soft voice she used with her horses.

When Grace finished, she covered him with a quilt and tucked in several hot-water bottles around his body. Then Grace picked up his damp jeans from the floor. From the back pocket, a wallet fell out and the contents spilled to the floor.

''What's his name?'' Melissa asked. She'd grown used to the weight and warmth of him against her and still stroked the soft hair along the side of his head.

''According to his driver's license,'' Grace said, stooping to pick up the wallet, ''this is Tyler Blackwell, thirty-three, 184 pounds, six-two.''

Tyler Blackwell. It had a nice sound.

''Lives in Fort Worth. Oh, no!'' As if the wallet had suddenly turned into a venomous snake, Grace dropped it. ''Missy, he's got a press ID.''

The words hung heavily between them. Grace held her breath while she waited for her reaction.

Slowly Melissa got up from the bed and moved to the farthest corner of the room. A chill colder than the hail stoning the castle walls iced through her. A reporter? Here? How dare he?

''Get him out of here.'' Melissa's body shook and her blood ran cold. Another reporter trying to advance his dubious career at her expense. The last two had created the witch and sealed her permanently from the world.

She wouldn't be easy prey again.

When Grace didn't move, Melissa paced the stone floor while she fought the quickening of her anger, the sting of tears. ''Now! I don't want him here.''

The idea of revenge crept unbidden into her mind. The poisoned thought fed on her anger and took on life.

White-hot fury swirled deep inside. Grace positioned herself between Melissa and the wounded man.

"Missy, he's hurt."

Revenge soured her mouth with its venom, spread like fire through her blood. He was hurt, but so was she. He had a life. Hers had been stolen from her. Not once, but twice. By people like him. She couldn't let that happen again. She had nothing left to lose.

This time she would fight back. This time it would be different. She stopped her animal-like pacing and gazed down at the broken man on the bed. No longer did she see the sensual lines that had so pleased her earlier. She saw her last chance to reclaim her peace.

Lightning clawed the sky. Thunder resounded, shaking the walls, matching the anger quaking inside her. Melissa spun on her heel and met Grace's stern look squarely.

"On second thought," Melissa said, "if it's a story he wants, let's give him one he'll never forget."

LIGHTNING AND THUNDER receded to low flickers and distant rumbles. Rain still crashed in fury against the windowpanes of Grace's spare room. Its rhythm mirrored the wild beating of Melissa's heart. She was tired of the pain.

In her mind she heard the child's sobs. They hadn't bothered her in years. Not since Deanna had showed her how to cage her anger and her sorrow with the horses. She wanted to cry, too, like the child she'd once been, but the years of conditioning wouldn't let that happen.

"You can't put him in the dungeon, Missy," Grace said. "It ain't right."

Anger's slow growl thrummed through Melissa's body. "Why not? He's ready to sell my soul for a story. Why not give him a story that'll fit right in with the trash he writes?"

"You don't know that." Grace sidestepped, hiding the stranger from Melissa's view. "You don't know he was even heading here."

"What else is there around here? The thriving metropolis of Fallen Moon?" Melissa waved her hands at the buttressed ceiling. "I don't think he's here to admire the architecture." She resumed pacing the far side of the room to keep from exploding.

A part of her realized that her anger resulted from her encounter last summer with Brent Westfield. He'd wormed his way into the castle under false pretenses. One of her paintings had sold for a fantastic amount at a charity auction sponsored by James Randall, Dee's father. She'd succeeded despite her condition, and that success had come as a pleasant surprise. For once she'd been normal. Pride at her accomplishment had let the reporter's interest in her work lower her natural defenses.

She cringed at the memory. The interview she'd never given, filled with lies and bizarre innuendoes, had hurt more deeply than she'd admitted to anyone. That the people of her own town had let the lies feed their imagination almost bled her dry.

"You can't put him in the dungeon when he's hurt," Grace said, her voice gentle.

"His kind always survives," Melissa scoffed, knowing Grace was right.

Grace crossed her arms over her ample chest. "My eyes might not be so good, but some things you don't need to see to know. Mark my words, Missy, you're making a terrible mistake."

When Melissa didn't answer, Grace caught her shoulders and shook her. "You keep him caged like that and you're no better than the townsfolk who pass judgment without knowing any of the facts. Let him go."

"No," Melissa said firmly. Her body shook. Her anger's poison filled her veins and she couldn't stop it. "I can't, Grace," she pleaded, wanting Grace to understand the desperate need she had to assert dominion over her tiny world. "I have to show them once and for all that I'm not a witch, that I need to be left alone."

"Are you sure that's what you want, child?"

No, it wasn't, but she'd learned long ago certain things couldn't be changed and certain prayers were never answered. And if she had to choose between being a freak and being alone, she would go with loneliness.

This man couldn't fulfill her dreams, but he could put an end to the witch. "That's the way it has to be."

Grace rolled her eyes in exasperation. Ignoring her, Melissa moved away to gather the contents of Tyler Blackwell's wallet from the floor. She riffled through the items, noting with interest that his wallet held no pictures—not even of his Lindsey. Why? Was this man as alone in the world as she was? Suddenly she had to know. She wanted to know everything about him. Adversaries needed to start the battle on an even footing. He knew about her, she had no doubt; she'd find out about him. Melissa tucked the wallet back in the jeans pocket, retaining only his driver's license.

"He'll have to see a doctor for that head of his," Grace said.

Melissa stood up. "Send for Adam. After Adam's seen him, put him in the dungeon."

"Missy—"

"If he's hurt that badly, Adam'll have him transported to a hospital. If he's not, he has a lesson to learn." Melissa handed Grace the driver's license. "And see what Dee can dig up on Tyler Blackwell."

"Missy—"

"Tell her to bring me her report as soon as she has it."

Melissa leaned on the foot of the bed and stared at the unconscious man. "It's my decision. I'll live with the consequences."

"I don't think you know what you're getting into."

AN HOUR LATER Melissa made her way down the steep steps of the northeast tower to the cell where Grace had installed Tyler Blackwell. Grace tucked a blanket around the unconscious man's body, now clad in sweats belonging to Grace's son, who was away at college.

"How's he doing?" Melissa asked, stopping at the open cell door.

"Doc says he'll be all right." Grace kept fussing with the blanket. "His body temperature's back to normal. He woke up once, then fainted."

"Maybe he's tired." Melissa grabbed one of the cold steel bars, worried despite her best intentions about the man's unconscious state.

"And maybe they're right to call you a witch." Grace put a hot-water bottle at the man's feet, then turned around to face Melissa. "He woke up long enough to tell Adam he didn't want to go to no hospital. I tried to make him see the light, but he's just as stubborn as you are." She shook her head. "You two deserve each other." She jerked her chin toward Tyler. "He needs to be watched till he comes to, and I'm too old to do it."

"I'll keep an eye on him. I'll come get you if he wakes up."

"You do that. Wake him every hour and make sure he ain't seeing double."

Grace departed with a huff that left no doubt how she felt about Melissa's actions. A twinge of guilt niggled at Melissa's conscience. Then the anger stirred again. *He's a reporter!* a voice in her mind exploded. *He wants to hurt you like the others.*

She heard the abandoned child's sobs echo somewhere in the past. They wrenched her heart and nearly dropped her in a pool of self-pity. Turning from the pull of memories took everything she had. The pain, the loneliness—both hurt so much.

She forced her attention back to Tyler Blackwell. He looked beautiful. So innocent and peaceful. But Melissa knew she couldn't trust the appearance of innocence or beauty. No one ever came to Thornwylde Castle without a reason.

She moved into the cell and checked on the reporter. His breathing was even and his skin felt warm. Suddenly his brows knit together and his face contorted itself into a mask of pain. She snapped back her hand. *What did I do? What should I do? I don't know what to do with a sick man. He's not sick. He's just bruised. This is what you get for letting your anger get the best of you.* Before she could run to call Grace, his face returned to its calm state.

He's a reporter, she reminded herself. *He wants to hurt you.* With her heart pounding, Melissa stood and moved away from Tyler. She wouldn't let him. Not this time. He wanted the witch, she'd give him the witch. Then she'd show him she wasn't a gorgon—just a simple woman.

The scene set, Melissa returned to Tyler Blackwell's bedside. She tucked the blanket around his shoulders. Then she sat beside him, watching and waiting. Every hour she woke him. Each time he called her Lindsey. Every cry to the unknown woman touched her soul and scratched at her resolve.

When the first light of dawn eked through the dusty

window, Melissa felt the stranger stir. Slowly she rose and left. As she closed the barred door, it squealed.

She turned the lock and pocketed the key. "My dear Mr. Blackwell, welcome to your worst nightmare."

"HEY, SAL, HOW ARE the biscuits today?" Ray Lundy asked. Breakfast at the Parker Peach had been a part of his routine since he took on managing J.R. Randall's stables three years ago.

The redheaded waitress turned and smiled.

"Hey, Ray, you're late this mornin'." Sally Warren grabbed the coffeepot off the heater and headed to the corner table where Ray took a seat. He doffed his battered cowboy hat and laid it crown-side down on the vinyl seat next to him.

"Hear about the fire at Granger's barn last night?" His eyes strayed over Sally's hourglass figure squeezed into a cotton-candy-pink uniform that was half a size too small. He licked his lips, then forced his gaze back to her freckled face.

"What happened?" Sally asked, interest glowing in her eyes.

"They say it was the witch."

"No!" Sally eyed the kitchen window, then placed the coffeepot on the table and sat down across from Ray.

"Yep. Granger, his wife and his daughter's Girl Scout troop all saw her ridin' away on that black stud of hers." Glad to see his juicy gossip having the desired effect, Ray sampled the coffee, added a heaping teaspoon of sugar and a small container of cream.

"What reason would she have to do that?" Sally placed her elbows on the table and cupped her chin in her hands.

In the background Ray heard the clatter of dishes being washed, the scuff of a spatula scraping grease off the grill and Joe's sharp bark at a kitchen helper. With the break-fast rush over, all Sally's tables sat empty at the moment. Besides, he'd timed his arrival just right; he knew she was due for a break. He had her rapt attention—for the next couple of minutes.

"Granger said his cows wandered over to her pastures a few weeks ago," Ray said. "She wasn't too pleased. Had her henchwoman tell him to keep his cows home or she'd do it for him."

"You don't say."

"Yeah. Good thing his stock was out, but the barn's a total loss."

"You know, that really doesn't sound like her. She's never bothered anybody before."

"What about the hex she put on Harris when he shot that deer on her land last spring."

Sally gave him a quizzical look.

"The next week the roof on his house caved in."

"Oh, come on, Ray, there was a tornado spotted during that storm. She had no control over that."

"Maybe, maybe not. What about Andy Stone?" Ray took a deliberately long sip from his cup. "I hear tell he saw her face last week when she was out ridin' and hasn't been able to talk since."

"For heaven's sake, Ray. Andy's got laryngitis."

"Are you sure?" Ray saw her thoughts waver. *She's so transparent.*

"Then there's the disappearin' animals," Ray contin-ued. "The Strykers' dog and the Andersons' cat. Even old Zeke put in a report he had a goat missin'." Ray sweetened his coffee with another spoonful of sugar. He loved the way the spoon clinked in time to Sally's thoughts. "You know the full moon's comin'. A witch's moon."

Ray saw Sally study him. They'd known each other since grade school. He liked to play with people, and she knew it. He hoped she wouldn't realize he was playing her for a fool. Knowing Sally as well as he did, she'd jump at the chance to be the first to repeat the juicy gossip. That was why he'd picked her. Ray recognized the instant she made up her mind.

"Well, I gotta get back to work or Joe'll have my hide," she said. "The usual?"

"The usual." Ray smiled a satisfied grin. He'd planted the kernel of doubt. Sally Warren's loose tongue would spare no time in sharing the rumors. Everything was going according to plan.

Chapter Three

Tyler's first thought was that he was dead. Then he tried to move and knew that if he was dead, he'd gone to hell. Nowhere else would such pain be allowed. His whole body throbbed. Something sharp dug into his rear and his guts hurt from sleeping on his back.

He willed his fuzzy mind to clear. Where was he? Why couldn't he open his eyes? He vaguely remembered a woman talking to him. Had he imagined the soft fingers on his skin when they'd unbuttoned his shirt, or the strong yet gentle hands that had held him as someone bandaged him, or the musical voice that had soothed him every time he awoke during the night? The floating image of a green-eyed angel buoyed on his closed lids. Warmth had surrounded him.

A dream, Tyler thought, as he shivered under the thin blanket. It had to be a dream. The narrow cot grew unbearably uncomfortable beneath him. He had to get up. If only his body would cooperate. Water dripped somewhere to his right—a sharp, slow, echoing clank. The wind moaned at his feet. The clop of horse's hooves on cobbles resounded above his head. *All that's missing are the scurrying rats,* he thought. He forced his head up to look around, then let his head flop back on the flat pillow.

There were bars instead of a door. Why wasn't he surprised?

I'm in the middle of a nightmare, and I'll wake up any minute now. He willed the warmth back, the soft hands, the gentle voice. It was no use. Reality kept intruding. The night came back in slow pieces. His promise to Freddy. The accident. Camelot. The castle. Why had he ever thought of the castle as Camelot? Somehow he'd ended up stuck inside a medieval dungeon. This wasn't the way he'd expected to start this assignment. She must be as crazy as the tabloids said she was.

He didn't like the idea of being at anyone's mercy. Not after Lindsey. And especially not at the hands of a nutcase like Melissa Carnes. He was the pursuer, the one who put on the heat, not the other way around. It was time he set the record straight.

Professional pride, if not his male ego, jolted him into action. He regretted his sudden move when pain resonated throughout his body.

Tyler saw at once that the medieval atmosphere was carefully orchestrated. The drip came from a faucet turned on just enough to let one drop at a time clang into a metal bucket. The barred window was open a crack, allowing the wind to moan through it, but not the fusty air to dissipate. The walls needed no dressing up; their stone starkness, wet with morning dew, was enough to depress anybody. He glanced at his wrist and found it bandaged and his watch missing. By the weak light filtering through the dusty window, he judged the time somewhere just after dawn.

He was dying of thirst and the dripping water didn't help. He hobbled over to the faucet and twisted it shut. The rust color inspired no confidence the water was drinkable. He made his way to the bars. Hanging on to them, he looked down the lightless tunnel. He could see nothing but black on either side.

"Hello," Tyler called into the darkness. "Is anyone out there?" The moaning wind was his only answer. He hobbled back to the bucket, emptied the water with a splash on the stone floor and carried it back to the bars. He banged the empty pail against the bars.

"Anyone out there?"

"There's no need for all that racket."

A hulking giant seemed to magically materialize before his cell. He stopped the noise. She held a tray heaped with food. The odor of freshly brewed coffee set his stomach growling. He couldn't remember the last time he'd eaten. He forced his gaze off the steaming platter and back to the dark-skinned woman.

"Where am I?" he asked her.

"Where did you wanna be?" Intense black eyes bored through him. Maybe Freddy was right and his niece's life was in danger.

"Why am I here?"

She shrugged. "You tell me. You're the one who insisted you had to stay."

Tyler didn't like the course of this conversation. "Is this Thornwylde Castle?"

Her impenetrable stare accused him of unknown crimes, but her face remained blank.

"I want to see Melissa Carnes," he commanded.

"She don't see no one till she's good and ready."

"I need to see her." Why was this woman making things so difficult? His request was simple enough. It deserved a simple answer. The headache pounding at his temple shredded through what remained of his patience.

"Don't you know, one look at her face and you'll turn

into a pillar of salt?'' He saw the amusement dance in her coal-black eyes.

''I'll risk salt over these accommodations.'' Maybe changing the subject would dispel the idea that he was dealing with a brick wall.

''She ain't too pleased with your presence, either.''

''Let her tell me herself.''

''She will.'' The big woman set the tray down by the door. ''When she's ready.''

A heavy set of keys jangled as she fumbled with the lock. Tyler thought of pouncing on her as she bent to pick up the tray, but to keep his promise to Freddy, he needed to stay here, not be shown the door before he'd even seen the woman he was here to protect. He silently sneered. *Some protector.*

The woman handed him the tray. Breakfast smelled good and he was ravenous. ''She told me to feed you gruel.''

He lifted the cover from the plate. Beneath lay eggs, bacon, hash browns and the biggest peach muffin he'd ever seen. He cast her a sidelong glance. Was this draconian woman an ally? While balancing the plate in one hand, he gulped down the glass of orange juice with the other.

''Best-looking gruel I've ever seen.'' His most genial smile was rewarded by a steely glare.

''Don't get too comfy now.''

''Fat chance!''

She waved two fingers in front of his face. ''How many fingers you see?''

''Two. I'm fine.'' He sat down and dug into the mound of scrambled eggs.

She grunted and left, keying the lock closed behind her.

''Tell Miss Carnes I'd like to see her.'' He bit into the muffin.

''She knows.''

A cacophony of various aches and pains stirred by his activity soon joined the pounding in his head and overtook his hunger. He placed the tray beside him. Sitting on the edge of the cot, he held his head in his palms and pressed the heels of his hands against his temples. What the hell had he gotten himself into?

''Any chance of getting some aspirin?'' he asked as the woman started up the stairs.

She paused and nodded. ''I'll see what I can do.''

Tyler forced himself to finish the breakfast. He'd need strength to face Freddy's witch of a niece—when Her Royal Shrewness deigned to see him. After he was done eating, he pushed the tray beneath the cot, then lay down. Sleep would take the edge off the pain. And maybe when he woke up, he'd find it had all been just an awful dream.

''GOOD JOB, Ray,'' the voice on the phone said. ''Rumors are flying from the café to the courthouse.''

Bright sunshine streamed through the stable door. The day wasn't halfway done and already Ray had more than exceeded his expectations. Everything from now until midnight was gravy.

''Thought you'd be pleased.'' Ray puffed on his cigar, a satisfied grin on his face.

''Keep the tongues wagging.''

You think you're ridin' high, you little priss, but I'm in charge of the show. You ain't gettin' me to do nothin' I don't want to be doin'. I've got position.

Ray took another puff on his cigar, anticipating another gain of material that would lead to the win that was right-fully his. Everything was going according to plan. That the witch had so easily taken in the reporter proved a bonus. "Hey, ever hear of a guy named Tyler Black-well?"

"Tyler Blackwell?" There was a catch in the voice.

Ray's grin widened. *Gotcha.* The chance at redemption, he'd discovered, made for good motivation. "Yep. Seems he landed on Melissa Carnes's doorstep last night."

"Well, well, what an interesting development." A pause, swarming with possibilities, followed as the contact processed options. "I can get him Tyler Blackwell's head on a platter as an added bonus." The phone clicked off.

"Yeah," Ray said, extinguishing the cigar under the heel of his boot. "What an interestin' development." No one knew how to play pawns the way he did.

BEFORE DEANNA RANDALL came to her, an endless parade of nannies had flowed through the castle as if it had a revolving door. The pent-up rage Melissa had harbored since the accident was flung full force on each new and unsuspecting arrival. They never stayed for more than a week. Most never made it through the first day. Melissa's unruliness drove her stepmother crazy and afforded young Melissa the only source of satisfaction she knew. Sable Lorel Carnes would have gladly sent her ugly stepdaughter to an institution and never given her a second thought, but William Carnes had just enough guilt to grant his daughter her wish to stay home.

Melissa was almost ten when Sable hired Deanna. Deanna was newly graduated from college with a degree in education, and she was a nice change of pace from the dour matrons Sable usually chose. She was full of the enthusiasm of a new teacher bursting with fresh ideas. No one had bothered to tell Deanna that Melissa had the man-

ners of a wild animal. Nor had anyone told Deanna she
had the right to refuse the job.

Melissa still remembered the day they met. She'd sat
huddled on the window seat in the room where her stepmother kept her hidden. Sable disappeared as soon as
she'd shown Deanna the room, not wanting to be around
when the fur started flying. Deanna hesitated as she entered the room. Her long blond hair, caught in a barrette
at her nape, flowed like liquid gold over one shoulder.
Her round face and rosy cheeks made her look more like
sixteen than twenty-one. But her starched white shirt and
conservative navy skirt branded her as the latest nanny,
and Melissa was ready to do battle.

"Hi! I'm Deanna Randall," she'd said in a gentle
friendly voice. Melissa simply glared at her from across
the room. When Deanna started moving in her direction,
Melissa flung a wooden toy horse at her. Deanna ducked
and kept on walking.

"Go away! I don't need you," Melissa screamed, putting her all into the performance.

"I thought we might be friends." Deanna had stopped
six feet away and lowered herself to Melissa's eye level.

"I don't wanna friend!" Her hostile stance dared the
new nanny to argue.

"I'd like to teach you wonderful things." The woman's
voice was silky smooth, inviting.

"Why should I learn?"

"Because learning is growing and growing is what living is all about." Deanna had talked to her like a person
instead of an animal to be ordered about, then shoved
back in its cage.

"What good is that gonna do me? I'm gonna be stuck
in this room for the rest of my life."

"That's up to you, isn't it?" Deanna smiled. Not a

condescending smile, but one that accepted Melissa's right to make her own decisions.

Melissa sprang from her seat. She stood, fists balled, directly in front of Deanna.

"Look at my face! See how ugly it is?" She turned her head and offered Deanna an unobstructed view of the mangled left half of her face. Deanna reached out and touched the still-tender burn scars.

"I can see inside you, and I see a beautiful soul."

Melissa had been stunned. No one had touched her so gently since the accident. Her looks had repulsed all of the previous nannies, and they hadn't bothered to hide it. Deanna had touched her softly and told her she was beautiful. Melissa hadn't known whether to hit her or to cry. So she'd done both. As her love-starved soul pounded the new nanny, Melissa had dissolved into tears. Deanna had gathered her in her arms and held her close. She'd sobbed as only a heartbroken child could.

They'd been friends ever since. Not that Melissa had made it easy for Deanna, but Deanna had thrived on the challenge and had made Melissa's life alive with laughter, learning and love.

They'd been inseparable until Deanna married Sam Ziegler five years ago. Sam and Deanna had since had two beautiful children, and Melissa's time with Deanna was reduced to one night a week and daily phone conversations. Melissa allowed herself to visit her two godchildren only when Sam was absent.

Tonight Melissa was determined to push Tyler's arrival on her doorstep last night and his presence in her dungeon out of her mind and concentrate on the movie Dee had brought. *Ghost* was Dee's favorite and she'd brought along the required box of tissues.

Dee lay sprawled on the sitting room's comfortable

couch while Melissa sat cross-legged on the plush cream-colored carpet using the couch leg as a backrest. A bowl of popcorn was propped on several cranberry-and-forest-green throw pillows within easy reach of both women.

Patrick Swayze slid his hands provocatively over Demi Moore's body while "Unchained Melody" played in the background. The actors' eyes glowed as they savored each other's bodies. And though Tyler looked nothing like Patrick, and she in no way resembled Demi, Melissa saw him there on the screen, touching her like that. Ridiculous, of course. Only Dee could stand the sight of her face. Only the horses could stand her touch.

"Is love really like that?" Melissa asked, eyes glued to the TV as she popped a handful of popcorn into her mouth.

"Like what?" Deanna answered lazily, her attention also directed at the screen.

"Serious and strong and raw and, I don't know, so intense." What was real? What was movie magic?

"Sometimes."

"Does it happen with all men or only when you're with a special one?" She had nothing to go on to analyze the strange feelings Tyler stirred in her.

"Why do you ask?"

"Just curious." Melissa chewed on another handful of popcorn. "Do you realize I'll be thirty next month and I've never even been kissed by a man?"

Dee sat up, reached for the remote control and switched the movie off. "What's going on in that head of yours, Melissa?"

"Nothing." Melissa picked up the bowl of popcorn and balanced it on her knees, refusing to look directly at Deanna. She concentrated on each kernel she picked, chewing it longer than necessary and swallowing it untasted. How could she explain lustful thoughts about a man who wanted to hurt her when she wasn't even sure what lust was?

"Come on, Mel. I know you. I know something's eating you."

Melissa continued her ritualistic choosing of popcorn, thinking of the man under lock and key in her dungeon. Now that Tyler Blackwell was fit, though bruised, she wasn't sure what she wanted to do with him. Dee was right, she should have shoved him out the portcullis at first light. But that would only have enhanced her witch image. And that, she'd decided as she'd watched him last night, was the last thing she needed.

Now, watching this movie of two people in love, she knew she wanted someone other than Dee and Grace to see her as a person—to see her as a woman. But how to achieve that when people tended to see only the scars?

"I'm just wondering about love between a man and a woman," Melissa said finally, not knowing quite what she wanted Dee to tell her. "How does it come about? How do you know when you've got it? What does it feel like?" She put the bowl of popcorn aside and faced Dee. "Is it like in the movies?"

Deanna shook her head. "Oh, boy, I don't know how to answer that. Why this sudden urge to find out?"

Melissa shrugged, then stood and walked to the window. Nothing but blackness in all its shades. After Dee left, she would go for a ride and gallop away all these crazy sensations sliding through her.

"Because I feel empty inside. I want a husband and children. A normal life—like yours. And I know I can never have that. I guess I'm going through an early mid-life crisis." She laughed halfheartedly, then turned to stare once more at the darkness. "How long does it take to get pregnant?"

"What!"

"Well?"

Deanna flushed. "We covered that in basic biology."

"Would one time be enough?"

"Are you considering artificial insemination?"

Then something seemed to click in Deanna's mind. She gasped and spilled the bowl of popcorn with her foot as she sprang up. "He's still here! Tyler Blackwell's still here! I thought we agreed letting him go was best all around. Dad says his being here can't be good. He's a dirt-digger, Mel. He doesn't stop until he gets what he wants." Deanna sucked in air and put a hand over her heart. "You're not planning on sleeping with him, are you?"

"Are you mad!" Melissa brushed away the half-sketched thought. "The man is out to ruin me. Of course I'm not going to sleep with him." She sneered and slapped her left cheek. "Do you really think he'd want to take someone like me to bed? Or that I'd even know how to seduce a man?"

Gently Deanna wrapped one arm around Melissa's shoulders. Melissa hated the pity in her friend's eyes.

"You know that's not what I mean," Dee said softly. "It's just that he's not another of the battered creatures you like to take in. He's much more dangerous."

"I know that." Melissa knew it with her mind, saw it with her eyes, felt it in the strange sensation shivering down her back. Shrugging off Dee's hand, she sat down and pressed the remote to restart the movie. But there was also something about Tyler Blackwell, about the pain in his voice, in his eyes, when he called to his Lindsey, that touched her deeply.

"I don't want to see you hurt."

"I know." But Dee, in her own well-meaning way, had also never encouraged Melissa to venture past these castle walls. All the field trips but one had been James Randall's idea. Because of his generous donations, he'd had museums and galleries opened after hours just for her. And as dangerous as Tyler Blackwell was, his words could open a whole new world to her. The only way she could think to achieve that was to hold him prisoner until he saw past the witch.

Patrick Swayze kissed Demi Moore, and she arched back in ecstasy at his touch. After wondering all night and all day what she was going to do with her unwanted guest, Melissa had her answer. The only question left in her mind was whether she would have the courage to follow through on her brash decision.

"MR. BLACKWELL?"

A woman's voice pierced through layers of drowsiness, and Tyler winced as he propped himself up to answer.

"What...? What time is it?" he asked, his voice hoarse with sleep. "Who are you?"

"I'm sorry to wake you up, but I need to talk to you. I'm Deanna Ziegler, a good friend of Melissa's." She looked at her watch and added, "It's about two in the morning."

"Two a.m.!" Tyler sat up. He was wide awake now and annoyed. "What the hell are you doing here at this time?"

"Visiting. For Melissa it's only midafternoon—she keeps quite different hours from most people. I want to know what your intentions are."

"Intentions?" His eyes adjusted to the night and he stared unbelievingly at the small woman peering at him through the bars of his cell. She sounded like a father facing his daughter's suitor. By the moon's soft light, spilling from the high window, he guessed she was about forty. Her hair, gleaming white and her smooth Germanic features drawn tight with worry betrayed her age more than the well-proportioned figure clad in fuchsia exercise pants and flower-print T-shirt.

"I'll arrange for Grace to let you go in the morning. I suggest you leave the second you get the opportunity," Deanna said.

Tyler guessed that "Papa" had judged him to be an unsuitable prospect. Who was Grace? The woman who brought him his meals?

"I can't." He rubbed the sleep from his eyes, then leaned his elbows on his thighs and cradled his head in his hands. The angel of his hallucinations with her heavenly voice and jewel-green eyes had revisited him in dreams a man like him had no right to have. The angel was so far removed from the tabloid witch that he *had* to reconcile the two and find which one was real. Maybe he was doomed to repeat his mistakes, he thought, as the need for answers once again reasserted itself. How did he expect to find a new path if he followed the same old road?

"What do you mean you can't?" Anger rose and turned the woman's soft features surprisingly hard. "Melissa's been through hell and can't take any more of the kind of pain you bring."

"I'm not here to hurt her."

The knuckles of the hands gripping the bars whitened. She shook her head. "She doesn't need the kind of notoriety your work brings. It'll change the quiet atmosphere she's used to and needs to survive. You're an investigative reporter, and I'm telling you there's nothing here to investigate or report.''

"I'm not going to hurt her," he repeated flatly. Family feuds had a way of burning anyone foolish enough to cross the battlefield. Freddy had to know that or he would have come to the rescue himself.

"Maybe you really don't mean to, but you have to understand, Melissa isn't like the people you're used to interviewing.''

"I don't imagine she is.'' How could she be after spending her life alone in a place like this?

"Put yourself in her place. You're eight years old and you're disfigured in the same accident that kills your mother. Imagine growing up without love, with scars that today even the best plastic surgeon can't make disappear because they're too old and set. Imagine being kept in a room all alone—just because your family thinks you're too ugly for anyone to see. Imagine what that does to the psyche of a child, and then tell me that your words won't hurt her.'' She jerked at the bars. "Go back to your editor and tell him you can't do this story.''

"I can't do that.''

"You have nothing to lose, Mr. Blackwell. You'll get other chances. The last reporter who did a story on her nearly killed her with his words. She's had enough pain to last her a dozen lifetimes. Leave her alone. Go,'' Deanna pleaded.

Deanna's fierceness spoke of loyalty and love. Freddy wanted Tyler's reason for being here to remain a secret until he could corroborate it, but he'd also said that to get to Melissa he had to go through Deanna. Nothing short of the truth would work here. "Freddy Gold sent me.''

She snapped back as if the bars were suddenly electrified. "Why would Freddy Gold send a reporter? He knows how she feels about them."

"To do an article on Eclipse."

"Freddy doesn't send reporters. I send him Melissa's copy over the Internet."

Freddy, Tyler thought, had probably never gotten around to asking his secretary to call Deanna about the article on her stallion. Were Rena and the baby okay? "He thinks she's in danger."

"From what?"

Tyler sighed. Freddy's hunches had garnered him untold scoops, but sometimes they were a pain in the butt to explain. But if he was to stay, he had to convince Melissa's guardian that his presence was needed here. "He received a warning that someone wants her harmed."

"Who?"

"I don't know. That's why he sent me here. He knows Melissa won't talk to him, won't even pick up the phone when he calls. He knows she won't accept his help except through a business transaction. That's why he thought she'd go for an article about her horse now that show season is under way. His secretary was supposed to call."

"She didn't."

The thing about Freddy's hunches was that they were usually right. And if Freddy thought danger lurked around Melissa's castle, then there was probably something to it. Sometimes the intuition proved nothing more than a leaky faucet. Sometimes it was the shot that killed the woman you loved. But it was always worth checking out.

"I promised Freddy I'd keep her safe. That's all." That was everything. And it was too much. Especially when she'd managed to haunt his dreams in less than a day. He rubbed at the pain pounding in his forehead. "The story is just a cover. I won't write one word about her. Call Freddy—he'll verify my claim."

"She's as safe as she can be behind these walls. The last thing she needs is an intruder—a reporter—with a hidden agenda." Deanna made an exasperated sound. "The best thing you can do for her is leave. I'll look out for her. I've been keeping her safe for a long time."

"Then maybe a fresh set of eyes is warranted."

Deanna's face hardened. "I come from a powerful family. I can make sure you never work again."

"The name Ziegler doesn't ring a bell."

A drop from the leaky faucet pinged onto the brick floor. A gust of wind moaned through the half-opened window. The concert of crickets outside suddenly stilled.

"Try Randall, as in James Richmond Randall."

"Randall Industries?"

"The very one."

The hair on the back of his neck bristled. Last year a trail of creative accounting, colored profits and corruption had led to Randall Industries before it ran cold.

Old instincts he thought had died with Lindsey revived. Danger had a scent, a taste, a feel of its own, and it slithered through him in a sticky cold that threatened to turn to black. He got up from the cot, shrugged off the unwanted feelings creeping down his spine and shuffled to the gate. He held the bars right above Deanna's hands and looked straight into her pale blue eyes, gleaming in the moonlight.

"Even J.R. Randall can't take something away from nothing. But you, how will you feel if the warning Freddy got is true and something happens to Melissa?"

Deanna swallowed hard. "She's safe here."

Money makes people do unspeakable things.

Did Freddy know Deanna was linked to Randall Industries? Was that why he'd sent him here? What chance did Melissa have against someone who thought nothing of murder to keep an illusion afloat?

"She's in danger, Ms. Ziegler, but not from me."

"I will not let you harm her."

"Then help me keep her safe."

Chapter Four

Tyler's worst hangover paled in comparison to the freight train barreling through his head. He tried to hold very still, but somehow the bruises on his body felt as if they were being pressed in turn for doneness.

Grace returned several times during the day. First with a bottle of extra-strength ibuprofen, his laundered clothes, soap and a set of towels, then with lunch, and finally in midafternoon with the remnants of his personal effects from his Jeep—minus his Swiss Army knife, razor, cell phone and Palm Pilot.

She inquired more than once if he wanted the doctor to look at his head again. He refused, knowing instinctively that once he left the witch's castle, she wouldn't allow his return. The faster he got to the bottom of the situation here, the sooner he could go. He didn't like the way his promise to Freddy was drawing him back into a past he was trying to forget.

He closed his eyes. The image of Lindsey's blue eyes widening with shock, of blood blooming on the bodice of her white dress, exploded on the black screen of his lids. He moved too fast as he sought to escape the bloody vision. Pain rattled through him as he came to a sitting position. Wiping a hand over his face, he forced himself to concentrate on his current situation.

What if Melissa wasn't the innocent lamb Freddy thought her to be? What if she was involved in a partnership with Randall Industries?

Then this time, he wouldn't miss the mark.

He was willing to bet that, for all Melissa Carnes's witch reputation, his skills were honed to a sharper edge—even with the wasted year to dull them. When he knew ahead of time he had to be patient, he found it easier to quell hasty actions and keep focused on the goal. And his goal was to wipe the slate clean between him and Freddy, to start fresh on a new page.

He rolled his shoulder, dragged his hands through his hair and massaged the back of his neck. A chilling feeling crept into his being, burrowed under his skin, and made evil seem to lurk in every shadowy crack in the stone wall, in the suffocating heat that settled and thickened the must, in the dankness that seemed to coat his skin like slime.

And if he wasn't careful, he thought, it just might swallow him whole—just as it had after Lindsey's death. The whiskey demon whispered to him and Tyler felt the pull of it from head to gut. *Think of something else. Think of what you're supposed to accomplish here. Think of the story.*

As evening darkness infused his already dim cell, the jangling of keys announced an arrival—but not Grace. Not Deanna. The footsteps were too light, too airy. Melissa Carnes. Patience was paying off.

"About time," Tyler mumbled.

He knew she was there, could feel her watching him from the shadows. He hated the fact his pulse kicked up a notch at her arrival. Leaning back on the unyielding hardness of the stone wall, he waited. The one who spoke first was always at a disadvantage.

"Does the dark frighten you, Mr. Blackwell?"

The melody in her voice took him by surprise. Given her reputation, her possible connection with Randall Industries, he'd almost expected a cackle. "Not particularly. What about the light that scares you?"

Her throaty laugh echoed in his cell. "You haven't done your homework, then."

"I know about your burns, if that's what you mean."

"And here I thought you were going to bring up witchcraft," she said. "Photophobia."

"Pardon?"

"One of my eyes was damaged by the heat of the fire and remains sensitive to light. Doctors have cautioned me to stay out of the sun because my skin has lost its ability to defend itself." He could hear the defensiveness in her voice. "And most people would rather I cloak myself in shadow so that they're not subjected to the sight of my ugly face."

"I'm not most people."

As his eyes adjusted to the darkness, Melissa took shape on the other side of the bars—a pitch-black outline against the dark gray of the stairwell. Her ghost-white fingers stroked the black creature—a cat?—in her arms. Her long-sleeved black T-shirt showed off the slimness of her body, the swell of firm breasts. Ebony hair flowed under the black shawl covering her head, face and neck, leaving only her steady gaze exposed.

"Which begs the question—what brings an award-winning investigative reporter to the redneck town of Fallen Moon, and more precisely, to Thornwylde Castle?"

Tyler shrugged. "What takes a reporter anywhere? An assignment."

"Honesty. Refreshing." She smacked one hand on the wall. "Your cards, Mr. Blackwell. Spread them on the table. Games don't amuse me."

"You've been playing a mean one since I got here."

"I've been trying to decide what to do with an unwanted guest."

He stretched his legs in front of him, crossing them at the ankle, then folded his arms over his chest. "What did you conclude?"

The slow stroking of her long fingers on the cat's fur didn't change. A shiver of recognition rippled down his torso. He knew exactly how they felt against his skin—gentle and warm. With a sharp hitch of his shoulder he shrugged away the disturbing sensation. A reporter's job was to get beneath the illusion and expose the truth. She was no angel.

"What do you want from me?" she asked with caustic interest, studying him across the murky darkness.

Power and pain. He could hear both in her voice, sense the fragile mask of tough over hurt little girl. Freddy didn't want her to know the true reason he was here, but this time Freddy was wrong. To gain her trust Tyler had to give her a measure of truth. "Your uncle sent me."

"I write my own copy for the articles on my horses. We communicate through his secretary."

"He's starting a new column called 'Texas Tales.' It's a series on Texas legends. People from Texas who've made it big."

Her fingers paused in their stroking of the cat. "Then you have the wrong Carnes. My father is the one who managed to build an empire from nothing. I merely spend his fortune."

"Your father passed on."

"He would still make a better story than me."

Sometimes the shortest distance between two points was the long way around. "What about your paintings? They're unique collector's items. They must afford you a decent income. Then there are your horses. Your stallion's success warrants a feature."

She said nothing. The soft purring of the cat sounded like a well-oiled chain saw.

Without quite knowing why, he found himself imitating her clipped regal tone. "Then, of course, there's your reputation. Some say you're a witch, the devil incarnate. Others say you're merely a harmless recluse. Yet others claim you're an agoraphobic who's turned into a vengeful neurotic." He paused. "But that's what you expect, isn't it? Persecution." Was that why she'd fallen prey to Randall's schemes? Innocent victim or willing participant?

The cat bumped its head against her stopped hand.

"If you don't believe any of those reasons," he said, watching every flicker in her shadowed eyes for signs of deception, "then there's always the truth."

Fingers laced over his lap, he waited.

"Truth," she said finally, her fingers resuming their slow stroking of the cat. Tyler almost purred.

"Freddy got a warning that you might be in danger."

"A warning?" The cat arched to keep its head in contact with her hand.

"Do you play chess?"

"Yes."

Why didn't that surprise him? She had the mind for it. And the time. "He received an article about the mason who broke his leg doing repair work on one of your towers and a bishop from a cheap plastic chess set."

Silence deepened and the shadows seemed to curl around him.

"Freddy wants me to find out who sent those items and keep you safe."

"Safe?" she said, sneering. "What can be safer than a fifteenth-century castle with walls six feet thick, a moat and a drawbridge?"

No point sugarcoating the situation. "According to Freddy, a bishop works on the diagonal and makes long moves. Working from a distance on the sly. Isn't that your relationship with Randall Industries?" He sensed more than saw her tension.

"Really, Mr. Blackwell, you take your work much too seriously. There truly isn't a conspiracy around every corner. James Randall is a friend and patron of the arts. Look at all he's done in the area with his charitable donations." Her strained laugh held none of its previous lilt. "A bishop has relatively little value. It can't win a match by itself."

"Exactly." Tyler noted that her gaze was level and her voice was steady. If Randall was using her, she didn't have a clue. So maybe it did all boil down to a family feud, and he was just letting his own past failures interfere with his present task. "Sometimes a billion-dollar trust fund is enough to make a bishop think he has a chance at the prize."

"My money? You think someone wants to harm me for my money?"

"Money is the number-one motivator for crime. Who benefits if you die?"

"The same people who benefit if I live."

"Do you know that women are more likely to hire a surrogate to kill for them?"

"Are you insinuating that my stepmother wants me killed?"

He shrugged. "If the shoe fits…"

"Wicked stepmothers went out of style with the Brothers Grimm, Mr. Blackwell. I happen to get along with mine just fine."

He had to reel back the urge to stand nose-to-nose, toe-to-toe with her, to retain an air of calmness in the electricity snapping through the air. "Then why are you stuck in this dusty museum in the middle of some hick town while she and your half sister are living it up in a mansion in Dallas?"

"By choice."

"Your birthday is a little more than three weeks away. If you die before you reach thirty, your stepmother and sister split your father's holdings. If the trust reverts to you, then you can do as you please with it. Your stepmother and sister are then at the mercy of your generosity."

"They're my family. They know I wouldn't deny them their share of my father's fortune."

"Do they?"

"If that's all you have—"

Tyler kicked the steel bucket by the cot. The sound resonated across the room like a gunshot and startled the cat that dug its white claws into its mistress's black-clad arms, making her flinch. "You haven't heard a word I've said. Someone has set a game in motion, and you're somehow the objective."

Melissa returned his steady gaze unblinkingly. For an instant he was a kid back in Pennsylvania, playing chicken with one of his stubborn sisters. *First one to blink is a rotten egg!*

"I'm not a princess in a castle, waiting to be rescued,"

Melissa said. "I don't need some knight in tarnished armor to conjure up a conspiracy because he needs a new victory to prove to the world he's still a hero."

Forgetting his resolution of cool calm, Tyler stood up. The cot scraped back with a sound that would have pleased a medieval torturer. "No, you're a recluse in a castle, shutting out the world. You can't shut this out, Melissa. Your lifestyle makes you easy prey."

"Why are you doing this?" she asked. "What do you have to gain by coming here and disrupting my peace?"

He wondered at the tremor in her voice and felt a nudge of sympathy for her. Not knowing was always the worst part. Answers didn't come until you pushed past the fear. He should have remembered that after Lindsey. "I owe Freddy."

Her short sharp laugh jabbed through the darkness. "Don't you know by now that some debts are too costly to repay?"

He knew only too well. "And sometimes your word is all you have."

She sliced an arm through the air in an arc. "I'm supposed to accept this improbable theory of yours based simply on your word?"

He shrugged, knowing he was asking her to take a lot on faith. "You've checked my background."

"Right down to your ambition playing a part in your wife's death."

He disguised his wince with a shrug. "Then you know I don't go for yellow journalism."

Melissa leaned forward over the cat, her gaze piercing. "But I also know that times have been hard for you. You haven't been able to hold a job for very long. Your alcoholic stupor has all but wiped out your promise of brilliance. Your bank account is overdrawn. Your utilities are about to be cut off. You're operating in the red, Mr. Blackwell. A perfect position for the lowering of standards.'' Her voice was bitter ice. ''I'm not a witch. Just a woman. There's nothing here that would interest your readers. There's no monster hiding around the corner wanting to eat me alive, except you and your poison pen.''

He was the intruder into her little world and he hadn't come bearing good news. He swallowed the knot of anger tightening his throat and forced his tense limbs to relax, his voice to sound even. ''Even the most complete report can't tell you what's in a man's soul. I don't want to hurt you. That's not how I work. Keeping a promise, Melissa, keeping you safe, that's why I'm here—not your scarred face.''

The purring stopped abruptly, replaced by an indignant yowl as Melissa unconsciously grabbed a handful of black fur. The irate cat bit her on the knuckles and leaped from her arms, landing on the stone floor with a soft thud. It flashed up the stairs and into the shadows.

Her skirt rustled as she stalked closer to the bars. Her eyes glowed an eerie green. He now understood how she'd earned the witch label. In their feral heat, her eyes looked old—as if she'd already lived a thousand years, suffered a thousand deaths.

''Aren't you afraid I'll use my black magic to turn you into a toad?''

He cocked his head and gave her his best Bogart grin. ''You could always kiss me back into a prince.''

Eyes narrowing, she stepped back. ''You want to know what it's like to be me, Mr. Blackwell?''

''Tyler. Yes.'' And he *did* want to know her. In the short while he'd spent with her, he'd seen her vulnerable as a child, as tough as a mongoose. Against all odds, how had she found the grit to succeed? How did she deal with the isolation? What made her paint those enchanting yet frightening watercolors? He truly wanted to know.

"Fine, come along, then." She twisted a key in the lock, then spun on her heel and headed for the stairs. "I hope your ribs are feeling better."

He followed, trying his best to ignore the symphony of aches that movement revived. "They're fine. Where are we going?"

"To do something you're an expert at. Shovel manure."

SOFT NICKERS of welcome greeted them as they walked through the opened stable door. The scent of hay, horses and leather took Tyler back to his teenage years and his bid to attract a girl's attention by learning to ride. He never got the girl, but did spend four summers eventing. How far back had Melissa traced his history?

She stroked the velvet muzzle of a chestnut mare. "This is Breeze," she said. The smile that surely graced her lips reached her eyes, warming something cold in his gut. "Do you know anything about horses?"

"A thing or two."

"These are American Warmbloods. I have Breeze and Eclipse shown."

"Breeze took the United States Dressage Federation Region Nine Reserve Championship in both Grand Prix and Intermediate Musical Freestyle last year. Eclipse took the USDF Sporthorse Breeding Horse of the Year Award. A couple of Eclipse's progeny also placed well."

"You did do your homework."

"That's me, a regular Boy Scout."

She slanted him a curious look. "I also have four broodmares, a retired gelding and a yearling out at pasture."

The black horse in the next stall sampled the ends of her hair. With a hand she signaled the stallion to back off. Without hesitation, he obeyed—not out of fear, but what passed for genuine respect. Tyler got the impression the powerful horse would willingly do anything to please his mistress. And for some reason that show of softness annoyed him.

Once she'd reasserted her dominance over Eclipse, she offered the stallion her hand. He played his mobile black lips over her open palm, gobbling up the sugar cube and making the tiny treat last as long as a bucket of oats. When he was through, his eyes begged for more, but he seemed to know better than to mouth the pocket of her skirt where the tasty treats resided.

"That's it. No more. You don't want your teeth to rot in your head, now, do you?"

Her laugh was free and it ruffled through Tyler like a warm breeze. He half turned away, inadvertently hitting his bruised ribs with his arm. He silently cursed at the ring of pain. That was better. He couldn't let her cast a spell over him as easily as she seemed to have done with the horses.

"You let a stallion stay here so close to a mare?" he asked, brushing away a thread of unease.

"He's well behaved." She opened the stall door. All of her attention focused on the horse as if she was communicating with him brain to brain, she led Eclipse without a halter into the aisle. "Besides, Breeze isn't in season right now."

A black cat meowed as it wrapped itself around Melissa's ankles. Eclipse bent down and sniffed at the Persian, but otherwise didn't move from the position Melissa had left him.

"Selma! There you are." Melissa scooped the cat up in her arms. A loud purr rewarded her. "Find any mice?"

The witch and her familiar. Maybe the rumors were true. What *would* it be like to be caught under one of her spells? He frowned. "What do you want me to do?"

Amusement lit her eyes, making the green dance like a sun-warmed lake and his gut tighten. Maybe he did have some sort of internal damage, after all. She disappeared into an adjacent room and came back with a pitchfork, shovel and wheelbarrow. "The manure pile is out back. I'm sure you can find it on your own. You know what to do?"

"Yeah." He took the pitchfork and shovel and looked down the concrete aisle at the eight stalls. His ribs hurt just thinking about lifting a forkful of manure. "All of them?"

"Of course. Even a witch must take care of the familiars who surround her. It's truly a glamorous life." She grabbed a bucket of brushes. "Be careful of Breeze. She likes to take chunks out of the stableboy."

Like horse, like mistress? "That why you had to cage extra help?"

"No, it's final-exam week, and he needs the time to study."

Did she really have regular help, or was she trying to make him believe she wasn't as alone as she seemed?

One thing for sure. She was testing him. And if he was going to get anywhere with her, he would have to do what she'd done with Eclipse—establish himself as lead horse in this strange little herd.

THE TRAUMA Melissa had suffered so long ago had attuned her to the vibration of pain. Though Tyler tried to hide it, she sensed the bruising ache each of his movements cost him, felt its echo in her own body, admired his resilience. But the best lessons about life she'd learned from the horses. Clear communication came from trust and obedience. The first few encounters with a new horse were the most important ones in establishing this balance. Actions spoke louder than words.

Tyler had to see that this was her world. If he was to intrude, he would have to follow her rules, bend to her will, see things through her eyes. Only then would he get a true picture of her.

Eclipse's shifting feet told her that if she didn't concentrate on her task more carefully, she could easily put a chink in years of patient training. She switched brushes and managed to give Eclipse all her attention—for a few minutes, anyway. She fanned the stallion's tail and raked a comb through it. Then Tyler's movements down the aisle drew her gaze.

Two days' worth of beard gave him a rakish look. She wanted to touch it. Would it be soft like a horse's muzzle or as prickly as it looked? Even the bruise on his forehead didn't detract from his beauty, but rather endeared him to her. Every time he lifted a forkful of manure, the muscles under his T-shirt flexed, making her wish for pencil and paper. Her gaze drifted over his lean hips, down his long legs, and she wondered at the tingle inside her at the sight of the clean lines of his body. Artistic delight in his physical perfection, she told herself, and combed out Eclipse's tail.

How would it feel to press her body against a man's hard planes, mold herself to him, have him fill her with his passion? She shook her head. She'd definitely watched too many of Dee's movies. The comb lay still in her hand. Eclipse curved his neck to look back at her.

"Are you going to admire me all night or are you going to pitch in?" Tyler asked.

The sheen of sweat reflected in the barn's low light accentuated his masculinity. She swallowed hard and disguised her unease with a clearing of her throat. "I'm making sure you're doing the job right. My horses are accustomed to a high standard of care."

She traded the comb for a hoof pick, and narrowing her gaze, she bent to pick up one of Eclipse's hooves.

"Probation?"

She didn't answer, didn't like the way he seemed to read her so easily. She *was* trying to determine how far she could trust him, how badly he needed his interview, how best to handle him. Deceiving humans was easy enough, but horses were too sensitive. Nothing got past them. He was handling fussy Breeze remarkably well. She didn't want to like him.

Honesty? Integrity? Did he have them? If they were part of his character, then had he brought the truth with him? Did someone truly want to harm her?

Was he right? Had her isolation made her easy prey for someone who might want to eliminate her? No, as much as she and Sable had issues, they understood each other on the matter of money. Was his story of a warning simply a way to to gain her trust?

An edginess itched under her skin. Had she learned nothing from her experience with Brent Westfield? As intriguing a specimen as Tyler Blackwell was, he was still a reporter. A good one. One with a reputation to rebuild. If she let herself fall for his manipulations before he could give her what she wanted, then she deserved to remain a witch for the rest of her days.

Melissa tossed the hoof pick into the brush bucket, then

patted Eclipse's neck. She needed to run. "Want to go for a ride?"

"I haven't ridden since I was a kid."

She glanced at Tyler over her shoulder. He leaned against the stall door, much too at home in her private space. "I wasn't talking to you. You're cleaning stalls."

"I don't think it's a good idea to go out until I've had a chance to check things out."

"Is that so?" This was a battle of wills. They were establishing control. She had too much to lose; she couldn't let him win.

"Why take a chance before you know what you're up against?"

His solidness, despite his bruises, the clear intensity of his dark gaze, seemed to offer something just out of reach. She licked her suddenly dry lips, trying to understand what was happening to her, trying to dull the burning desire to let him be the hero of her own romantic movie. "Why narrow my world before I know if there's even a reason to?"

A gust skipped down the aisle, stirring bits of wood chips that skittered against the concrete like hungry termites.

"Do you want to die, Melissa?"

The question hissed, heavy with the venom of an oft-contemplated option. Breath choked in her chest. Something keened inside her. She wanted wind in her hair, against her face. She wanted wide-open spaces and speed. She wanted freedom. "I want to live. That's all I've ever wanted."

MELISSA LED HIM into the darkened castle as easily as if it were day. Maybe she sensed she'd revealed too much of herself with her answer, or maybe he'd let his pain show too much. Whatever the reason, she'd cut his stall-cleaning duty short. And they seemed to have reached a draw.

"This castle was built in the fifteenth century in the Yorkshire region of England," she said. "At one time it belonged to Sir Alasdair Thorne. Have you heard of him?"

"No."

"He was an alchemist. Legend has it that he discovered how to turn lead into gold, but was so paranoid someone would steal his secret that he wrote it in code and left it somewhere in the castle. Even after death, he wanted to protect his findings. He's said to still haunt the castle."

"Trying to scare me?"

She chuckled. "Is it working?"

"I've been to hell," he said, thinking of Lindsey. "Nothing scares me anymore."

"Pity. If you hear the stirring of chains in the deep of night, you'll know it's only the old alchemist chasing his dreams of gold." She started up a narrow flight of stone stairs, dimly lit by the kind of tube lighting seen in theaters and airplanes. Up, not down. Where was she leading him?

"My father wanted a castle from Cornwall where our ancestors originated, but had to make do with this one."

They made their way through a series of suites fitted with antiques—mostly sixteenth-century, she informed him. He took her word for it. Even with the tube lighting, everything looked like black lumps in gray soup.

"You can explore these rooms to your heart's content by daylight and revel in my father's good taste. He spent a lifetime collecting the perfect contents for each of these rooms." Her voice was tour-guide crisp.

"Does that mean you're letting me stay?"

"It means I'm still thinking about it. Your Jeep's at a garage in Weatherford. The filling station in Fallen Moon hasn't had a mechanic in over two years. I'm afraid the damage to your vehicle is fairly heavy. If you need to leave, Grace will drive you into town."

"I'm not planning on going anywhere."

"The southwest and southeast towers are sealed—I can't ensure your safety if you choose to explore them. One holds a dry well, the other is an old storehouse that I use for hay in winter. My quarters are in the northeast tower, and you're not welcome there. You should see the stained-glass windows in the chapel on a sunny day. They're quite a sight."

She stopped before a heavy wooden door but didn't open it. "Here we are. You'll find a lamp by the bed, three paces to the left."

"No dungeon tonight?"

Her eyes glittered even in the dark, and he found he liked the fighting look. Whatever Freddy thought, this woman was far from meek.

"Did you know that dungeons were originally used to protect political prisoners from harm?" she asked.

"No." He cocked his head, suddenly wondering who was playing who and for what stakes. "Why am I still here?"

"They provided secure accommodations for these prisoners because they were men and woman of equal status and therefore had to be treated honorably. Chivalry had a very strict code of conduct."

A warning. He was the enemy. She didn't trust him. He could understand that. His stay was probationary because she wanted something from him. What, he couldn't fathom. But that she did gave him an advantage.

She unlocked and opened the door, then handed him the key.

"You're not locking me in?"

"No."

"Aren't you afraid I'll leave before you can get whatever it is you want from me?"

"Good riddance." She waved him into the room. "Sleep well, Mr. Blackwell."

With a swirl of skirt, she sailed away as regally as any queen. Tyler smiled at the starch in her step. Definitely not meek. He found himself pitying the person who wanted to tangle with her.

He patted the wall until he reached the night table, fumbled for the lamp and clicked it on. Faint light bathed the room in a soft glow.

She was letting him stay. He'd crossed the first hurdle. He was feeling pretty good about his accomplishment until he turned around to look at the room. His smile widened. She'd won the first round, after all.

The scenes on the tapestries were so graphic they unnerved even him. A sinister assortment of knights in full armor engaged in bloody battle surrounded him on three sides.

An immense bed of carved walnut took up most of the room. Gold tassels trimmed the crimson bedcover. Triangular panels, edged with gold and painted with cherubs whose angelic faces were wrenched with pain, fringed the canopy. Upon closer inspection, the carvings on the bedposts revealed gargoyles enmeshed in snakes with elaborate skins. A huge medallion topped the headboard. There, a carved chain surrounded the most demonic face he'd ever seen.

Beyond the bed stood a walnut wardrobe with veneer panels. Scythe-armed skeletons guarded the contents.

On a traveling trunk covered with leather and decorated with nailwork, he spied his duffel bag, and beside it the Swiss Army knife, cell phone, razor and Palm Pilot Grace had earlier confiscated. The heavy crushed-velvet drapes were pushed aside and the window stood open, letting in the clean night air. He picked up the cell phone and plugged it into an outlet to recharge.

"You have a warped sense of humor, Miss Carnes."

Tyler peeled back the bedcovers, stripped off his clothes and climbed between the sheets. The physical labor had not only revived his aches and pains but drained his energy.

"The joke's on you, Melissa. I'm so tired the devil himself couldn't scare me tonight."

She was up one, but they'd just begun to dance.

Chapter Five

Melissa was used to being alone, especially in the past few years with Dee spending most of her time with her husband and children, and Cedrick, Grace's son, away at college. Even Grace's days followed a different rhythm than her own.

Coming out of the kitchen on her way to the stables and seeing Tyler sitting in the gazebo in the courtyard stopped Melissa short. The unexpected curl of anticipation at seeing him there made her cling to the shadows.

The blazing sky was fading to purple, wrapping the courtyard in a comforting quilt of darkness. A stiff breeze rustled the oak's leaves and stirred the wind chime that hung from a branch. The sweetheart-quartet tune was familiar, as was the scent of roses perfuming the air. But not the sight of the man sitting in the gazebo, horseshoed by lush red, pink and white blooms. Selma, a creature of comfort, had coiled her feline body into his lap. The contradiction of Tyler's watchful relaxation filled her with curiosity and an odd kind of contentment. And that wayward contentment had her frowning and pursing her lips.

She had just decided to ignore him when the distant popping of gravel on the road penetrated her preoccupied mind. The grating of the portcullis at the gatehouse announced that the visitor was no stranger. Soon a set of headlights cut across the courtyard.

Her sister, Tia, dressed in a body-hugging red sundress, emerged from the equally bright-red sportscar and blew a kiss at the unseen driver behind the tinted glass. "See you later, Drake."

She waved at the departing car, then spun toward the kitchen door, long brown hair flying around her.

"Melissa?" she called at the top of her voice.

Melissa smiled. There was nothing subtle about Tia. That was what Melissa liked about her sister—no pretension. What you saw was what you got. Which only made Tyler's claim of a family conspiracy to dispose of her seem that much more ludicrous. Tia had never cared about Melissa's looks, and the castle was a source of solace for the young girl from whom Sable expected so much.

"Melissa? Where are you?" At the sound of Tia's voice, Selma snapped her tail, hissed and struggled out of Tyler's lap. Tail waving from side to side, the cat disappeared out the postern door. Selma preferred a calmer approach than Tia's whirlwind.

Usually her sister's visits were like a ray of sunshine, but Tyler's presence complicated things. Tia's lack of subtlety often made social situations embarrassing—providing Sable with a constant source of irritation. Tyler would surely take Tia's brashness the wrong way and fuel his conspiracy theory with it. The only way to salvage the situation was to keep them apart.

Melissa moved out of the shadows to intercept her sister, but she was too late. With Selma's hurried departure, Tia swirled in Tyler's direction. "Melissa? Is that you?"

"No," Tyler said. There was much too much interest in that simple word.

"Male? How interesting." Tia's hips swayed provocatively as she sashayed toward him. "Melissa doesn't have any friends, especially male ones." At the gazebo stairs, she held her hands and handbag behind her and swung coquettishly from side to side, making sure he didn't miss any of her tantalizing curves. The once-over she gave him resulted in a glow of approval and had Melissa tightening her fists. "My, my, aren't you a handsome one. Where did she find you?"

"Passed out at her front gate." Tyler leaned back on the gazebo frame, stretching out his long legs before him. His smile seemed amused at her sister's overt sexuality. Melissa ground her teeth and walked faster.

Tia raised an eyebrow in curiosity. "Ah, yes, my dear sister does tend to collect strays." She flopped in a very unladylike manner on the bench beside him.

"Tia Carnes," she said, extending a well-manicured hand to him. He took it and skimmed his lips over her knuckles. Tia blushed and giggled at the Old World gesture. Melissa frowned. "Tia as in the Egyptian princess, not the Spanish aunt."

"Pleased to meet you, Tia."

A mischievous glint gleamed in her big brown eyes. She leaned forward and whispered, "Have you seen her face yet?"

"Tia." Melissa's voice pierced the night. The racing of her heart and the prickle of sweat on her brow had nothing to do with Tyler and everything to do with her fast walk to prevent disaster. She hugged her sister, hoping to draw her away from Tyler. No such luck. Tia held her ground. "How nice of you to visit."

"You're keeping secrets, Mel," Tia teased. She remained seated and squeezed Tyler's knee, staking her claim to the handsome male. Who could blame her? Who could blame him for appreciating the attention of a beautiful female?

"There's no secret," Melissa said more harshly than planned. "He was hurt in a car accident and ended up here."

"I see." Tia arched one eyebrow. "End of conversation."

Of course Tia would notice the unwarranted edge to her voice and pout. Melissa softened her tone. "I saw your car drive away. Are you staying the night?"

"Here? No. Drake has business nearby and couldn't stay. I just wanted to drive out with him. Thought I'd stop by and say hello." She beamed a smile at Tyler and all but batted her lashes. "So glad I did. Mother's at some charity thing in Weatherford. She'll be by in a bit to pick me up."

Oh, great. Tyler would get to meet Sable and feed his conspiracy frenzy. *Stay calm. You can deal with this. Keep it all light and airy.* "I take it this Drake is your latest flame."

Tia blushed like a proper Southern belle. "Oh, Mel, he's so-o-o dreamy. This time it's the real thing. I'm in love!"

This from the girl who only minutes ago had shamelessly flirted with a man she didn't even know. Melissa laughed gently. "Um, that's what you said last time, too."

Forgetting Tyler, Tia swiveled toward Melissa, put both her hands over her heart and sighed. "It's different this time. I've never met anyone like him. He's so…oh, Mel, he's just perfect. Sweet, attentive, strong. Even Mother can't find fault with him—he's from old money. Oil or something."

Melissa slanted Tyler a triumphant glance. *See?* she silently told him. *She has no need for my money.*

Tyler raised an eyebrow as if to say the jury was still out on that conclusion. Tia's mention of money seemed to give him ammunition for rather than quell his off-base theory. She had to get Tia out of the way. "Do you want to go out for a ride?"

"Well, I won't be staying that long." Tia looked down at her lap and smoothed the skirt of her dress. "Since I'm here, anyway, I thought I'd see if you'd do me a little favor."

"Oh?"

"I need a teensy loan to see me through the month."

Tyler's grin was gloating. Great. They were going from bad to worse. "Tia, you just got your allowance."

Tia frowned as if she were a child denied candy. "What do you need it for? You never leave this place."

"That's not the point."

Tia reached for Melissa's right hand and trapped it between both of hers. "I want him, Mel. I want to be sure I get everything right. I saw an image consultant yesterday and she said the best way to build a wardrobe is to buy everything at once to make sure all the pieces match. She's taking me shopping next week. And if you think about it, it's actually going to save us money in the long run." Tia's gaze pleaded. "I'm working really hard at being proper. I want to please Drake."

Package presentation. Melissa hated Sable for teaching Tia that outer beauty and charm were more important than the true beauty Tia's guileless personality gave her. "He should be showering *you* with gifts."

Tia's brow furrowed. "Don't make me beg, Mel." There was a cold edge to her voice and a belligerence to her stance. If this kept up, Tyler would definitely think Tia was out to get her.

"How much?"

Tia's voice brightened. "Only a few thousand, and I'll model every piece for you. You'll see it's money well spent. This image consultant has a really good reputation." Tia dug into her purse and drew out a card. "Check her out if you want. You've heard Sable talk about Jane Harrigan? Flora and Augustus Harrigan's daughter? You know the horse-faced girl with no chest? Well, once Christie was done with her, Jane bowled over the country club at the annual ball. Would you believe she's getting married? To Colm Hempfel of Hempfel's Department Stores, no less."

They chatted for a while about Tia's plans for the summer, Tia's new love, Tia's life. Melissa listened attentively, asking all the right questions, wishing for once that Sable would hurry and fetch her daughter. All the while Tyler's gaze drilled deeper and deeper into her, itching like a rash she couldn't reach. How skewed were his perceptions of her sister? How much damage control would she have to do?

The conversation finally sputtered to an end, and Melissa almost sighed her relief.

"Did Grace do any baking today?" Tia asked.

Melissa smiled. Tia was always one for forbidden fruit. Sweets weren't permitted in Sable's kitchen. Bad for the figure. "Chocolate-chunk pecan brownies."

"Oh, her brownies are simply the best." Tia frowned, then gave a careless shrug. "I'll diet tomorrow." She got up, rolled her hips sexily as she glided down the gazebo steps, then turned and cocked her head. "Would you like to join me, uh… I'm sorry, I don't know your name."

"Tyler. Thanks, but I've already sampled more than my fair share of Grace's brownies today."

"Pity." Tia waggled her fingers at them and left. The sway of her hips told them that she knew Tyler was watching every move and that she was enjoying his attention.

"She's barely twenty-one," Melissa said, crossing her arms. Biting her lower lip, she wished she'd held her tongue.

"She's not my type."

"Looks like you're enjoying the view."

His grin was all male. "Admiring and touching are two different things. I'm bruised, not dead."

No, he was very much alive and much too distracting. Just when she thought she could earn a reprieve and head for the stables, Sable's car rattled over the wooden drawbridge and its headlights flooded the courtyard.

The black Lincoln Town Car stopped by the chapel. Sable exited, long tanned legs first. She moved toward the gazebo with precise grace, eyes darting in all directions as if she expected some unseen monster to pounce on her at any moment. She'd never liked the castle, and once she'd married William Carnes, it had taken her less than two months to convince her husband to live in the city.

"Where's Tia?" she asked. No, "Hello, how are you?" Just, "Where's Tia?" Tyler would make a big deal out of this, not understanding that she and Sable actually respected each other—even if they didn't care for each other personally.

"In the kitchen with Grace."

"Chocolate?"

"Brownies."

Sable shook her head. "She knows sweets ruin her complexion."

"She can restrain herself to one." And would eat it in miniature bites to make it last as long as she could. Watching Tia eat was a treat in itself.

"Let's hope so." Sable waved a hand toward the kitchen. "I'll, uh, go get her and we'll be on our way."

As he had with Tia, Tyler watched Sable's elegant figure disappear into the kitchen. Even at fifty-one Sable could turn men's heads.

"So," Tyler said, circling his keen gaze back to her. Was he comparing? How could she help but fall short? She toyed with the shawl covering her face, arranging it so that no skin showed.

"So what?" Melissa bent and fussed with the roses surrounding the gazebo. Maybe she should go back inside, find the pruning shears and gather a bouquet for her quarters.

"We have motive."

She straightened and cut him with a glare. "We have nothing."

"Your sister's been here for what? Forty-five minutes?"

Melissa shrugged. "So?"

"She didn't once ask how you were doing, how you were feeling, how your life was going. Neither did your stepmother."

"It's not like this is a hotbed of activity. Nothing ever happens here. They know that."

He stood and stretched, reminding her of a predator stirring before a hunt. "Tia's charming, totally self-centered and obsessed with money. Like daughter, like mother?"

That languid flexing of muscle caused a flutter low in her belly. "You're wrong. There's a difference between pampered and predatory. Besides, neither plays chess."

"They don't have to. The warning came from someone else. Someone who knows them."

"Someone who says he wants to protect me?" She

swallowed the bitterness burning her tongue. "Something Freddy Gold made up?"

"Freddy doesn't have the time or the inclination to make something like this up right now."

No, Freddy was always too busy for family. He'd made that abundantly clear over the years. Her finger caught on a thorn, breaking the skin. She folded her finger into her palm, putting pressure on the shard of pain.

Tyler stepped off the gazebo and moved to stand next to her. "I'm sure Tia's allowance is generous, yet she wanted more."

"She had a good reason," Melissa said, shrugging a shoulder and concentrating on the roses. "She's beautiful. Why not show off?"

He reached for a spent blossom and nipped it off with this thumb and forefinger. The petals floated through his fingers. "But you don't have access to the trust fund until next month. Does she realize her teensy loan is coming directly from your pocket?"

"Like she said, what use is it to me?" He was much too sharp. And much too close. She didn't like the tension coiling in her stomach or the way the heat of his body seemed to seek hers. She bent down and sniffed a half-opened rose, letting its perfume obliterate Tyler's clean male scent.

He reached across her, making her step back only to find part of his body blocking her escape. His solid presence made her skittish, but she couldn't move without touching him, and she feared the jolt and recoil that would cause. He plucked the bloom whose fragrance she'd just sampled. With a swift movement of fingers, he stripped the leaves and soft thorns, then he stretched his hand toward her. She turned her face away. He captured her chin through the shawl. Her hands came up and grasped his wrist to push him away. The unexpected softness of the skin there seemed to fuse her fingers in place.

Their gazes met, sharp and heated. Her mouth opened to take in more air and found none. Every line of his face, every shade of color in his dark hair became etched in her mind. He slipped the flower's stem between the material of the shawl and her hair. She closed her eyes and cursed herself for her thundering heart, for not slapping his hand away, for not running. When he bent his head toward her, she shivered.

"Do you realize," he whispered, his deep voice vibrating in her ear, "that the teensy loan you're advancing your sister could be the down payment for your own murder?"

Her eyes snapped open. She shoved his wrist away and scrambled back as if she'd barely escaped the jaws of a shark. A shark, she reminded herself, who was hungry for a story. Hungry enough to conjure up something out of nothing—just as Brent Westfield had done. She snatched the flower from her hair and tossed it into the bushes. "Really, you're being ridiculous. Does Tia look like the type of woman who could even think of such a scheme?"

"She looks like the type of woman who's self-absorbed enough, greedy enough, to dispose of any obstacle between her and the money that fuels her extravagant lifestyle."

"You're wrong."

"She's spoiled and wants more."

"She's young and knows there's more than enough."

"Don't underestimate the lust for money."

Remembering his recent ambition-caused failure, she flung it back at him. "Speaking from experience?"

He acknowledged the hit with a slight nod. "I've cornered a lot of rats in my line of work. And always there was money at the bottom.''

''This time you're wrong.'' He was on the move again, slow and sure like a cat on a mouse, making her arms and legs twitch with the need to run. ''Tia and Sable lack for nothing.''

''Except control.'' His voice was a low growl. ''How do you think they feel having to come to you for every penny they want, having to explain themselves, their needs, their desires?''

Though Melissa wouldn't admit it out loud, she did hold the power in this odd little family. And worse, she liked it. Did Tia and Sable resent her hold over them enough to want her dead? She turned and started toward the stable. ''You're wrong.''

Tyler's fingers clamped her shoulder like talons, holding her in place. ''Then stop fighting me and help me prove it. The sooner we rule them out as suspects, the sooner we can move toward the truth.''

''What if you're wrong?'' She glanced at him over her shoulder. The moon's light accentuated the beauty of his features, sending a wave of disappointment coursing through her. ''What if there is no one out to get me? What if it's all a figment of Freddy's imagination?''

''Then you'll have a good excuse to go chew out Freddy and maybe make up whatever went wrong between you. He's family, too.''

A GOOD GALLOP on Eclipse would help dispel the tension stringing her tighter than a bow ready to release its arrow.

Sensing her mood, Eclipse pawed the wood chips in his stall. Melissa grabbed the rainbow-colored rope from the tack room across the stall and pulled it over the stallion's head and onto his neck. After leading him into the courtyard, she vaulted onto his back effortlessly. By the time she'd made it out the postern door to the open fields where it was safe to gallop, most of her anger had dissipated and she was content to let the rhythm of Eclipse's powerful walk lull the rest of her tension away.

What did Tyler Blackwell know, anyway? He was a washed-up reporter trying to rebuild a shattered career. Tia and Sable and she didn't have the best of relationships, but it worked for them. Freddy was the one who'd abandoned her to the hyenas and forced her to forge these tenuous bonds. What business did he have meddling with situations he understood nothing about? Had he made up the warning with the chess piece? What could the mason who'd started to repair the towers have to do with anything?

No one else even knew her. Her business clients dealt with Deanna. Grace took care of managing the household. The people of Fallen Moon didn't exactly welcome her, but they were happy enough to leave her alone, if only to ensure she paid her town-supporting tax bill on time.

Who would know her well enough to send Freddy the article and chess piece? Dee and Grace both would have come to her with their suspicions of harm before going to Freddy—especially if Sable or Tia were involved.

No one had any reason to scare her, except it seemed, the uncle who'd sent a reporter, of all people, to "protect" her and thereby buy his way back into her life. He was too late for that—by twenty years. She'd needed him then. She didn't need him now.

She didn't need anyone.

Eclipse's choppy walk echoed the turmoil of her thoughts. She forced herself to smooth them out. This was her favorite part of the day, and she wasn't going to let Tyler Blackwell or Freddy Gold ruin it.

A strip of woods surrounded her land. She'd purposefully let the saw briars and thorn bushes grow wild, not allowing any room between the towering oaks and diminutive mesquites for curious onlookers to trespass. If the macabre shadows the whole created weren't enough to keep people out, then the threat of copperhead snakes, black widow spiders and scorpions that bred in the tangled mess usually were. The only way from here to the neighbor's fields beyond was through a maze only she knew existed. No one dared cross her front gate except the local teenagers, and they were harmless.

Melissa loved the forbidding landscape she'd created. Creepy from the outside, paradise on the inside. Flat open land for riding, a pecan grove to the south of the castle, a peach orchard to the west and a pond and scattered oaks in the pastures for the horses made up her world—her very own little Camelot inside Hansel and Gretel's haunted forest.

At the edge of the woods, she stopped Eclipse, stroked his silken neck and found herself scanning the trees for shadows that didn't belong. Damn Tyler Blackwell. She didn't want to believe him. Sable and Tia would *not* plot against her. She was sure of that. They'd talked about the trust fund. They'd talked about her intentions. They knew she planned to share.

What about Freddy? Did he have anything to gain by scaring her? According to her mother's wishes, Freddy would inherit the Gold part of the estate she'd left Melissa should Melissa die before he did. She'd invested all of that into the horses. But that was nothing compared to what Freddy had earned on his own. On the surface he seemed to lack for nothing.

What about Tyler? Could he have started this whole warning scare to revive his dead career? A prize-winning reporter known to keep digging until he got what he wanted made Tyler Blackwell a risky adversary or a helpful ally. Which was he? He hadn't wanted to dig for a long time, and maybe his skills had dulled during the past year. Was that the reason Freddy had sent him? To ensure his failure? If the warning was true, if someone did want to harm her, was Tyler a help or a liability?

The play of light and shadow across the planes of his face fascinated her. The shape and flex of muscles and tendons in his arms and hands intrigued her. His brown eyes flecked with gold spoke volumes—far more than he knew—and captivated her. In them she'd seen intelligence, depth and raw pain. But also determination. Out in the courtyard, in the soft light of the moon, her fingers had itched to sketch him as feverishly as they wanted to hit him. She didn't like the confusion he'd brought in his wake.

Melissa urged Eclipse into a trot and into the briar maze.

Her primal awareness of Tyler irritated her. Beguiled her. Was it simply because he was male? No, Brent West-field, the conniving reporter who'd betrayed her faith, had stirred no such curiosity in her. She shook her head. Another stupid fantasy, courtesy of Dee's romantic movies. She'd have to insist on a mindless action adventure for next week.

Eclipse snorted his displeasure at the slow pace. Melissa waited until they had stepped out of the maze before she urged him into a canter. They flew over the top of a hill onto a wide meadow. In the middle of the field stood an unexpected knot of people. Melissa brought Eclipse to a halt and backed into the shadows of the surrounding trees.

She rubbed Eclipse's neck as she took in the scene. A

man, a woman, three children of various sizes, a telescope. The Andersons and their brood. Their discussion was lively and they hadn't noticed her.

The man pointed toward a constellation. "See those five stars that look like a *W?* That's Cassiopeia."

"Wow!" a boy exclaimed. "I see them. I see them."

"My turn, my turn!" A girl jumped up and down. "I wanna see!"

The woman distracted the child by pointing up. "See those three stars in a row? That's Orion's belt."

When the baby fussed in his mother's arms. She cooed at him, offering a breast.

Melissa's heart contracted, and familiar longing melted through her as sweet and sticky as honey. A baby. A little boy, a little girl, of her own. Bonds of love, not obligation.

Another fantasy best forgotten.

She signaled a turn on the haunches, then hugged the edge of the woods back to the mouth of the maze.

The sound of a branch cracking had Eclipse pricking his ears forward. Melissa halted. In spite of the night's warmth, a cold shiver snaked down her spine.

Her gaze scoured the shadows. What was she looking for? A man with a gun? A telltale bead of red like in the movies? She could see nothing in the dark. No slithering shadow. No laser sight aimed at her heart. Not even the glowing yellow eyes of a wild animal.

Just ordinary night noises. And she'd let Tyler's theory mutate them into murder.

She set Eclipse into a walk. She'd been afraid Tyler's proposed article would eat away another part of her soul. What he'd done was twice as ingenious. Already, with just a few words, he'd shrunk her small world by half. What was next?

She couldn't let him do that. Her life was too narrow

already. If she let him steal any more of it, then what would she have left? She plowed back into the maze toward home and emerged in the pecan grove.

The play of moonlight through the pecan leaves delighted her. She nudged Eclipse into a trot and started chasing the light patterns. The easy grace of Eclipse's movements, the majesty of his bearing, the power flowing through his sinewy muscles, slowly filled her body and calmed her mind until a soft melody took over and made her one with her horse.

Dancing among the light and shadows, fear and danger, time and place, dissolved.

TYLER HOBBLED out the small wooden door near the rose garden as fast as his still-aching ribs would allow. What was she thinking of, traipsing out in the open like that? How could she have gone and made herself a perfect target, knowing there was someone out there who wanted to harm her?

Was she just stubborn or plain stupid? That was what happened when someone received no socialization. When he caught up with Melissa Carnes, he was going to teach her a thing or two about manners.

He thought he'd scared her into the relative safety of the stables. His tactical error had been giving her space to absorb the seriousness of her situation. Instead of considering his own theory of relativity, as he'd hoped, she'd escaped to the very last place she needed to go—riding outside the castle walls.

He wanted to strangle her, and he didn't understand why he should care so much about her welfare when she obviously didn't.

As he climbed over the white board fence to take a shortcut across the pasture, he shook his head. Maybe he'd been out of the game too long. Maybe the rules had changed.

No, he decided as a broodmare ambled between him and her foal, it was the situation that warranted a different approach. Melissa wasn't a criminal who needed rope to hang herself. She needed boundaries to keep her safe.

And whether she liked it or not, her safekeeping was his responsibility. Whether Freddy's hunch proved right or wrong had no bearing on taking precautions.

Tyler scanned the woods for the spot where he'd seen her disappear, but could find no opening in the snarl of briars and trees. With the moon nearly full she should have been easy to follow. Where had she gone? Dressed all in black and riding a black horse, he could only hope she would make a difficult target for anyone who had harm in mind.

Not having her in sight had him stalking the length of the woods with teeth gritted. Night sounds surrounded him—cicadas, some creature foraging, the occasional snort of a broodmare out at pasture. A bat skimmed the treetops and screeched, making him silently swear. From somewhere on the other side of the dark tangle came the soft footfalls of a horse.

When he found her, she was going to get an earful. For one thing, she wasn't as delicate as Freddy thought her. He had a feeling people tended to pussyfoot around her because of her condition. But as far as he was concerned, this was political correctness carried too far. Someone had to tell it like it was. This might be her little world, but for now *he* had to take charge. She'd just have to live with that fact until Freddy discounted the warning or they found out who had something to gain by disposing of her.

The snap of a dry branch stilled him on the spot. Its echo crazed the night like aberrant thunder. The scent of something nasty wafted to him on the breeze, revving his adrenaline. He had to find Melissa and fast.

Something moved in the gloom. Just a shadow, he told himself as he watched the purple-black blur on the pitch-black skeleton of briars and branches. Then it moved again. Coyote? No, too large. Deer? Surreptitious footsteps crackled dry brush. Too heavy to belong to night creatures. Too light and creeping to belong to someone with a right to be there. The sense of danger had his scalp crawling, his senses heightening. Tensing against the coming confrontation, he took a few steps toward the shadow moving away from him in the woods.

Behind him Melissa exploded out of the woods.

He whirled, ready to shout to her when something stopped him.

The wind became the only sound of the night. It caught the edge of her shawl, uncovering her head. Another invisible tug sent the silk floating out behind her, forgotten. Moonlight gleamed blue ribbons on her dark hair. Lithe figure astride the powerful horse, she made the stallion dance without appearing to ask for anything. The horse wore no saddle, no bridle. Only a rainbow rope she wasn't even holding hung around the horse's neck.

Like a whisper, they wove in and out of shadows. From the horse's footfalls came music. Woman and horse moved in perfect unison. Moonbeams flitted on hair and mane, caressed womanly curves and equine haunches, rippled through a tail held proudly. Every movement was fluid, graceful. Half pass. Pirouette. Passage. Serpentine.

Magic.

His muscles relaxed. His pulse slowed. The cloak of threat disappeared. He'd been chasing crooks and exposing lies for so long he'd forgotten the world could be a beautiful place.

He'd never seen anything so magnificent.

The sight of the liquid waltz sliced something sharp right through his gut, stealing his breath. Something deep and primal. Something pure. It sent a surge of emotions rushing through him, and he wasn't sure what to do with them. So he watched and lost himself in the magic.

The reason for the beauty of the dance soon struck him. The horse wasn't an obedient creature bending to his mistress's request. He was a partner, enjoying the dance as much as she. Could he hear the music of his footfalls? Did it sing in his soul? It must, for even from this far a certain joy resonated from both beast and woman. The witch had him completely under her spell.

Then a report exploded, breaking the trance that held him in place. Before he could think, he was running.

But just like what happened with Lindsey, he was too far away to reach Melissa in time.

Chapter Six

Heart pounding, Melissa reacted instinctively to the sharp crack that rent the night. Stop, drop and roll. The drilled-in command had nothing to do with guns, but it was the first thing that sprang to her mind. She was halfway down Eclipse's back to the ground when someone tackled her the rest of the way, knocking the wind right out of her. Staying close to her, Eclipse pranced nervously. The attacker's viselike grip tightened threads of panic that rippled through her in their adrenaline cocktail.

Wheezing in fast, sharp breaths, imagining Tyler's cold-blooded assassin, she fought off the weight pinning her to the ground. As she bucked and kicked, the edge of her boot connected with a hard shin, drawing a curse out of the madman. Her elbows connected with ribs, making him hiss. Her fist reached for his hair and pulled.

"Stop moving," he growled.

Tyler, not an assassin.

She let go, deflated. From her squashed position, she heard a second report, then a series of choked sputters that identified the perpetrator of the shot as a bad muffler. The popping of gravel on the dirt road on the other side of the woods sounded like a truck pulling a horse trailer. Just the Quarter Horse ranch down the road.

As relief coursed through her, she forgot all about the imaginary assassin and became horrifyingly aware of her exposed face. Scouting for her fallen shawl, she felt her pulse start to gallop once more. Hatred of her accident was hot and fluid and all encompassing. The years no longer divorced her from the pain. She felt it sharp and hot, throbbing through every line of scar on her face, arm and leg. The child's cries echoed in her mind, stuck in her throat. All he'd see was the witch. Clawing at the ground for traction, she tried to squirm out of Tyler's hold, to go anywhere but here, but his arms only tightened around her.

"What do you think you're doing?" She fought his hold.

"Don't move."

"Let go of me, you jerk." If he hadn't woven all those conspiracy theories for her, she would have known the difference between a backfire and a gunshot and not fallen to the ground like a scared eight-year-old. "This is all your fault."

"I told you riding out here wasn't a good idea."

"I was perfectly safe until you tackled me."

"It could have been a gunshot."

"It was a muffler. Get off me." She pushed against him, felt him tense.

"Stop. Moving."

Something about the strained tone of his voice stilled her. "What's wrong?"

"Ribs," he choked out.

Great! He'd gone and hurt himself playing hero.

He sucked in a breath and rolled off her, then lay on the ground beside her. She didn't know if she should slap him for scaring her or send for help. Except slapping him would require facing him, and she couldn't do that. Not yet. "Serves you right. What were you thinking?"

"That I'd take a bullet for you and save your sorry hide. Though why, I don't know."

"My hero." She let sarcasm drip from her voice as she scrambled to her feet. Take a bullet for her? He hadn't really thought that, had he? She went to Eclipse and stroked him to calm him down, to calm herself. Draping her hair over the left side of her face, she risked a glance at Tyler.

He was whiter than the moon under his tan and the frown pleating his forehead looked painful. She wanted more than anything to find her shawl, cover her face and hide in the shadows, but the torment twisting his face had her kneeling beside him, keeping her good side toward him. She wasn't a witch. He had to learn that before he could see past the ravages of fire on her skin. She reached toward him, then drew back, not knowing what she should do. "Did you break anything?"

"I don't think so."

"Can you get up?"

He closed his eyes and swallowed. "Give me a minute."

"I'll get someone to help you." She sprang up, but he grabbed her wrist and held her in place.

"No, I'm fine."

She wrenched her wrist free. "You're in pain."

"It'll pass."

"More like 'pass out' from the looks of you."

He rolled to one side and, using his elbow, pushed himself to a sitting position. "You need to get back inside."

"It was just a car backfiring."

"I heard someone in the woods."

"That was just me."

He shook his head. "Someone on foot."

She remembered the crack of a branch, the sense of evil that had crawled down her spine. Had someone really been there? "Just an animal."

"No."

Not wanting to dwell on the possibility, she focused instead on the sweat beading his forehead. She didn't like the glassiness of his eyes, either. She needed Grace or Deanna. They would know what to do. What if he *did* pass out? "There's no way you can walk."

"You go. I'll follow."

He was carrying this macho stuff too far. "Oh, that'll look real good, especially if you pass out and get bitten by a snake. The town would have a field day if you died in my pecan grove." She slid an arm around his waist to support him. There was no way she could carry all that lean hardness back to the castle. "Up you go."

He bared his teeth in a painful wince. She cringed with him. "Are you okay?"

He nodded.

"Eclipse feels like an overstuffed chair. If you can get on him, I'll lead you back."

"I'll w—"

"There's a time for heroics. This isn't it." Hair still hiding her face, she turned and faced him, letting him hang on to her shoulders. Leaning forward, she cupped her hands for him to use as a stirrup. "Up you go."

One of his hands gripped Eclipse's mane. He hissed in a breath as he raised his foot to her interlocked hands. "Ready?"

"Ready."

She boosted him up, and he landed heavily on the horse's back. "Okay?"

He nodded, bracing his left side with an arm. In silence

she led Eclipse slowly across the pecan grove, the pasture and into the courtyard. Tyler was in pain because of her. Maybe there was someone out to hurt her. Maybe there wasn't. But that didn't alter the fact that even with bruised ribs, he'd still thrown his body over hers to protect her. He'd been willing to take a bullet for her.

The heat of shame filled her. If this was simply another way to gain her sympathy, it was working. Big-time. And the last thing she wanted to do was feel anything for a reporter.

Back in the courtyard, she kept her head bent as she helped him slide off Eclipse's back. Once he was steady on his feet, she slipped to Eclipse's off side and screened the marred half of her face with the horse's dark head.

''You need a doctor.''

Cradling his ribs, he shook his head. ''No doctor. I'm not leaving.''

''Go to an emergency room, then, and have your ribs X-rayed.''

''Nothing they can do for it, anyway.''

He reached for the snarl of hair clouding her face. Heart thundering against her ribs, she grasped his wrist to push it away. His finger strained against her hold and traced the outline of her face, pushing the hair aside.

Tears welled in her eyes, tightened her chest. Rasping breath scratched her throat. Anger rumbled through her limbs, creating explosive tension. ''You want to see?'' she asked between clenched teeth, tilting up her chin, breathing hard. ''Then take a good look.''

She turned and let the moonlight illuminate the red ridges and dark splotches that sculpted her skin into a grotesque mask fit for a horror movie.

He was looking at her strangely—not with revulsion, as she'd expected, but almost as if what he saw fascinated him. She wanted to escape, to fly across the courtyard to the safety of her quarters, but the intensity of his gaze transfixed her. She would not cry. She'd already cried too many tears for her sorry state.

Slanting forward, he gently touched his lips to hers over the horse's head, lingered there for a moment, then leaned back.

The gentleness of the whisper-touch took her breath away, had her blood coursing madly through her veins, heat spreading like dreaded fire from head to toe. She touched two fingers to her lips, wanting to hold the sensation in until she could examine it.

"What was that for?" The bite to her tone came from confusion. What did he want from her? One minute he was badgering her; the next he was playing hero. Now he was acting as if her scars didn't matter. She didn't like the gnawing confusion, the spin of yearning. Not one bit.

"The way you ride," he said, a slight hitch cracking his voice, "I've never seen anything like it."

She sucked in a quick breath when she realized with a start that, out there in the moonlight, he'd caught her bared soul when she'd let Eclipse dance through the pecan trees.

Most people who were subjected to the sight of her face treated her like a monster or pretended too hard not to see the obvious, silently counting the seconds until they could leave. They never got past the surface appearance. But in Tyler's eyes she could see indifference to the scarred skin. It was as if he truly didn't see the jagged landscape of her face and, instead, saw something else. With a fist she kneaded the bruise on her heart. *He's a reporter. It's part of the game.*

Swallowing hard, she turned away. She'd known him for only a few days, and yet it seemed much longer. She wanted him to leave. She needed him to stay. "You need a doctor."

"No, I'm fine. I just need some ibuprofen."

"Let's go," she said, pivoting. Why were her hands shaking? Why was her stomach pitching? Why couldn't she make sense of Tyler Blackwell?

He'd been willing to take a bullet for her. No one had ever done that. Where was the harm in helping him? Wouldn't that simply disprove his conspiracy theory? Why was she fighting this so hard? She started to lead Eclipse toward the stables. "I'll get some ice and ibuprofen for your ribs, then we can start."

"Start what?"

In chess it was always better to play an offensive game than a defensive one. She'd let her fears make her forget that simplest of strategies. Tyler wasn't her soul mate— that was fantasy talking. But he was here because he was driven to find the right order of things. That was what had made him good at his job and also what had broken him. And now he needed to find his feet again. So did she. "Looking for the truth."

SHE WAS A CREATURE of habit and played while others slept. With the Andersons stargazing, the situation was even better than planned. No need to play more than a pawn with this move. The true measure of power, he was learning, was letting others do as much of the dirty work for you as possible.

The whole town was already in a flap about the witch. Just today at the Parker Peach, he'd heard the old preacher plant the seed of fear that, with just the right chemistry, could lead to an old-fashioned witch hunt. His errand tonight would give the rumors a nudge and send protective parents in a tizzy.

Now all he had to do was convince Tyler Blackwell to stick around for a while. He needed someone who would understand betrayal to record the rise of the righteous and the fall of the corrupt. According to his boss, Blackwell made the perfect candidate. Someone had cheated him out of his due, too.

Ray stopped the truck just out of sight of the castle and took out his high-powered binoculars. One clue. Would Blackwell understand it? Ray slipped on latex gloves, then took the bag from the seat beside him.

"WHERE DO WE START?" she asked him.

The ibuprofen was finally kicking in and the ice pack over his ribs had just about numbed his side. Tyler sat at an old pine board table in the castle kitchen that had once been a scullery. A cup of coffee steamed before him. Melissa sat across from him, shawl once again in place, nursing her own cup of coffee. She'd dimmed the lights so that the table, chairs and cabinets glowed a mellow warmth, and the stone walls and empty hearth recessed in shadows. A plate of brownies staked the boundary between them. Her stiff body, her green eyes peeking over the edge of her shawl, both declared Keep Out louder than any billboard.

He hadn't meant to kiss her. Hadn't expected that simplest of contact to stir something inside him so deeply. The distress in her eyes, the fear and anguish so bright and raw, had unfurled a wave of sympathy in him. He'd needed to let her know he wouldn't hurt her and had sensed on a gut level that words would mean nothing.

After watching the magic she'd wrought in the moonlight, he could never think of her as ugly. She wouldn't believe that, either. He knew, too, that his dead heart had nothing to offer someone with such a beautiful soul and regretted adding to her suffering; regretted, too, the chink the connection had caused in his own protective armor. Passion distorted. He'd learned that the hard way. And to get through this assignment, he had to concentrate on facts to keep his vision clear.

"First," he said, wincing as an ice cube shifted in the makeshift pack he held over his ribs, "we make a list."

She retrieved a pad of paper and a pen from a desk tucked in an alcove and returned to the table. "A list of what?"

"Let's start with what we know."

"Okay." She poised the pen over the pad. "What do we know?"

"We know that Freddy received a warning about your welfare." He waggled a finger at the pad, wishing he could pace. Action made thinking easier. "Write down 'Freddy Gold.' Under that put 'newspaper article about mason and chess piece.'"

"Or made up a warning," she mumbled as she wrote.

Even upside down, her script was bold and artistic. He frowned at her right hand, at the long fingers, the short nails. A working hand. He noted the hint of green paint at the edge of the nail of her index finger and wondered at the subject of her current painting. His frown deepened and he forced his attention back to the facts. "What reason would he have to lie?"

She shrugged. "You know him. You tell me."

"His wife is going through a difficult pregnancy. Trust me, he doesn't have the time or the energy to make up a false story."

She quickly doused the hint of surprise. "Not even to give a down-and-out-reporter friend another chance to repair his career?"

A flicker of pain zagged through her eyes. He realized

then that both she and Freddy were burdened by their past and neither quite knew how to change the situation. They needed each other, and maybe this assignment would end with a reconciliation, if nothing else. "He cares about you. And the fact you won't talk to him hurts him."

She shook her head and waved away his comment. "It's too late."

"It's never too late." Something he needed to remember himself. And for that second chance he needed to concentrate on facts.

He gestured toward the pad of paper. "Turn to another page. Write down 'Melissa Carnes.' Under that write 'trust fund.' Are there restrictions to the trust fund?"

"Control of the fund reverts to me on my thirtieth birthday. When Tia marries, there's a sum set aside for her to put toward a home of her own. The castle belongs to me and the mansion belongs to Sable."

"Okay, write Tia's name on another page and the amount she'll get." He consulted the chart in his head and went on to the next player. "What's Sable's story?"

"What do you mean?"

"How come your father didn't leave any of his fortune to his wife?"

Melissa sneered. "My father married Sable knowing that money was her first love. He was also ashamed of his horror at my face."

"You don't need the veil, you know," Tyler said, angry with himself for wanting her comfortable enough around him to forget to wear her shield against the world.

A quick hitch of breath betrayed her anxiety. She bent over the paper and her voice hardened. "He wanted to be sure I'd be taken care of. He also knew I had a good head on my shoulders and wouldn't squander all he'd worked so hard to earn."

"Like father, like daughter."

"No." She looked up, and the blazing green of her eyes ignited a degree of frustration he couldn't explain. "I don't care about business, and I don't care if I ever add another dollar to his fortune."

"How did he earn his fortune?" *Facts, Blackwell. Stick to the facts.*

She shot him an annoyed glance. "I thought you did your homework."

"I want to hear your take on it."

She sighed heavily as if the task was a chore, but he sensed she wanted to examine every angle, too.

"He started out as an engineer," she said. "A school project earned him his first job. Then he discovered he was better at nurturing the ideas of others into products than coming up with his own projects. So that's what he did. He provided the space and the leadership to nurture ideas and bring them to market—everything from consumer products to medical instruments to industrial machinery. The rest, as they say, is history. Carnes Design became synonymous with solving problems."

And William Carnes's name was written all over local and business history. It was too bad he couldn't have used his legendary people skills with his own daughter.

"Who has access to the castle?" Tyler asked.

She stared at him accusingly for a moment, then bent again toward the pad of paper. "Sable, Tia, Grace, Cedrick and Deanna. And I trust all of them."

"Cedrick?"

"Grace's son. He's away at college right now."

"Are you sure?"

She aimed her pen at him. "Don't even go there. Cedrick was practically raised here. He's a hard worker and wouldn't even think of harming anyone, let alone me.

Besides, I'm paying for his education. Why would he want to hurt me before it's all paid for?'' As Tyler opened his mouth, she put a hand up to stop him. ''No, it's not charity. He earned it with years of shoveling manure.''

Her gaze was as fierce as a tigress's protecting a cub. ''What's he studying?''

''Veterinary medicine at Texas A & M in College Station.'' Genuine pride beamed in her voice.

Passion blurred facts. Why was he having such a hard time remembering that? This time he couldn't make that mistake. ''Write him down, anyway.''

Her gaze was sharp and lethal, but she nevertheless wrote down Cedrick's name.

''Tell me about Grace.''

She hesitated, stuttering the end of the pen against the table. ''Leave Grace out of this.''

He shrugged. ''I can always do a background search. It'll save us time if you just answer my questions.''

''Grace is the most loyal person I know.''

''I'm not questioning her loyalty. I just want to know how she fits in the puzzle.''

''She fits like a stone in the wall. She's as much part of Thornwylde as I am.''

The ice pack—now more water than ice—gurgled when he leaned forward. ''What brought her here?''

She sighed testily. ''She killed her husband.''

He raised an eyebrow. Grace's height and bulk were impressive, and he had no problem believing she could easily squash most men who got in her way. But since he'd arrived, he hadn't seen anything but gentleness from her—even when her employer had ordered her to feed a prisoner gruel.

''Her husband was a minister who preached peace to his congregation and wreaked chaos in his home. Grace took his abuse until he turned his hand to their son. Cedrick still limps from the horrible shattering of his leg that day. And Grace was in the hospital for months recovering from the beating he gave her before he finally had the decency to die. She spent seven years in jail for her crime. When she got out, no one would hire her.''

"So you did."

Her forehead knitted as she underlined Grace's name. "I got the better end of the bargain."

The witch and the outcast. That bred loyalty. Had Grace sent Freddy the warning, knowing he would help, while seeking to preserve her status in the household? He made a mental note to speak with Grace in the morning. "What about the mason from the newspaper article?"

"Grace hired him and supervised him. I don't deal with outside workers." She looked up at him, slanting him a cutting glare. "And they'd rather have it that way."

"What happened?"

"I'm not sure. He was repairing the southwest tower and all seemed to go well. Then one morning he fell off the scaffolding and broke his leg. The EMTs had a hard time calming him down. He kept mumbling something about the devil being inside the castle walls and saying the place was cursed. He refused to come back, and Grace hasn't found anyone willing to finish the job."

Finally a hint of something concrete. "Was there anything in the wall that would warrant that kind of reaction?"

She shook her head. "Not that I know of. All I could see were signs of aging. Mold."

"I'll check it out in the morning."

She snorted. "Make sure you call the paramedics before you do, so they're there to catch you."

He almost smiled at her show of spirit. "I'll take that

under advisement." As he took the pad from her, their fingers grazed. The tiniest spark flashed from knuckle to knuckle, making him frown at the speed it traveled from finger to gut. Flipping through the pages, he cleared his throat. "Where were we? Right, Deanna."

"You're determined to discredit everyone who's close to me, aren't you?" Temper warbled through her voice as she snagged the pad of paper out of his hand.

Sensing the checked slap, he grudgingly admired her restraint. He was, after all, forcing her to look with new eyes at the few people she depended on for her survival. The results were bound to give a picture she might not like. "Facts are cold, Melissa. They have no emotions. I'm just trying to put them down on paper so we can look at them objectively."

"It feels as if you're trying to tear my world apart."

She looked so forlorn that he wanted to hold her in his arms and reassure her. Objectivity, he reminded himself. That was the only way to get through this without failing. He rose, dropping the melted ice pack on the table.

"Do you need more?" she asked, pointing at the bag.

"No." He shuffled to the coffeemaker and refilled his cup. "Who do you know who plays chess?"

"I do. Dee's father."

Coffee splashed on the counter. "J.R. Randall?"

She nodded.

Here's where the interview could get tricky. "He comes here?"

"No, we play through e-mail."

"What's your relationship with him?" Ignoring the mule kick of pain with each step, he walked to stand beside her and poured coffee into her cup, watching for signs of deceit.

"He's like a father to me. When Dee told him about

my interest in art, he did everything he could to encourage me.'' Unlike her own family, who it seemed hadn't even noticed. ''He bought some of my pieces and displayed them in his offices. He arranged for my first showing.''

''And for the charity auction last year.'' If she was lying, she was doing a damned good job of it.

She dismissed his comment with a shrug. ''He's a very civic-minded person. He sponsors a lot of charities in the area.''

''What do you know about his business?'' Tyler returned the pot to the coffeemaker. Was Randall using her without her knowledge?

''Nothing.''

Drinking from his mug, he leaned his backside against the counter. ''Do you own stock in his company?''

''I own a lot of stock in a lot of companies.''

''Including his?''

She swiveled in her chair to meet his gaze head-on. ''Including his. What difference does it make? Randall Industries is a good bet. Ask any stock analyst.''

He didn't answer, but added a mental note to go over the facts he'd gathered on Randall Industries last summer and see if he could connect with some of his old sources.

''Who else in my entourage do you want to disparage? The horses, perhaps?''

Her tone was light, with a touch of royal uppitiness, but he sensed the deeper dread that he would indeed tear her world apart with his questions. ''Let's call it a night. I need to go to Fort Worth tomorrow. Check on some sources.''

She crushed the pen in her fist. ''Can't you do that from here?''

''Even with all of today's technology, some things need face-to-face.'' She slept during the day and would be safe enough until he returned. He'd put Grace on alert just in case. "You'll let me back in?"

"You started this, not me."

Temper again. Here was a woman used to getting her way in spite of the restrictions her lifestyle entailed. He had to hammer back the thought of taking her along, opening the world for her. He wasn't a knight—just a guy stumbling back to life. And as she'd said, she was no weak princess imprisoned in a tower. If she wanted the world, it was right there for her to take.

"And I'll see it through to the end, Melissa. I promised Freddy, and now I'm promising you."

She gave a careless shrug, but it didn't fool him. She had too much to lose.

"When are you leaving?"

"First thing in the morning. I'll be back before dark." He added lightly, "Need anything while I'm in town?"

Melancholy dulled the green of her eyes as she rose, handed him the pad of paper and stowed the pen in its proper drawer in the desk. "Just answers."

He wanted to hold her again, to reassure her that he was tearing apart her world in order to put it back together on a stronger foundation. He shook his head and drained his coffee into the sink. *Don't go there, Blackwell. Keep to the facts. Facts don't get you in trouble.*

But as he braced his arm against his aching rib to make his way back to his nightmare room, he knew he was already in too deep.

Chapter Seven

The nights in late May were still cool. These perfect evenings wouldn't last much longer, reflected Melissa as she threaded her way silently up the tower stairs that led to her quarters. The closer she got to her destination, the slower her pace became. Uncertainty oscillated through her, causing her to stop and start.

This was all Tyler's fault, she thought as she touched her lips once more.

Fire. Tyler's kiss had been like fire. Melissa hated fire. Fire had taken her mother from her. Fire had robbed her of a normal life. Fire was dangerous. And now it flowed through her veins, hot and hungry. And worse, even knowing that going toward that flame would leave her singed, she wanted more.

Since her stay at the burn hospital, drawing had been her therapy. One of the nurses had suggested the activity to keep her left hand flexible while the skin grafts healed. But never, not once, since that night had she ever drawn people. Animals, yes, monsters, but never people. Now because of him, she couldn't seem to stop. Every time she picked up a pencil, it insisted on drawing a likeness of Tyler Blackwell.

In her studio she stood before the slanted board propped

on a large white table and snapped on the light above it. The lush shades of green in the landscape showed her love of nature. When she painted, she tried to look past the obvious and create something new and unique. Over the years, what had started as physical therapy had also grown into psychological therapy. In the transparent and painstakingly applied layers of colors, in the details of branches and leaves, of grasses and flowers, of rocks and earth, she'd learned to camouflage her monsters. Giving them life in her work seemed to trap their power to haunt her.

But in the past few days, the vision that had driven her to start this piece had seemed to mutate. In the wake of the storm covering two-thirds of the panel, a rainbow emerged, and eyes—human eyes—were peering back at her. Human features were taking shape with each stroke of her paintbrush. An ear here. A mouth there. A nose.

Cups filled with brushes and pencils, tubes of paint and an array of sketches were strewn over the desk, awaiting attention. Melissa found she couldn't pick up any of them. Her body reverberated with nervous energy. Her fingers itched to draw. But she didn't want to apply another layer of paint. She didn't want to see whose face would take shape in the splash of rainbow.

When the phone rang, she let out a grateful sigh. Before she could even say hello, Dee's anxious voice came on.

"Are you all right?"

"Why wouldn't I be?"

"Something's going on and I don't like it."

Had Dee somehow sensed the confusion Tyler had ignited in her? Melissa wrapped an arm around her waist and strode to the window. "I don't know what you're talking about."

"The gossip."

Melissa's shoulders relaxed. "When did you start caring about gossip?"

"I don't, but what's going around right now is vicious, Melissa. Someone seems to be deliberately stirring things up."

Melissa shrugged, but couldn't seem to get the sound of a cracking branch out of her mind. Tyler said he'd heard footsteps in the woods. She still found it hard to believe that anyone would want to hurt her. Sable? Just for money? She shook her head. "It's the time of the year when kids—"

"No, there's talk of hexes and devil worship. They say you spilled a cauldron filled with foul-smelling stuff on the courthouse steps. They say you stopped the clock in the tower—something that hasn't been done for a hundred years. I'm worried, Mel. People are starting to talk about protecting their children and doing what's best for the town. If it was just one or two people, I could shrug it off. But a mob? People who are afraid do stupid things. They let the crowd sweep them along. I don't want you out riding by yourself."

She gave a dry laugh. "You want me to take Tyler along?"

Melissa could hear the hard beat of her heart in the interminable pause.

"I thought we agreed he should leave," Dee said in a starched voice.

Had she hoped for Dee's blessing? "He's helping me."

"Helping you? With what? Melissa, it's just a smokescreen. For heaven's sake, I thought you were smarter than that. You've been burned before—"

"And I have the scars to prove it." She ran a hand over the left side of her face.

"I'm not kidding, Melissa. Whatever Tyler Blackwell

says, he's not your friend. And someone could easily hurt you out there and no one would know until it's too late. I want you to be careful.''

''I'm always careful.'' Careful not to be seen. Careful not to be hurt. Careful not to be touched.

Maybe too careful.

What had she gained by shutting out the world? Certainly not peace.

''That's not good enough,'' Dee said.

''What? You want me to stay locked in my tower like some Rapunzel?'' She was pacing now, a tight nervous line, twitching like a fish on a hook with every slap of her boots on the stone floor. ''Don't you think I've done that for long enough? Don't you think I deserve the truth?''

''I think you deserve to be safe. Stay in, just until the gossip dies down and people regain their sanity. I want you to hire security guards to patrol the grounds.''

''No, Dee. I can't. I'm not going to let anyone take away what I have left.''

''I'm not talking forever. Just for now. I don't want to see you hurt.''

''Join the club.'' She stopped pacing and took a long breath.

I thought I'd take a bullet for you.

I promised Freddy, and now I'm promising you.

Melissa still found it difficult to wrap her mind around such statements. He was a stranger to her. She was a stranger to him.

But loss bound them. He needed to find answers as much as she needed to open doors. Could Dee understand? No, Dee with her sweet family and her freedom wouldn't comprehend such a nebulous bond or how it could tie two strangers together. There was no point discussing it.

"Is Sam okay with you going to the show next weekend?" Melissa asked.

"He's fine with it. We were going to make the trip a family affair and take the kids along."

A family affair. Melissa scratched at the itch of jealousy just under her skin. "When are you planning on leaving?"

"I don't think I should go."

"Eclipse needs the points."

"He can get them at the next show."

How could she make Dee understand that while her world was falling apart, she needed to hang on to the few unchangeables in her life? Horses—Dee had brought them into her life as ballast when Melissa was cast adrift in self-pity. She needed that one remaining piece of stability. "No, it's set. He deserves the chance to shine. I'll expect you tomorrow to ride him and get ready."

"Tomorrow is Emmy's preschool graduation."

Four-year old Emmeline with her blond curls and her pixie grin. Melissa smiled at the image of the little girl and her fascination with Aunt Mel's colors. "Oh, you should have told me earlier. I'd have drawn her a card. You'll take pictures?"

"Of course." Glad to divert the conversation, she led Dee into talking about the exploits of Emmy and her two-year-old brother, Austin. Usually Melissa loved living vicariously through Dee's family, but tonight it seemed only to highlight the emptiness of her own life.

After they said goodbye, she sat on the window ledge and craned her neck toward Tyler's room. The windows were dark. She could imagine him sleeping; see his long lashes caressing his golden skin.

With a jerk, she ripped her stare from Tyler's darkened

window. Her gaze came to rest on the crumbling tower. This castle had been her home for more than twenty years. It was her haven, her safeguard against the world. With the stone walls, the moat and briar fence, she'd always felt safe here. But like the crumbling mortar around those tower stones, her image of her home was growing brittle and gray.

Her gaze strayed back to Tyler's window. He held the key to her future, and she didn't want to give him that much power over her.

The child's cry came again, pelting her like rain, making her wish for an umbrella for her heart.

He was leaving in the morning. And part of her was afraid he wouldn't come back. How would she find the door?

As it turned out, Tyler hadn't needed paramedics to catch him, because he hadn't had to climb the tower to retrieve evidence. No one had cleaned up after the mason's fall, and stone bricks still lay haphazardly on the ground. He examined the black markings on the stones as he stowed them in a box in the back of Grace's car. He could see how the black squiggles might look like mold to Melissa. He could also see how a superstitious man might make evil eyes, horns or snakes out of the black scrolls.

"Make sure she doesn't go out anywhere," he said to Grace as he closed the car door.

"I've been taking care of her longer than you have, son."

"I know. But she can be stubborn."

Grace barked a laugh. "You got that right."

"I'll arrange to have your car brought back to the castle after I get mine from the garage." He slid in behind the wheel. "Thanks for lending me your car. I didn't want to leave Melissa alone."

Heavy arms crossed, Grace grunted her response.

"I should be back before dark," he said.

Grace said nothing but disappeared inside the gatehouse. As the iron gate started to move, a package propped against a bar fell over, catching Tyler's attention. He got out of the car.

Outside the gate, he glanced left and right. The rising sun cast a golden-pink hue over the awakening countryside, gilding trees, grass and road. Birds twittered reveille. Bees homed in on dewy Indian paintbrushes, golden waves and winecups. A deer scented the air, lifted its white tail and sprang into the woods.

Still scanning the area, he crouched and, using the tail of his shirt, picked up the plastic bag. Lifting it high, he examined the contents. His throat constricted and the bag fell from his suddenly numb fingers. A spoke of sun highlighted the crinkles on the bag, magnifying the bleeding wound on the white chess queen and the black obituary headline.

"Mr. Blackwell?" Grace said. "Everything all right?"

Standing up, Tyler shoved the bag into his jeans pocket. He gave the landscape one last scouring glance, then turned back to the car. "Make sure Melissa stays put. Don't open the gate for anyone."

Grace scowled at him. "I know how to run my business."

"That's the only reason I feel comfortable leaving her." He rummaged through his wallet and pulled out a card. "Anything, and I mean anything, looks out of sorts, you give me a call at that number."

Grace jammed the card into the pocket of her apron. "I've been taking care of my girl for a long time."

"She needs you now more than ever."

He cranked the engine to life and slammed the stick into gear. "I'll be as quick as I can."

This was no longer a game. By throwing Lindsey into the equation, someone had pushed the wrong button. The obituary also reminded him of unfinished business. He had a long-owed debt to pay back.

THE CLOCK BY HER BEDSIDE glowed a red 9:33 a.m. when Melissa first heard the commotion in the courtyard. Grace wasn't in the habit of raising her voice. Something must be wrong. The horses? No, they were all out at pasture. Melissa frowned as she shook the haze of sleep from her mind. Was Tyler back already? Her heart skipped a beat and a flood of anticipation surged through her. He'd only been gone a few hours, and she missed him already. No, not him, she told herself as she slipped on a pair of black jeans. Just what he could do for her. And why would Tyler's return make Grace fuss so?

Melissa finished dressing in a hurry and wrapped a shawl around her head as she rushed down the stairs and into the courtyard. She blinked at the sharp pain in her left eye the sunlight caused and wished she'd grabbed sunglasses.

Grace, hands on hips, blocked the main gate entrance with her big body.

"Give me a good reason," Grace demanded.

"This warrant gives me the right, and if you don't move, ma'am, I'll have to take you in, too."

"What for?"

"Obstruction of justice."

"You go right ahead and try." Grace puffed out her chest and gave her best impression of a mountain.

"What is going on here?" Melissa peered at the sheriff

around Grace's unmoving bulk. The rack lights on the sheriff's car blinked in a frenzy, and a deputy stood poised on the other side ready to respond. The sheriff's legs were braced against Grace's verbal assault, but he held his ground.

"I'm afraid I'll have to take you in for questioning, ma'am."

At an early age Melissa had been forced to learn the subtleties of law, the games lawyers played to win their cases, the ways to safeguard herself from unwanted questions. "Am I being charged with anything?"

Sheriff Tate cleared his throat and shifted his weight. "Cruelty to animals and vandalism."

"Excuse me?"

"Well, ma'am, an altar with a sacrificed goat was found in the clearing between your land and the Andersons'. And a witch's star was painted on my front door with goat's blood."

"So naturally you concluded I was involved." Sarcasm oozed from her voice. How dare *anyone* accuse her of animal abuse! She took in all the beasts people dumped at her door. She nursed them. She found them good homes—well, Grace did.

He shuffled and cleared his throat again. "I'm afraid I have to ask you a few questions."

"Ah, you want to know if the witch has prayed to Satan recently. I would hope, Sheriff Tate, that you would have more backbone than to fall prey to idle gossip."

"Ma'am, I'm just doing my job."

She was tired of this, tired of people spooking at every shadow, thinking every roadkill was her fault. "Then I suggest that you get out there and do just that. You won't find anything incriminating here."

"I'm glad you agree because I also have a search warrant for the premises.'' Sheriff Tate's right hand unconsciously fingered the gun at his belt.

"Where's your probable cause?"

"Ma'am, I saw you ridin' away from my house myself."

"You what?" Melissa clutched Grace with both hands. "When?"

"At midnight."

She and Tyler were in the kitchen at the time. "That's impossible. I was home then. I haven't gone out since the shot—"

"Shot?"

She shook her head. "Never mind. I didn't do whatever it is you think you saw me do. I spent the night at home."

"I have a warrant for your arrest, ma'am." The sheriff lifted his left hand and waved the paper clenched in its grasp. "It would be much better if you came willingly."

She stared at him, then at the car with the blue and white lights flashing. Their frenzied pulse matched her own. Sweat coated her skin. Her throat went dry. Her hurting eye watered. "I can't."

"I'd really rather not have to use force."

She couldn't stop shaking. "The car."

Grace understood and wrapped her body around Melissa, trying to shield her from the two men. "She can't ride in no car."

"She doesn't have a choice." He took a step toward them.

Grace tightened her hold on Melissa, taking her breath away. "Don't you dare lay a hand on her."

The deputy's rifle clicked into a ready position.

"Threatening an officer is a federal offense, ma'am." The sheriff gritted his teeth.

"I ain't threatening," Grace said. "I'm warning."

Melissa swallowed hard, fought the pressure building in her chest. The last thing Grace needed was an encounter with the law. With her record, even a minor offense could land her in jail, and selfishly, Melissa wanted her around. She pushed away from Grace's protective arms, swayed. "It's all right, Grace, I'll go."

"Missy—"

"He's right, I have no choice." The pounding of her heart drowned out Grace's answer.

The sheriff drew out handcuffs. Her vision narrowed.

"Please, Sheriff, no cuffs," Grace said. "It'll make things worse."

"I've already said I'd cooperate." Melissa was going to throw up.

"It's policy."

"I'll go with you."

"No, Grace, I need you here. Find Dee." Tyler. He was her alibi. "Tyler."

Cold metal clamped against her wrists. The sheriff urged her forward. The deputy opened the door. The squawk of the voices on the radio sounded like spiders devouring a fly. The sheriff pushed against the top of her head and folded her in the back of the squad car. Nausea billowed at the assault of the scent of sweat. "You have the right…"

As her vision blurred, the world tilted off its axis, spun. *Mama! Mama!* The godawful crunch of metal. The silence. The explosion of colors. Black smoke. Dark orange flames. White flashes. The heat. The smell of burning flesh. Oh, God, the smell. The child in her screamed, and Melissa heard no more.

Chapter Eight

The problem with alcohol was that once it got in your blood, it was hard to get out. You craved it the way you once craved food or sex or even breathing. Whiskey had been the only way to drown out the memory of Lindsey's blood and Lindsey's helpless gurgles as she'd died in his arms.

In the past few months, he'd almost banished the ghosts, if not the guilt, but the wreath of black roses hanging on his apartment door, after the bleeding queen and the obituary of this morning, revived the thirst, the yearning for oblivion. "Happy Anniversary" proclaimed the black ribbon flapping in the wind. A thousand little knots tied his muscles, making him crave the magical spirits that could unwind them.

With caution he opened the door and stepped inside. The place was more utilitarian than showy. It consisted of one large room that served as both kitchen and living room. To the right was a door to the bathroom and one to his bedroom.

The first thing he saw was the liter of whiskey waiting for him on the table, along with a single glass. He licked his lips, could taste the earthy flavor of the dark amber liquid as if he'd taken a sip. His hands shook as he walked to the devil on the table and reached for the glass. Even as part of him understood it wasn't the liquor he wanted, part of him needed the excuse to dull the sharp boomerang of pain.

At the sink he filled the glass with water and gulped it down as if he'd just spent a week in the desert. But the water only seemed to make him thirstier, to deepen the hankering. He threw the glass across the kitchen and watched it shatter against the refrigerator.

Let it go, Blackwell. Let it go.

He circled his apartment, searching for other signs of intrusion and found none. All the while the bottle called to him, spinning its invisible threads, drawing him closer and closer. He shook his head. Who? Who knew? Who had access? In the pantry he found old granola bars and devoured three before he realized they wouldn't stave off the kind of hunger shredding him. His gaze was pulled toward the bottle. Turning away from it, he raked both his hands through his hair. Why? Why the setup? Why now? The shaking intensified and Lindsey's dead eyes stared at him accusingly.

With a growl he ripped the bottle off the table. He strode to the sink, unscrewed the top and started to pour the contents down the drain. The spirit fumes spiraled up like a genie promising wish fulfillment, making him dizzy with its dark attraction. Watching the liquid splash against the sides of the sink, he felt desperation claw at his gut. He was pouring out salvation. He was pouring out the sweet blanket of nothingness. He was pouring out the fortress against further emotional damage.

He couldn't do this. He couldn't help Melissa any more than he'd been able to help Lindsey. What had made him think he could?

One gulp, that was all he needed. To steady his nerves.

He lifted the bottle to his lips. The cold glass clanked against his teeth. The cool liquid burned down his throat and into his stomach. He wanted, no needed, more. A glass, that was all. Where was the damn glass? Desperately he wanted the darkness to shroud the ugliness of his soul.

As he spun toward the table, he saw the pawn. The white piece was on its side, a bright slash on the dark surface of the wood. His stomach dropped as if he was coming down from the highest peak of a roller coaster.

If he gave in to the whiskey demon, Lindsey's murderer would win.

Again.

OH, TO BE A FLY on the wall! A chuckle filled the empty room. No matter. News of the sheriff's visit would soon sweep the local grapevine.

The pen checked off another item on the list. The next step was to get an unwilling conspirator to cooperate. For that he needed another pawn. It shouldn't be too hard. The guileless little twit was in love.

FREDDY CHOMPED greedily on a loaded slice of pizza and let out a satisfied groan of pleasure as the forbidden food slid down his throat.

"Does Rena know what you're having for lunch?" Tyler asked with a smile that hurt the corners of his mouth.

"She thinks I'm having a turkey sandwich on whole wheat, heavy on the sprouts, with a side order of carrot sticks and an apple." Freddy shot Tyler a playful warning glance. "You tell her otherwise and you're fired."

"Bet you'd have snuck in a few beers if you thought you could get away with it."

"Yeah, it's tough being the boss. Always got to set the good example."

Freddy's swivel chair squeaked as he angled it to get a better look at Tyler. He was dying to ask questions, that was plain to see, but Tyler had no intentions of giving him many answers. The whiskey devil was still hot on his heels, and Tyler wasn't sure that, in spite of a morning pounding pavement, he'd quite outrun him yet.

"So," Freddy asked, "what have you come up with?"

Tyler plopped his half-eaten slice on the cardboard box lying between them on the desk. "How are Rena and the baby doing?"

"Rena's doing great and the baby's holding his own. And as much as I'd like to go on and on about them, I'm not going to let you distract me. Find anything yet?"

"Nothing more than crumbs." Frustration hummed along his nerves. "I can't stay at the castle and dig at the same time. The Internet provides only so much. For the rest I need contacts."

"I can arrange for the legwork. Just let me know what you need."

"I need information on Tia Carnes's new boyfriend for one thing. Drake's his first name and, according to Tia, his family is old money—oil."

Freddy scribbled himself a note. "Done."

"Something's too pat. It's like someone left a trail of crumbs for me to follow. It's pretty and just enticing enough, but my instincts say it's leading nowhere."

"What kind of crumbs?"

"Financial crumbs. Sable's spending more than she has and is using creative juggling to keep the balls from falling all around her. She can't hold out much longer before Melissa finds out."

"Gives her motive."

"That it does. But..."

Out of the corner of his eye, Tyler saw Freddy reluctantly push away the piece of pizza he was working on, lean his forearms against the edge of the desk and level Tyler with his most even gaze. "It seems to me your instincts served you well in the past."

Until Lindsey.

"Do I need to remind you about the box of awards at the bottom of your closet?" Freddy asked.

Tyler shook his head. "Don't start—"

"What happened to Lindsey was an accident."

Tyler snorted.

"An accident, Tyler. How long are you going to beat yourself up over that?"

"As long as it takes."

A drive-by shooting. Gang-related, the police said. Lindsey was an innocent victim. But the black wreath on his doorstep on the morning of Lindsey's funeral proved them all wrong. Lindsey had died because of him. Her life was cut short because he'd just had to meet one more source, dig just a little deeper. It couldn't wait until morning.

He was thirsty again and drained the can of soda dry in one gulp.

I'll go with you, Ty, then we can still make the show in time.

A compromise. An error in judgment. An error that had cost Lindsey her life.

The image of the bottle of whiskey with its black label floated before his eyes. He crushed the can in his fist.

"Lindsey knew what she was getting into," Freddy said as if he could read his mind. "Don't take that away from her. She liked the chase as much as you did."

Except that this one hadn't been her chase. It had been his.

"So what are you going to do about the crumbs?" Freddy said, picking up the slice of pizza.

"Pretend I'm taking the bait and keep digging where I'm not supposed to." Driving, pushing, seemed the only way to keep one step ahead of the devil.

"And that would be where?"

"Randall Industries."

Freddy shook his head and drilled a finger into the desktop. "Melissa is the important one right now. Randall Industries is old news."

"Maybe not." And if he could get Freddy to pitch in some cash, maybe it would help loosen his contact's tongue. The guy was hesitating, weighing greed against fear. Tyler took out the plastic bag with the wounded queen and the obituary. "Someone wants me involved."

Freddy fingered the bag. "Where'd you find this?"

"Outside the castle gate." He took the pawn from his jeans pocket and set it up on the desk. "I found this on my kitchen table, along with a bottle of Jack Daniel's and a glass."

Freddy studied him closely. "You okay?"

Tyler shrugged. "Probably sent by the same guy who sent you your piece and article. Find anything on that?"

Freddy let out a frustrated breath. "No. I'll send these along with your brick samples to my guy, but it'll probably be as clean as the pieces I got."

"The message seems clear. To go forward, I'll have to go back."

"Randall has nothing to do with Melissa. He helped her get her career started. He has no reason to want to harm her."

"None that we can see."

Freddy's gaze narrowed. "This isn't about Lindsey, Tyler."

"No, it's about Melissa and keeping her from ending up like Lindsey." Tyler reached for another soda. "I've been eyeball deep in research all morning, and every time I hit a dead end, it has the Randall name on it. Did you know he had a geological survey done on his and Melissa's land last summer?"

"You're letting your past dealings with him cloud your judgment."

Tyler gave a brittle laugh. "You don't trust me so much now, do you?" He held up a hand, not giving Freddy a chance to answer. "I have to see it through. If I don't, then the devil wins and I'm going to drown. I won't let anything happen to her. I made you a promise and I intend to keep it. Even if it does mean covering old territory."

Freddy stared at him long and hard, then nodded once. "How's Melissa handling this?"

For the first time since he'd arrived in Fort Worth, tension eased. "She has one tough wall built around her."

"She's had to."

"What happened between you and her?" Tyler doodled mindlessly on the blotter with a finger.

"It's not important. You just keep her safe."

Freddy's secretary poked her head into the office. "Sorry to interrupt, but there's a call for Mr. Blackwell. It's the same woman who's been trying to reach you all morning."

"The one who wouldn't leave her name?"

"She says it's an emergency."

Tyler picked up Freddy's extension. "Mr. Blackwell? Thank God I found you."

"Grace?" Why hadn't she called his cell phone? Tyler glanced down at his belt and realized he hadn't turned the phone back on after shutting it off at the library. How could he have missed such an important detail? Tyler listened to Grace's frantic words and was moving before she'd even hung up.

"Call a lawyer," he told Freddy as he sprinted from the office. "Melissa's been arrested."

AFTER GRACE'S CALL, Tyler rushed to the courthouse. He argued and bullied and threatened until, with the help of Freddy's lawyer, Melissa was released. She was so still, so silent, so white. Standing there with her head bowed trying to hide her scars from the glare of the fluorescent lights with a curtain of hair, she looked defeated. The green of her eyes had turned yellow and dull. Her hands were neatly folded in front of her—right over left to hide the mottled texture of her burned hand. Worst of all her shoulders were curled into a defeated slump.

Seeing her like this hurt. He wanted her fighting. He wanted her sharp tongue cutting him to pieces. He wanted to see fire in her eyes.

Freddy was right. This wasn't about him or Lindsey. This was about Melissa.

What he had to do was give her something other than her fear to think about.

"Don't touch me," Melissa said as he led her out of the courthouse.

He tightened his hold on her elbow and bent down to whisper in her ear. "I'm going to hold you and you're going to let me. You scared the hell out of me. I need a hug, and you're all I've got right now."

He folded her into his arms. Her hands clawed at his shirt, pushing him away even as her head fell onto his chest. Tears choked her. But she never cried. Not when Mama was buried and she wasn't allowed at the funeral.

Not when Daddy married Sable. Not when they left her behind in her dark prison with a strange nanny.

Tyler's arms felt good around her, and a bit of the tightly wound tension eased. His touch, his scent, made her feel safe after the chaos and stink of the jail. But safety was just another illusion. This incident had shown her that. Tyler had almost made her believe there was a place for her in the world outside the castle. Now she knew positively that what she'd suspected was true. Her face would never allow her to glide through the outside world safely. There she would always be a side-show freak. The only place for her was inside those crumbling gray walls with her paints and her horses and her monsters.

A few minutes passed and he led her to his Jeep. A long, low moan keened inside her. A wave of nausea tossed through her stomach. "I can't."

"You don't have a choice. It's too far to walk." Carefully, as if she were a horse he was afraid would spook, he pulled down the top of the Jeep.

Did he understand about tight places? About fresh air? About the dark? She reminded herself to breathe. She reminded herself to leave her terror outside. She reminded herself she'd survived.

"I'll go slow," Tyler said as he eased her into the Jeep and fastened her seat belt.

He glanced at her as he turned on the ignition. The engine's growl reverberated through the soles of her feet, through the seat and seemed to jangle the very marrow of her bones. She was smothered. She had to get out.

As he eased the Jeep into gear, fear slogged through her as if it wore heavy studded boots. Dread held her death-still. And an all-consuming sensation—a notch short of full-blown panic—kept her eyes shut tightly and her arms wrapped around her middle. If she let go, she was sure she'd fall apart as she had this morning. This time they would have to sweep up what was left of her with a broom.

He reached for her arm, loosened its grip from her waist and took her hand. He didn't seem to notice the sweat coating her palm. She tried to pull away. He interlaced their fingers, locking their hands together. She didn't have the energy to fight both him and the panic, so she focused on keeping herself together and let her hand go limp in his. Soon the warmth of his fingers penetrated the ice in hers and she held on just a little more tightly.

"You know what?" he said entirely too brightly. She wanted to slap him. "I think this calls for a celebration."

She slanted him a cutting look. "Are you mad? What's to celebrate?"

"Plenty." His smile dazzled. She blinked at its brightness. "A dozen people saw you. You lived through it. They lived through it. This is a milestone for you, Melissa. My mother was a great believer in celebrating milestones."

"Then take *her* out to celebrate."

"Too far. Besides, it's your milestone we're celebrating." Driving with his knees, he reached toward the back seat.

"What are you doing?" She frantically tried to shake her imprisoned hand free. "You're going to get us killed. Get your hand back on that wheel right now!"

"Take the wheel," he said, letting go of her hand and twisting farther around.

"No!"

"If you don't, we're going to end up in the ditch. Been there, done that already this week."

"You're crazy!" she said, but took the wheel. Her heart

pounded. Her vision darkened and narrowed. How could he do this to her?

"To the left a bit. That's a girl. Now you've got it."

She swore creatively as she concentrated on keeping the wheels on the pavement. Sweat drenched her.

"Got it." He came up with a phone and dialed with his thumb. "Grace. We're on our way back and we're going to celebrate."

"Don't listen to him, Grace," Melissa shouted.

"Is there any way you can bake a cake? We need a cake." He glanced at her. "Chocolate?"

"If you bake anything, Grace, you're fired."

"Don't listen to her, she's just letting off a bit of steam. Of course she wants to celebrate getting out of jail. Does she have any dresses?"

"Forget it, I'm not going to your celebration."

"Anything in green? I think she'd look good in green." He paused and looked her up and down. "A skirt works. That works, too. You pick. We'll see you in a few minutes." He disconnected. "We're all set."

"How could your wife stand your overbearing manners?"

The jab hit its mark, but she felt no guilt. She wanted to hurt him. He was insinuating himself in her life, thinking he could take it over. He was mistaken.

"I think it was the dimples." He gave her a stunning sample of their disconcerting effect. "She said she found them hard to resist."

Melissa growled in frustration and tried to make him take the steering wheel. He leaned back and, splaying his elbows as he put his hands on the back of his head, said, "No, you keep driving. Want to sit on my lap?"

She ground her teeth and focused on the white line in

the pavement. "You're crazy. One hundred percent certifiable."

"Want to know what I found?"

"No." She decided she no longer wanted anything to do with Tyler Blackwell. All she wanted was to get back home, back to her quarters and back to the storm raging on her worktable. She had a slew of new monsters to bury in the fomenting clouds of her latest piece. She didn't want to think that her castle wasn't a safe place, either, that someone she knew wanted to harm her.

"I'll tell you, anyway." He told her about Sable's spending. He told her about Tia's spending. He told her about J.R. Randall's name turning up at every corner. Didn't Tyler know he was shaking her foundation to its core with his litany of bad news?

"Freddy's going to check out Tia's new boyfriend and the results of the geological survey Randall had done last year."

The mention of Freddy's name made her bristle. "I have a copy of the study. They found nothing worth killing me over."

"We'll see." Tyler kept talking, his voice becoming a soothing drone.

Before long, they arrived at the castle. Grace must have been waiting because the gate rolled up.

"Here we are." Tyler stopped the Jeep outside the stables, then turned to her and smiled. "Two more reasons to celebrate."

She sent him a scalding look, fumbled with the seat belt and scrambled out of the car. He reached for her wrist and gently held her back.

"You made the trip home without sedation. And you had your first driving lesson."

She realized then what he'd done. He'd kept her so

distracted, so angry, the panic hadn't had a chance to take root and bloom.

Damn you, Tyler Blackwell.

Thank you.

She was home now; she'd be okay.

"One hour, Melissa. If you don't show up in the dining room, I'm coming to get you. We have to talk."

Chapter Nine

An hour later Melissa hadn't shown up, so Tyler went to look for her. He wasn't going to let her isolate herself now that she'd had a breakthrough. Granted, she'd made it under unpleasant circumstances, but once she thought about it, she'd realize that everyone who'd dealt with her was too harried to see her as anything more than another piece of business on an already overfilled slate. Her scars had made her too self-conscious in public. What she needed to get over this was repeated exposure. Once they unmasked her secret tormentor, he planned on doing just that.

In the meantime he would get her used to baring her face to him. If he concentrated on her problem, the whiskey demon wouldn't catch up with him.

Tyler knocked on her door, but didn't give her a chance to answer. He simply walked in. "I hope you're ready."

She wasn't. Still dressed in the black T-shirt and jeans, she was petting Selma and staring out one of the windows of what he assumed was her studio. His heart gave a lurch. *Don't give in, Blackwell. She doesn't need pity. She needs tough love.* Love? The notion put a slight hitch in his step. Yeah, love. Not flowers and chocolates, but a mirror of reality.

Hearing him, she scrambled to reach the piece of silk draped over a nearby chair. He scooped it up before she could. Caught in the middle, Selma meowed her displeasure. Tail wringing, she walked regally out of the room.

He crammed the silk scarf into his pocket. "You don't need that."

Fury lit Melissa's eyes and she jerked her chin up defiantly. "Get out!"

"I'll give you a few more minutes to change."

She sat on the window seat, giving him a view of her stiffened spine and the back of her head. The soft waves of black hair made him want to run his hands through them, but it was too early, and he wasn't the right man.

He wanted to derail her fears, but he wouldn't break her heart in the process. He had too many demons of his own to sort out to give her what she needed in that department. But keeping his mind from dwelling on those deep-green eyes, his gaze from following the unconsciously sexy movements of her body, his fingers from touching the sleek mane of hair, was becoming more difficult by the day.

He'd made Freddy a promise to keep her safe, and that included safe from his own base nature.

Strolling around her studio, he took in the dozens of paintings stacked against the wall. The pretty pastoral scenes were rich in color and detail. They lured the viewer into exploring them only to shock him with their tortured undergrowth. He came to rest near her worktable and turned on the light. The layers of color before him looked as he imagined the dawning of the world must have. Parts of a storm were starting to take shape against a background wash. In the roiling of clouds, in the innumerable shades of gray, in the silent screams trapped in the waterlogged fury, she seemed to have captured the essence of his soul. The thought frightened. He didn't want to be sucked in. He needed to stay in control. "What will it be?"

"I don't know. It hasn't revealed itself to me yet." *Go away,* she willed. *I can't handle you right now.* She wanted to be alone. Ignoring even Dee's calls, she'd tried to lose herself in her work. When it refused to draw her in, she'd simply let the cloak of dark feelings settle on her shoulders.

She was so tired that all she wanted to do was crawl into bed and sleep. But sleep wouldn't come. When she closed her eyes, all she could see was the harsh light in the courthouse, all she could hear was the din of chaos all around her in that jail cell, all she could feel were the dozens of judging eyes staring at her, filling her with shame and dread.

She'd hoped Tyler would forget his threat and leave her alone—as any person with an ounce of decency would have. Yet part of her was glad he'd kept his promise. But that bit of self-betrayal served only to feed her anger. Refusing to look at him, she concentrated on the horses outside. The edge of a storm shoehorned the horizon; she'd have to bring in the horses before it hit. When a dark bank of clouds skimmed across the sun, Tyler's reflection developed on the window. Her eyes refused to obey her order to refocus on the mutating sky.

"Is that how you work?" Tyler asked, peering at her work with an intensity that made her self-conscious. Did he see the monsters? "In layers?"

"Yes. Images, colors, feelings, lines, shapes. They all come through me onto the paper in layers." And monsters. Horrible, screaming monsters with bloody heads and exposed skulls.

"Then what happens?"

Forgetting her bare face, she shot him a questioning glance.

"Obviously they take a lot out of you," he said, still staring at her work. "What do they leave in their place?"

"Hunger," she said without thinking. A psychic hunger that, when the work was finally done, left her limp for days at a time. A hunger for normalcy. A hunger for things she could never have. She let her head find her raised knees and hugged her legs. How had he known there was a cost? Did he understand? No, not even Dee did.

Tyler shifted position. His footsteps toward her quickened her pulse. His fingers on her shoulders made her tense until they massaged the knots gnarling her scapulas.

"What else?" he whispered.

Wasn't that enough? Her stomach shrunk to a tight ball and pain rolled through her body.

"Emptiness." Even to her, her voice sounded dead.

"How do you deal with it?"

Why was she talking to this man? Don't trust him. *Don't trust anyone,* a small voice reminded her. But the warmth of his hands on her cold skin and his honeyed voice drugged her sharp senses. "I ride."

"Yes."

That simple word said it all. He understood. The knots unwound one by one.

"I made dinner," he said, breaking the intimacy between them, leaving her feeling adrift. "We should eat before it gets cold."

"You cooked?"

"Nana Leonardo's very own secret recipe. Don't look so surprised."

Despite her need to remain morassed in anger, Melissa

found the corners of her mouth twitching. "Grace let you mess with her kitchen?"

"She can't resist my smile."

As if on cue, Grace walked in, carrying a heavy tray. "If you need anything else, you fetch it yourself."

"Thanks, Grace. You're an angel."

Grace grunted a response. "I expect you to clean up that kitchen."

"Yes, ma'am."

"Storm's coming," Grace said. "I'll get the horses in."

"No, I'll do it," Melissa said, jumping at the opportunity to end the false sense of kinship with this man.

Grace scowled. "I didn't drag that thing all the way up here for nothing. You eat every damn bite. I'll fetch the horses."

For Grace food was solace—her way of mothering, her way of loving. "Thanks, Grace. I'll check on them in a bit."

After Grace left, Tyler turned to Melissa. "Where should I set this?"

She didn't like the devilish look in his eyes. Or the way the five-o'clock shadow of beard gave him a rakish look. And his easy relaxed movements in her private space managed to churn restlessly inside her. "In the kitchen. By yourself."

"Don't be childish, Melissa. It doesn't suit you."

"This is my home. I'll do what I want."

"That's right. Isolate yourself. Feel sorry for yourself. Play poor pitiful me. What was I thinking? That we could share a decent meal, celebrate your victories and discuss your situation like two adults?"

When put that way, she did sound rather pathetic. "There's nothing to discuss."

She watched him warily as he cleared one of the small tables holding supplies and dragged it near the window. "On the contrary, there's plenty. Someone seems to want to harm you and that same person seems to want me to be here to witness it. You have to ask yourself why."

"What?"

"I found a queen and a copy of my wife's obituary this morning. Then I found a pawn in my apartment." On the table he laid out a lacy tablecloth, silverware and two domed plates, along with a salad, some bread wafting a divine garlicky scent and a silver candlestick with a red candle. She'd had nothing to eat all day, and her traitorous stomach had the nerve to gurgle.

"I think the message is fairly clear," Tyler said. "Somehow, I'm being played as a pawn in this twisted game."

He stood next to her, reached for her hand and led her to the table. "I don't like being played, especially not as a pawn."

With a flourish, he lifted both domes. "Fusilli di Leonardo. Ah, Nana would be proud."

Melissa hid her confusion by sitting down and taking a giant bite of the aromatic pasta. Might as well get this ordeal over and done with as soon as possible. "Is there really a Nana Leonardo?"

"Of course. And she's not of the sweet variety. Her tongue is acid. Her opinions cutting. Her praise rarer than water in a desert. When she's around, she's in charge and everybody knows it."

"Sounds like someone I know."

He flashed her his dimples. "What can I say? Leonardo genes are powerful."

"Tell me about your family."

He dug into his meal with gusto. "I was raised by a

brood of women. The men in our family don't seem to hang around very long. Maybe it's because the women are so strong. After Grandpa Leonardo died, Nana came to live with us. Dad checked out soon after. Heart attack. Can't say I blame him. Nana made his life a living hell. So it was Nana Leonardo, Mom, three sisters and me.'' Tyler reached for a slice of bread. ''Did I mention I was the youngest?''

She couldn't help herself, she laughed. ''That explains everything. I've heard the youngest tends to be a spoiled brat.''

''It's a wonder I'm sane with all that female hovering and manipulation.''

Remembering his way with horses, she asked, ''Where did you learn to ride?''

''Pennsylvania. One of my sisters evented and dragged me along to be her groom at shows. It didn't take me long to realize that stables were overrun with girls, and that girls who loved horses tended to be very passionate.''

She tried to ignore the fluttering of her stomach at his steady gaze and concentrated, instead, on the flavors of tomato and cheese melding so beautifully with the garlic, oregano and pasta. ''Why doesn't that surprise me? So why did you leave such a haven?''

''Actually I left *because* of all the females in my life. They were driving me crazy. They all wanted to run my life and each one of them was pulling me in a different direction.''

''So you escaped.''

Smiling, he shook his head. ''Barely made it out alive, too. A scholarship was an acceptable reason to leave, and I never looked back.''

Melissa twisted her fork in the pasta, feeling a pang of

regret she didn't understand. "Don't you miss your family?"

"Sure." He shrugged. "I visit a couple of times every year. But I'm always glad to be back."

"You're lucky to have a family that cares about you."

He looked up from his meal and his gaze seemed to reach right inside her. "I know. But sometimes that's as much a handicap as a family who doesn't care enough."

She nodded and swallowed around the sudden constriction in her throat. Too bad they couldn't somehow subtract their families' shortcomings and end up with one that cared just the right amount. "Was your wife suffocating, too?"

"Lindsey?" He placed his fork and knife just so on his plate and slid away a few inches. "No, she was sunshine."

And I'm shadow. Had she really believed Tyler could see her as a woman?

"When we met, we had the same goals, the same ideals. The job was exciting, and we fed off each other's enthusiasm." His features changed as he spoke, growing more serious, clouded. "We pushed each other to achieve more, to reach higher, to reach deeper for the truth."

"You loved her."

"I loved her."

"And you're here for her."

He shook his head. "No, I'm here because truth still matters. I forgot that for a while. I ran away from my ghosts, but they came back to haunt me, anyway." He looked at her thoughtfully. "Someone's gone through an awful lot of trouble to get you in trouble and to involve me in it. I have to know why. You have a chance to face one of your monsters, too." He jerked his head toward the pile of paintings propped against the wall. "And maybe they'll stop showing up in your art."

He saw too much. "Can't we forget about all of this for one night?"

"No."

She pushed her plate away and was surprised to see she'd eaten every bite. "I haven't done anything. The sheriff will have to drop the charges. There's no evidence. It's not a monster. It's—"

"A setup. The sheriff found a can of goat's blood in your tack room. The brush that was dropped by his front door is the same brand I saw on your worktable. The sheriff had to note that detail, too. They found foot prints that match your boots at the sheriff's house and near the altar. And the knife found beside the goat is the same brand Grace uses in the kitchen."

"But that's all it is, coincidence. You were here. You know."

"But it's my word against what the sheriff thought he saw. And the town seems bent on feeding his case with more witch sightings and more witch destruction. I don't like being manipulated, Melissa. I would think that, by now, neither would you."

"I keep to myself and I've never done anything to harm anyone."

"Which is why I think we should draw this person out and not wait for him to make his next move." He rose from his chair and stalked the room.

"How do you propose doing that if you don't even know who's behind all this?"

He stopped before the carved chess set next to her computer and stared at the men frozen in play. "Give him rope and let him hang himself."

"How—"

A horse's panicked trumpet splintered the night.

Melissa sprang from her chair to the window. "Oh, my God!"

"What?"

"Someone's in the pasture," she said, and turning she raced out the door and disappeared down the stairs.

"Melissa!" She heard Tyler cursing his sore ribs behind her. But she didn't dare slow down to wait for him. "Melissa!"

People who are afraid do stupid things, Dee had said. *They let the crowd sweep them along.* Is that what was going on in her pasture? How dare they trespass on her land? How dare they take out their anger against her horses?

"Grace!" Melissa called out in the courtyard. "Call the sheriff!"

Not waiting for Grace's answer, Melissa raced into the stable, grabbed the shotgun from the tack room and sprinted out the pastern door. Focused on the horses, she paid the driving rain no heed.

At the pasture gate, she skidded to a halt and wiped the rain from her face. The sight of three men beating on Grace with baseball bats churned her stomach. Grace was struggling to keep Journey and her foal out of the path of the blows, taking each whopping hit on her wide back.

"Hey!" Raising the shotgun, Melissa ran into the pasture.

Journey's struggles weren't making Grace's task easy. And Grace, bless her heart, was putting herself between the horses and the attackers just as she'd put herself between her son and her raging husband. Melissa couldn't let anything happen to Grace. Grace was her strength.

"Leave her alone!" Melissa shouted. Steadying her breath, she aimed at the tall man in the middle.

The three men froze, bats in midair.

"Thou shalt not suffer a witch to live," the squat, beady-eyed one said, thumping his bat against the palm of his hand.

"Burning for burning, wound for wound, stripe for stripe," snuffled the prune-faced gnome beside him as he waved his bat in an arc.

"Your sin will find you out," the tall, flame-haired one said, and brought his bat down on the back of Grace's skull. The crack was sickening. The mountain that was Grace crumpled as if she were a bag of sand. Journey and her foal galloped away.

Deliberately aiming high, Melissa pressed the trigger. "Next time I won't miss."

None of them moved. Melissa stared them down. The leader with the beady eyes and walrus mustache looked away first. The gnome beside him cowered behind his friend. And the flame-haired, wide-eyed lunatic who looked more like a witch than either she or Grace, spat. "Next time, we won't, neither."

Keeping the shotgun level, she moved toward Grace. The men backed away and once at the edge of the fence, scattered like rats in three directions.

Melissa squatted next to Grace and shook her. "Grace? Are you okay?"

Melissa peeled back the wet rain cape. Blood covered the top of Grace's hair and streamed down her face. "Grace."

It was then Melissa realized that Grace had donned the black rain cape Melissa usually wore. They'd called her witch as they'd beat on her.

The bitter taste of bile rose to her throat. They'd thought Grace was her.

TYLER REACHED THEM soon after the men scattered. He seemed to take an eternity to hobble back to the castle and bring the Jeep around to the pasture. An ambulance would take too long. Melissa wanted Grace helped now. Together they hefted Grace into the back seat and sped to the hospital. Melissa had been too scared for Grace to notice the confines of the car. And her concern for Grace negated her self-consciousness at her exposed face.

Another millennium seemed to go by before someone came back with the news that Grace was still alive. And at least another century crawled by before Melissa was allowed to see her.

"Ten minutes," the nurse warned.

Melissa went in and sat beside Grace. She hesitated before she reached for Grace's hand. Would Grace want her anywhere near her once she found out she was to blame for her condition?

"Do you remember that first day you walked into my studio?" Melissa said, squeezing Grace's hand, willing her to open her eyes and scowl at her. "You saw the painting I was working on. The one with the cougar attacking the horse. You asked me why. 'Why you got to draw such a bloody picture, Missy?'" She imitated Grace's voice. "And I asked you who you thought survived the encounter. I could see on your face that you thought maybe you'd made a mistake, that maybe I was as much of a witch as they said. You were afraid." Melissa licked her lips. "The truth is, I was the one who was afraid. I thought for sure once you got a good look at that scene, you'd leave and I'd be all alone again."

Melissa leaned forward on the chair. "Do you remember what I said?"

She stared at Grace's bandaged face and sniffed back

the itch at the back of her throat. "The one who wants to live the most. That's the one who survives."

She wanted to hug Grace so fiercely her body shook. "I never chose death, Grace. Neither did you. That's the easy way out. You and me, we've never taken the easy way out."

But Melissa knew she had chosen the coward's way. She had chosen not to face the monsters, but rather, cage them in her work. "You have to come back, Grace. You have to get better, you hear."

Her throat tightened, forcing her to gasp for her next breath. "Grace..."

Melissa felt a hand on her shoulder, and a familiar voice spoke words she didn't hear. She hung on to the knife-scarred hand of the woman who'd become such a dear friend.

"We have to leave, Melissa." Tyler's voice registered somewhere in her brain.

He pulled her out of the chair, and she tried to shrug away his hold. "I have to stay."

He twisted her around and shook her once. "Listen to me. You can't. They've placed you under house arrest."

"Me?" She blinked madly. "Why?"

"It's temporary until Freddy's lawyer can sort out this mess. The lawyers had to do a lot of fast talking to get that compromise."

He nudged toward the door. She grasped his arm and held her ground. "Tyler, you're not making sense."

"The sheriff believes you're the one who attacked Grace. That the men in the pasture were just trying to save her from your wrath."

"That's crazy." She shook her head. "How can the sheriff believe such a thing?"

The strain of the evening showed in the deep furrows

on Tyler's forehead. "The rain washed away a lot of evidence. It's your word against theirs. And you're not in the sheriff's favor right now."

"It still doesn't explain why they were on my land with baseball bats. Or even how they got there."

"They say you were the one with the bat, trying to beat the devil into her."

"That's ridiculous! Let's say the sheriff was right and I did want to kill Grace. How could anyone on the road even see into the pasture?" A burning rage spread from deep inside her. "And how come I don't have a scratch?"

"You're a witch, Melissa. Everyone knows witches don't bleed."

She shot Grace's unmoving form a glance. "I would never hurt Grace. Never."

Tyler wrapped an arm around her shoulder and led her out of the room. "I know, sweetheart, but right now we have to go unless you want to spend more time in jail."

She leaned against him. "It's not fair."

"No one promised you fair."

No, no one had. You'd think she'd have learned that by now.

"WHAT HAPPENED out there?" the contact asked with much too much huff for Ray's taste.

"A slight miscalculation." The drunken fools had fed too easily on the preacher's hatred and started off on their frenzy of justice too early. "But no harm done." The play was still going his way.

"Lucky for you. He doesn't want her hurt. Just gone."

"You can't have it both ways. Not if you want the whole cake and not just a slice. And we both know you've got a healthy appetite." Ray smiled, satisfied his hit had found its mark. Greed was such an easy sin to feed. "Is the other on board yet?"

A slight hesitation. God, how Ray hated people who thought they could sit on the fence and stay clean. Didn't they realize straddling doomed them to fall?

"Give me a few more days," the contact said.

"You're the one with the deadline, not me."

Ray cut the connection and let the fool ponder that. One way or another, in less than two weeks the attack was going to move into endgame. And the pawn was going to turn up big—right there on the front page for the world to see.

Ray savored the thought, the power. His. All his.

Chapter Ten

Once back at the castle, Tyler insisted on entering the premises before her, on seeing to the horses with her, on checking every gate and every window while she stayed safely inside.

Now that Melissa was on familiar ground in her own quarters, the surge of adrenaline that had carried her through the ordeal with Grace was fading fast, leaving a bone-deep tiredness in its wake. But her mind still reeled, and she couldn't seem to stop pacing.

Tyler walked through the rooms of her tower, checking, she assumed, for hidden gnomes carrying bats. She didn't complain once about his overprotective behavior.

"Everything looks okay." He stood at the door, those sharp dark eyes watching her. How much did he see? And though his gaze was intrusive, she couldn't bear the thought of shutting the door on it and being left all alone.

"Don't leave." She rubbed her arms to keep the cold from eating her alive. Even in the smothering heat and humidity brought by the storm, she could not stop shivering. "Please."

He nodded. "Do you mind if I use your computer?"

She shook her head. He sat at the small desk that held the unit and turned on the machine. Reaching across his shoulders, she typed in her password, allowing him access to the programs. The brief contact of forearms on shoulder, of cheek against cheek, sparked a sudden hunger that had her skittering away.

"I'm sorry," she said, resuming her pacing.

"What for?" His fingers sped across the keyboard.

"For locking you in the dungeon." She'd done it out of anger, but that was no excuse. Grace had tried to warn her, but she hadn't listened, and now the guilt was eating at her.

"I forgive you." His smile warmed her, but it did nothing to lighten the burden that weighed down her spirit.

"Do you know why I let you stay after your accident?" she asked, trying to center herself. Maybe confession was good for the soul.

"Why?"

He was staring at her again. The intensity of his gaze increased her pace. "I wanted to hurt you just like I thought you wanted to hurt me."

"That was never my intention."

"Then I wanted you to see me. The real me. Not the witch." She gave a short sharp laugh. "The only problem is, I don't know what the real me is." She cursed the croak in her voice. She didn't want him to feel sorry for her; she just wanted him to understand.

"I never saw you as a witch."

"The irony is that for years, that's exactly what I was. I went around blaming everyone for what happened. My mother. My father. Sable. Even Tia."

"You were angry."

And she'd felt trapped by the force of that anger, by the dueling Melissas who'd lived inside her—the one who needed to lash out and the one who needed to be held. "I took it out on everyone around me. Especially Dee and Grace.''

She stopped pacing and looked at him, rubbing her cold arms, shaking her head. She was as close to tears as she'd been in a long time and hated their weight. *Don't break down and cry like a baby.* "I don't want Grace to die. If she dies…''

"The prognosis is good.''

"Yes.'' Once Grace came out of her coma, the doctors would be able to assess the damage. But when would she? Would she be the same Grace? How long would they keep her in the hospital? Without Grace, how would she survive? There was no place for her outside, and now that Dee had a family, her existence inside these walls depended mostly on Grace. Outside. Just the thought made her shiver. Slowly she turned to face Tyler. He was still watching her with that keen gaze.

"Tyler, when you look at me, what do you see?'' Once the question was out, she held her breath, not quite sure she wanted a response.

He took so long to answer she thought her heart would jump right out of her chest. Then in the cozy light, his gaze softened and filled with compassion. He moved to stand in front of her, tilted his head and studied her as an artist might a subject. He raised a finger to her face. She fought the instinct to flinch and gave in to the warmth of his finger trailing the zigzag course of scars on her cheek. "I see pain. I see courage. I see strength.''

Emptiness, yearning, whistled through her, making her sway. "Do you see a woman?''

"Yes.'' He placed his hand over her heart. Something in her sighed. "I see a woman with a generous heart.''

"I want to know…'' She licked dry lips. "Make love to me, Tyler.''

Shaking his head, he took a step back. "Sex isn't going to stop the hurt."

Brashly she stepped forward and pressed her lips to his, lingering, absorbing the long slow shiver that rattled through her. Her fingers curled into the material of his shirt as she felt her blood heat. "I want to know…" she murmured against his lips. "I need—"

"Melissa…"

She placed a finger against his lips. "I need—"

"Not from me."

Anger, swift and cutting, razored through her. It always came down to the curse of her accident. "Because I'm ugly."

"No," he said, then tenderly brushed her lips with his. "Because I am."

If she were a generous person as he claimed, she would let him go. She would turn around and walk away. She would be happy that he saw through the scars to the deeper layers, that he was chivalrous enough to want to protect her. But she wasn't generous. She was selfish— needed to be to survive. With Grace hurt, and Dee busy with her own family, Melissa feared for her very existence. If he left her, she would be alone. And she couldn't be alone. Not tonight.

Eventually he would leave. She knew that. Once the danger was past, once he'd kept his promise, he would leave. But if she let him step away now, she would shrivel up. The darkness that lived inside her would suffocate her. That he cared for her, that she cared for him, made their union a sacred one. It felt right. It was right.

As she'd seen in so many of Dee's movies, she reached up and framed his head with her hands. She kissed him long and deep. So caught up was she in the swell of sensation that she lost track of the small voice buzzing a warning in her mind.

She touched by instinct, learning the hard lines of him as if he were a sculpture, reveling in the warmth of his chest, savoring his musky male scent, the heady taste of him.

"Melissa…"

And then the heat cooled when she realized she had no idea what came next. Clothes came off, and in Dee's movies, the screen always went dark right about then, cutting to later and the afterglow of lovemaking. The space in between was simply imagination. A pang of fear gripped her.

Without clothes, he would see that the melting of skin went beyond her face, that the fire had licked her left arm and left leg. He would see the rectangular scars on her right thigh and back where skin had been harvested for grafts. He would know then that there was nothing beautiful about her. Hot tears squeezed between her closed lids, wet the cotton of his shirt.

"Melissa…"

He kissed the line of tears, making them gush faster.

"Please, Tyler…" She wasn't sure if she was asking him to stop or to continue.

Rain tapped the windows, drumming as furiously as her heart.

He wrapped his arms around her, holding her against him. She felt the strong pulse at his neck beat beneath her cheek, the rapid hammer of his heart pound beneath her hand, the hard line of his body fusing intimately with hers. She no longer cared that he would find her ugly. In the dark he couldn't see the unappealing discoloration of skin or the distorted map of her scars.

And maybe in the dark she would be enough.

"I don't have anything to protect you," he said in a hoarse whisper.

"What?"

"Birth control."

The thought of fertility was a kick in the gut, a possibility, a miracle. A baby? *Oh, please, yes.* "The timing's not right," she lied. She would deal with the consequences later.

"I promised Freddy not to hurt you."

"It's too late." Had been too late since the first day.

His touch against her skin was alive with the same electric energy swirling in the air outside. As he bared her left shoulder and kissed the mottled skin, colors seemed to fly off the canvasses propped against the wall and whirl around her. When his thumb caressed her breast, the rainbow vortex spun into a blinding white light that electrified every atom of her body. The drugging kisses made her weak. The liquid heat pooling low in her belly made her bold. She pressed herself closer to him, twined her arms around his neck, dug her fingers into his soft hair. She wanted him to slow down. She wanted him to hurry up. She had no idea what she wanted, what she needed, only that he had it.

He lifted her off the floor and into his arms, then headed toward her bedroom down the hall. The sure strength of his arms around her made her feel feminine in a way she never had before.

When he placed her in the middle of her bed, he winced.

"Your ribs," she said, her hand hovering above the bruise beneath the shirt. The heat of him pulsed against her palm.

"I'm fine."

Bracing his elbows by her face, resting his body alongside hers, he gazed into her eyes. The look on his face was one some deep part of her had yearned for since the day her mother had died.

But falling in love wasn't part of the plan.

Lightning sparked against the night sky. Thunder drummed low and deep. Rain tap-danced across the windows. He was waiting, she realized, for permission.

The night was alive.

And so was she.

"Yes," she said. She brought his face to meet hers and kissed him. For all she'd gone through, she was entitled to a scrap of joy. Tomorrow would be soon enough for regrets.

HE SHOULD BE running and fast. If he had any brains left at all, he would get up and leave. But she had him so stirred up he wasn't sure he had any logical capabilities left in his brain. As those green eyes darkened under his scrutiny, his useless gray matter was skipping ahead to imagining himself deep inside her.

Her innocent desire, her sweet kisses, were putting him in an awkward position. The responsibility of it scared the hell out of him. Then there was his promise to Freddy. He'd sworn not to hurt her. All this would get her was a straight shot to heartache.

She had no idea what she was asking. And he didn't have the guts to refuse her. Not after watching her with Grace tonight. Not when she would take it as a rejection of her face and not protection for her heart. She had no idea how much he wanted to touch her, to take her. And there was no way she could handle the fervor of that hunger.

Breathing heavily, he curled his hands into fists, hoping

to gain an ounce of control. His voice just short of a croak, he said, "Melissa." God, where had his vocabulary gone?

Holding on to the collar of his shirt, she frowned. "Tyler? Not out of pity."

Pity? Where had she gotten that notion? This had nothing to do with pity and everything to do with lust. Slowly he rose. Deliberately he clicked on the small lamp at her bedside. Methodically he toed off his boots, peeled off his shirt and jeans, shucked off his shorts and socks. He stood naked before her, drinking in the fluid reactions flitting across her face. "Does this look like pity?"

She swallowed hard. "Oh, my, no."

"Your turn," he said, reaching for her hand.

She let him lift her to her feet. "What?"

He let go of her hand and jerked his chin toward her attire. "Take off your clothes."

Instinctively her shoulders rounded. "The light—"

"Stays on." He captured her chin in his hand and forced her to look deep into his eyes. "Either you trust me or you don't. The choice is yours, Melissa. We can stop now."

She shook her head. "No. I want... I need..."

"I won't let you hide."

She nodded again and sat primly on the edge of the bed. Her gaze latched on to his as she lifted the long-sleeved T-shirt off her body. The ghost-white skin on the right made a sharp contrast to the swirl of darker pink and purply-brown dapples on her left.

He saw the small shake of her hands as she watched him watching her. "Go on."

She reached back and unclasped her bra. His breath quickened as her lovely white breasts spilled out of their satiny cups. He couldn't help himself and reached for them. Her skin was as soft as the rose petals in her garden. "Beautiful."

Rising, she reached for the button of her jeans. He let her slide the zipper down, then spanned her hips with his hands and slipped the denim down the silkiness of her legs. With one hand, he threw back the rainbow-colored quilt and lace-edged sheet covering the bed. With the other, he invited her to lie down with him.

When her inexpert hands skimmed up to the yellow-green bruise over his rib cage, his stomach quivered. He swore softly at the tightening of his already overwound body, at the renewed fury of his desire.

She snapped her hand away. "Did I hurt you?"

"Sweetheart, you're killing me."

Their gazes met and held, and soon a smile of pure feminine contentment graced her lips. "That's good?"

He trailed his lips over her face, across her jaw, down her neck. "That's very good."

She touched him low, and raw need exploded. "Very. Good."

He ran his hand over her calf, up her thigh, then skimmed his thumb between her legs. She closed her eyes and gripped the sheet with her fists. She was wet and hot. Her hips moved to meet his touch. The soft moan deep in her throat had his system screaming for her. But he wanted to be careful with her, gentle.

He slipped his hands under her hips and cupped her bottom. Bringing his mouth a breath away from hers, he whispered, "Look at me, sweetheart."

She opened her eyes. Only a small halo of deep green crowned the wide-open pupil. The longer he looked, the more he saw. It was like being sucked into one of her paintings. The connection was more than physical and it took his breath away.

"Look at what you do to me," he rasped.

The groan as he entered her had nothing to do with the pain tattooing his ribs and everything to do with being lost. There were words that needed to be said, words she needed to hear, but he could not articulate the chaos jumbling inside him. "Melissa."

With a swift stroke he broke the barrier of her virginity, watched helplessly as her eyes clouded, her face contorted in surprise, felt her fingers digging into his hips.

Half-mad with need, knowing she needed time to adjust to his invasion, he kissed her tenderly, whispered the only word that his mouth seemed able to form—"Melissa"—over and over again.

And when he felt her soften beneath him, when her hips pushed once more against his, he gently thrust again, acclimating her inch by inch to the rhythm of love.

His senses were filled with the taste of her, the feel of her, the scent of her. Slowly she picked up the cadence, moving as one with him. The liquid waltz of body against body resonated through him. The song of it touched his soul.

"Oh," she said, and went still. Her eyes widened. Her body shivered. He clung to his frittering control. "Tyler?"

He whispered sweet nothings to her and held her as she rode the crest of her climax, then careened helplessly after her into the insanity of his own release.

So much for objectivity, he thought as he collapsed.

Without it, people died.

Lindsey.

He saw her now in his mind's eye, her blond hair shimmering in the sun, her blue eyes seeming to take in the whole world. Then the picture whirled and she was limp in his arms, blood staining the bodice of her dress. The godawful noise of her last breath filled his memory. And a dull ache kneaded his heart.

He couldn't allow his thoughts to follow that track. It would lead straight to the whiskey demon, and he needed a clear head to keep Melissa safe.

She deserved more than the taking of her innocence. But he didn't want a relationship. Losing Lindsey had nearly killed him. He wasn't going to risk emotions. Emotions blurred facts. And he needed to maintain what little edge he had to see this through.

Rolling onto his good side, he scooped Melissa against him, held her tightly and kissed her tenderly. She settled against him, her curves fitting perfectly to him. Her sigh of contentment echoed his own.

With his fingers he reverently traced the soft lines of her body. Then, spreading his palm over a stretch of reddened skin, he propped himself on one elbow. "How did it happen?"

She tried to turn away, but he gently held her in place. "Curiosity, Melissa, not judgment."

Her eyes softened and she nodded, settling once more against his body. "We were driving home—here," she clarified. "Mama had picked me up from my friend Jessica's house after a business thing at my father's office. They said she was drunk. I couldn't tell. It wouldn't surprise me, though. She hated hosting my father's cocktail parties. We were going down a Mixmaster overpass when we hit a retaining wall. I don't remember anything after that."

"There was a fire." He kissed her ribs and heard the sharp hiss of her breath.

"They say my seat belt came undone and somehow I ended up under the dashboard, instead of through the

windshield. The burns came from the engine fire. Someone pulled me out.''

''Your mother?''

''No, she was still inside.'' Melissa gulped.
''Trapped.''

With eyes and fingers, he was studying the contrast of
textures on her body when she put her hand over his.
''Does it bother you?''

''No,'' he said, gaze straight and true. The scarred skin
was tougher, shinier, slicker than the rest of her skin, but
no, the leathery feel wasn't unpleasant.

''That skin feels stiffer because it doesn't have pores.
There are no sweat glands, no hair follicles.''

''That's why you stay out of the sun.''

''Partly. My left eye is still sensitive to light.'' She
turned on her side, facing him. ''Dee tried to get me out.
Once. She took me to the Modern Art Museum in Fort
Worth. I trusted her when she said everything would be
okay. But it wasn't. I saw the elbow nudging, the finger
pointing, heard the whispering. People followed me with
their eyes, pretending they weren't looking at all. And
then there were those who came back for a second look
as if I was an animal at the zoo.''

She reached for him as if she needed the contact. Her
callused palms brushed against his chest. Electricity ser-
pentined down his torso. ''I couldn't stay. I didn't want
anyone looking at me. I didn't want anyone feeling sorry
for me.''

''So you hid.''

''And now—'' she shrugged ''—even this place isn't
safe.''

He held her close and kissed the top of her head.
''We'll find whoever's doing this to you, Melissa. I promise.''

Silently he swore. He'd gone and mired himself eye-ball-deep in emotions.

A perfect recipe for disaster.

THE LIBRARY at the Randall estate was *Architectural Digest* perfect. Everything was just so. No speck of dust was tolerated on the polished mahogany of the furniture. No book allowed to stray so much as a quarter of an inch from its position at the edge of a shelf. No cold ember of coal was permitted to soil the hearth of the fireplace. All reasons why Ray hadn't bothered to wipe the horse manure from the bottom of his stable boots and why he placed the dirty crown of his hat on the tapestry seat of the chair beside him.

The ritual was a daily one. Jimmy, as immaculate as the room in his dark suit, would have coffee waiting. Forehead pleated, white eyebrows knit, he would play his move on the gold-and-silver chess set. Then, as Ray pondered his own move, Jimmy would give his orders for the day. One rule of chess was silence, but people like Jimmy tended to ignore the rules.

Jimmy moved his king. "Give me an update on Black Witch."

The mare had pulled up lame after her last race, but had recovered enough to race again this weekend. Ray brought Jimmy up-to-date on the rest of his charges. Then he moved his bishop to threaten Jimmy's king and contained his smile. Jimmy would have to give up material to stave off Ray's threat. One of the joys of chess was pulling off a difficult attack. But for all his hard-ass reputation, the great J.R. Randall hated to take risks.

Without acknowledging the brilliance of Ray's move, Jimmy got up and headed toward the desk parked between two tall windows. Bright sunshine radiated around him like a halo. "Deanna is to attend a horseshow in Irving this weekend. Once she's on the show grounds, I want you to arrange for her truck to have engine trouble."

"Sir?"

"That seems clear enough. Dee will be out of town and I want her to remain out of town."

"Yes, sir." Gritting his teeth, Ray picked up his hat and crammed it onto his head. How was he supposed to be in Irving taking care of Deanna's truck and at Trinity Meadows shepherding three horses into the winner's circle?

"And Ray? Make sure neither my daughter nor the horse are harmed."

"Yes, sir."

The proverbial lightbulb went on in Ray's mind. He saw Jimmy's game spread out, every move outlined. Too bad Jimmy was attacking without having control of the center. That left him exposed to a counterattack that could split his forces. At this rate he was going to end up on the wrong side of a masterly win.

Chapter Eleven

Over the next couple of days, Melissa and Tyler drew up charts on large swaths of paper and hung them around the studio walls, adding facts as they came to light. But all their efforts seemed to lead nowhere, except in circles.

As Tyler once again tried to conjure something new out of the ether of the information highway, Melissa paced from chart to chart, examining the entries, making excuses to brush against him, to touch him. So far, what they'd gathered looked more like Swiss cheese than a blueprint to expose a villain. "We're missing something."

"Maybe we're looking at it from the wrong angle."

Melissa stopped before the chart topped with Tyler's name and studied the entries. "Tyler?"

"Mmm?"

"Your pawn. You said you thought it meant someone wanted you involved."

He shrugged as he typed. "Why send me a pawn unless they thought they could use me?"

"Maybe it was a warning." She placed her hands on his shoulders and squeezed, fearing that his presence here, guarding her, was putting him in danger. "Maybe they want you to stay away."

He brushed a kiss against her fingers. "Then their tactic backfired."

At what cost? Would whoever wanted to harm her plow through Tyler as they had through Grace to get to her? Melissa sat on a stool next to her worktable, reached for a drawing pad and a pencil. What did they want? Her money? Then why go through this complicated charade? Why not simply ask or take?

Tyler had been willing to take a bullet for her. Now she found she would gladly take one for him. To live while he died seemed the worst tragedy she could imagine. Is that how he'd felt about Lindsey? "Tell me about that day—the day your wife died."

"You don't want to hear."

Pushed by her nervous energy, the pencil scratched against the paper. Selma hopped on the worktable and begged for attention. When Melissa ignored her, the cat jumped to the windowsill and curled into a ball. "Tell me, anyway. What happened?"

Tyler spun the computer chair around. "You're not going to like the direction."

"I'm not liking anything about the situation." *Except having you in my bed.* She'd been an ostrich for too long. It was time to face reality head-on, even if she didn't like what she saw.

Tyler leaned forward, placing his elbows on his knees and dangling his hands between his legs. "I was working on a story about Randall Industries. They were the darlings of the year. Their earnings had shot through the roof and their stock was the one to buy. But things weren't adding up. The investigation was going nowhere. Then I got a phone call from one of their accountants."

"A disgruntled employee?" Being awake this early was a novelty for her, and she liked the way the bright sunlight played over Tyler's face, the sharpness it gave to his features. Her pencil raced across the page as she tried to capture his essence.

"No, he'd already found another job because he didn't want to get caught in the crossfire, but he also didn't feel right about what was going on. He told me that if something wasn't done soon, when the company collapsed, a lot of people were going to get hurt. Not top brass, but worker ants."

"Well, obviously he was wrong, since Randall Industries is still going strong."

"On the surface. Rot eventually shows."

"Either way, there's no proof. What happened next?"

Tyler blew out a breath. "He asked me to meet him. Lindsey wanted to go to a performance of Shakespeare in the Park, so I made arrangements to meet him nearby. I was going to go ahead and meet her there, but she thought driving two cars was ridiculous and talked me into letting her tag along." A cloud of pain darkened his face. Melissa wanted to kiss it away, but kept her left hand moving over the paper, instead. "And someone shot her."

As Melissa imagined the sunshine that was Lindsey fading, her pencil slowed. Suddenly she felt sorry for the woman she'd never met. Her life was taken for nothing, and with it, something vital in Tyler was stolen. "While you were talking with the accountant?"

Tyler nodded. "I didn't get enough out of him before. At the sound of the shot, he fled."

"Do you think it was a setup?"

Tyler squared his shoulders. "From the look on his face, no. No one's heard from him since."

"You've tried to find him?"

"Lester Collins seems to have disappeared off the face of the earth. And no one's talking."

Had he paid the same price Lindsey had? What could have been so important to hide that lives were made disposable? Melissa put down her pencil and crouched in front of Tyler, holding both his hands in hers. "It's not your fault, you know."

He shook his head. "I knew this was an explosive case. I should have insisted I meet her at the park. If I had, she'd still be alive."

"It still hurts." She wanted to crawl into him and take away the grief.

He nodded, his gaze on a place that didn't include her.

The pain would always be there. She was a fool to think she could ever make him forget. How could she compete with the ghost of the wife who'd owned his heart, still did? Swallowing thickly she asked, "Why would someone want you to relive that agony? How would that help them get whatever it is they want from me?"

He dragged a hand through his hair and expelled a gusty breath. "If we knew that, we'd be ahead of the game."

And in a position to do something about it. She didn't like being in defensive mode. A popping of gravel on the road caught her attention. She cocked her head. "Dee's here. We need a break. Let's go watch her ride."

"SHE DOESN'T MAKE him look half as good as you do," Tyler said, leaning against the white fence as they watched Dee ride. Eclipse's muffled footfalls on the soft ground of the roped dressage ring didn't sing as they had for Melissa. His movements, though still extraordinary, didn't create a sense of awe. And Dee's petite figure seemed to perch atop the horse whereas Melissa's had become part of the horse.

"Good enough to win Horse of the Year last year."

Her smile was more brilliant than the shades of orange washing the evening sky. She wore no shawl—hadn't since he'd rescued her from jail. Her long black hair fluttered in the breeze, teasing his arm. He wanted her—again. He couldn't seem to get enough of her. And that couldn't be good—for either of them. After that first time, he'd made sure to have condoms available. He'd done enough damage without bringing another life into the mess.

"*You* should show him," he said.

Frowning, she shook her head. "I want them to see him, not me."

"They would see magic." As he had.

She blinked, and in those bewitching green eyes, he saw a world of vulnerability. His heart contracted. He slipped an arm around her waist and refocused his attention on the horse going through its paces in the ring.

Lindsey's death still had him raw, and the memory of her threatened to engulf him. She'd been his world, and his do-whatever-it-takes-to-get-the-story attitude had cost her her life.

He had no right to feel the things he did for Melissa. She would never leave this castle, and he realized with a pang that he couldn't stay. He'd made her no promises about the future; she'd asked for none. Yet he felt as if he'd somehow failed her.

It was all so confusing. But he was a reporter. His job was to make order out of chaos, to expose lies. For that he needed to think clearly. He had to unravel the snarled ball of wool in front of him before Melissa ended up just like Lindsey. Figuring out the maze of his complicated emotions would have to wait.

Still, he couldn't escape the feeling that time was running out, that if he didn't do something soon, history would repeat itself. He didn't want the responsibility, but Freddy had put it squarely on his shoulders.

For self-preservation, he needed a breather. With distance, he could get a grip on objectivity. Melissa would be safe here with Dee for a bit. He leaned down and brushed his lips against her forehead, lingering for a moment. "I have some calls to make."

What did he have to offer her?

Nothing at all.

MELISSA WATCHED him leave and felt a sense of loss—as if a cloud had scudded over the sun, stealing its heat. Someone temporary shouldn't feel so permanent. She was beginning to depend on his presence, his touch. This from a woman who'd prided herself on her independence. But Tyler's arrival and Grace's attack had changed that perception. She needed more than these gray walls and wasn't sure how to go about getting it—whatever "it" was.

Dee halted in the center of the ring and saluted the imaginary judge sitting at the top of the ring, then loosened the reins as she petted Eclipse's neck and headed toward Melissa. "How did he look?"

"He needs more engagement in the back."

"He doesn't like the double bridle and stiffens up on me."

"Lighten your hands." The advice was old hat. Dee did her best, but Tyler was right, she couldn't ride Eclipse as well as Melissa did. Dee didn't have the deep connection that came with long hours of companionship. "What time are you picking him up on Friday?"

"I thought we'd leave early. It'll give us time to get settled before we perform."

"Good. I'll wait up for you."

Dee dismounted. Her face was set, disapproving. "You slept with Tyler."

It wasn't a question. "He gave me an enchanted evening." No need to mention mornings or afternoons. It would only make Dee worry more.

"You're heading for heartache."

Melissa searched Dee's eyes for a bit of softness. "Can't you be happy for me?"

"Mel—"

"You have it all, Dee. The husband, the kids. You get to live out there, do what you want. What do I have? I know it's a fantasy. I know it isn't going to last. Just let me enjoy it while I can."

"I don't want to see your heart broken."

Melissa raised her hands helplessly. "Don't you see? It already is."

Dee reached through the fence and hugged her. "Oh, Mel."

TYLER HEADED UP to Melissa's tower and watched her from the window as he dialed Freddy's number. The distance provided no relief. He wanted her here, touching him. Shaking his head, he turned away from the outside view.

She was driving him crazy, and that was no way to get through this. But the harder he tried to get a grip, the more slippery it became. Breath he didn't know he was holding huffed out of him.

He asked about Rena and the baby, and Freddy obliged before getting down to business. "The black substance on the stones you brought isn't mold. It's burned on as if someone etched them with a torch."

"Do you know the history of the castle?" As Tyler spoke, he ripped a piece of paper from the roll beside

Melissa's desk and taped it to the wall. He grabbed a marker and wrote "Castle," then the information about the stones.

"William Carnes imported it from England. It's supposed to have belonged to Sir Alasdair Thorne who is supposed to have studied under Nicholas Flamel, the famed alchemist. The centuries don't match, though."

"Is there anything to this alchemy thing?" For someone who didn't believe in anything he couldn't see, the whole concept seemed half a bubble off level. But just because he didn't believe in things like astrology and numerology didn't mean that others couldn't. And keeping an open mind would allow him to see the whole picture.

"As far as I know it's legend."

"Did your guy make anything out of the marks?" Tyler asked, trying to recall the shape of the scrolls. Melissa would. She could have drawn them for him straight from memory.

"He'd need a bigger sample to see a pattern, but yes, he seemed to think they might be letters or symbols of some kind."

"For an alchemy recipe?" Tyler spun on his heel and headed for the far window. The crumbling tower stood in the corner. What if the answer was in the stones?

Freddy sighed. "I doubt it. Alchemy is more of a philosophy than an actuality—transforming the base metal of ignorance into the gold of wisdom."

"But what if someone took it literally? What if someone really thought these burn marks led to a recipe for riches?"

"You're thinking of Randall again."

Tyler scanned the timeline. "Look at the facts, Freddy. This whole thing started after the mason inadvertently unearthed the markings on the stones." He raked a hand through his hair, remembering the lead article of the *Wall Street Journal* that morning. "Randall's in trouble. Even Wall Street is starting to ask questions."

"Randall's a practical man. According to alchemist belief, the most important part of success in alchemy is the alchemist himself. Only virtue can transcend the spiritual world to appear in the physical world. There's nothing divine about Randall."

"Except in his own mind. How do you know all this?"

Freddy bellowed a laugh. "I'm a master at trivia."

Tyler smiled. You could always count on Freddy to know some arcane bit of knowledge—or at least where to get a lead on it. "What about the rest? Anything on Sable or Tia?"

"Sable has a full calendar and she's keeping the guy I have tailing her on his toes. But so far, she hasn't done anything to warrant a second look. Other than being inordinately happy, there's nothing to report on Tia, either. She's going through money like water—but it's all going for new clothes."

Tyler was drawn to the opposite window. Below, as the sun was sinking into the trees, Melissa and Eclipse danced. His breath caught. He shook his head to loosen the grip of the spell. "What about the boyfriend?"

"Drake West. I'm still waiting on the background check."

Tyler frowned. "Why does the name sound familiar?"

"West Oil."

"Didn't Randall's sister marry a West?"

"I'm betting we'll find some relationship."

Tyler shook his head. "I don't like it."

"You don't like Randall, and you're letting it cloud your judgment."

"Because I don't like Randall, I'm making sure I have

facts to back the hunch.'' Tyler fisted a hand and wanted to punch at something, anything, to dispel the frustration winding him tight. ''It's happening again, Freddy. It never stopped.''

Freddy was quiet for a moment. ''Are you sure you can handle the situation?''

''Yes.'' He had to. For Lindsey. For Melissa. For his own sanity.

''Your job is to watch out for Melissa. I'll do the digging from now on.''

''Fred—''

''I mean it, Tyler.''

Tyler closed his eyes and swallowed his anger. ''Looking out for Melissa means I can't ignore what's going on around here. There's a town going crazy around us. There's someone stirring the pot. And every stone that gets turned—even by you—seems to have Randall under it. You can fire me, but I can't quit.''

Freddy was right. He was too involved.

GOLDEN LIGHT spilled over the room as he threw the wall switch by the French doors leading to the patio. The air-conditioning dried the sheen of sweat from his skin. He walked straight to the discreet bar near the desk and reached for the bottle of twenty-five-year-old single-malt scotch. The cork slipped out of the glass neck with satisfying ease, and he poured generous fingers into a crystal glass. The rich peaty taste went down smooth.

He wandered to the walls of books, barely glancing at the gold-etched lettering on the leather bindings. His hand homed in on the album. As he eased into the carved and gilded wooden armchair covered in silk damask, the pages cracked open to the right spot.

There they were—William and Royal. So young. So

foolish. Didn't take long for both of them to learn that trust ought to be given only in small measures. One idea had led to a kingdom, and the rightful creator had been discarded like garbage. Someone had to pay.

He looked around the well-appointed room, at its comfort, at its richness, at its glamour. This was his. It rightfully belonged to him. And the feeling of power warmed him more than the expensive scotch.

In a few days, the crude was going to blow. But this he would protect. By any means. The riches—gold and oil—in and under the castle also belonged to him. He wouldn't stop until he had all that was his due.

He returned the album to the shelf and placed the glass square in the middle of the desk.

God willing and the creek don't rise, everything would go smoothly. The course of action was set. The scribe would record the events because he couldn't do otherwise. The legal battle was all but won—the proof of wrong right there for all the world to see. No one would dare hold what belonged to him once the truth was exposed. How could they?

And then, since William had up and died before the debts were squared, his daughter would have to atone for his sins.

Chapter Twelve

On Thursday members of Reverend Palmer's church staged a demonstration on the public road near the castle's driveway. Since they weren't trespassing, the sheriff said his hands were tied. They brandished Satan-exorcising placards all day and left them planted on the soft bank of the moat as they faded into the night, chanting hymns.

On Friday they were back bright and early, holding hands and praying for her eternal soul while the sun burned off the thin fog. Dee picked up Eclipse and left for the beehive of activity that was the show grounds, leaving Melissa stung with a tiny bite of envy. The reverend's fire-and-brimstone words followed Dee in and out. She ignored them.

As the truck and trailer exited through the front gate, Tyler's words replayed in Melissa's mind. "*You* should show him." Was there even a remote chance that judges and spectators would see Eclipse's brilliance and not focus on her ugly face? "They would see magic."

No, that was just another pipe dream.

She rubbed her stomach, thought of the possibility of a child already growing there. Closing her eyes, she fiercely prayed that at least one of her fantasies would come true.

Not long after Dee left, Sable stormed the castle, clipping one or two of the faithful in her rush. Never had Melissa seen her stepmother so flustered. She wore no makeup. Her hair wasn't tied into its usual chignon. Her clothes didn't match—as if she'd simply thrown on the first blouse, skirt and shoes she could get her hands on. With the engine still running, the car door winged open. Sable wasn't out of the car before she started shouting for Melissa.

Frowning, Melissa left her chores in the stables, called to Tyler, who was out by the crumbling tower collecting bricks, and hurried toward her stepmother.

"What's wrong?" Melissa asked, catching Sable on the fly.

"Tia's disappeared!" Sable exclaimed in a shrill voice.

Melissa tried to calm her, but Sable kept unraveling before her. "She's probably with one of her friends," Melissa said. "Have you called Drake? They seem inseparable these days."

Hands flying, eyes darting, body undulating, Sable seemed on the verge of becoming airborne or collapsing. "He told me he hasn't seen her since last night."

"Did he seem worried?"

Sable shook her head. "No. No, he didn't. He said she'd planned a shopping expedition with Christie."

"Well, there you go." Melissa tried to usher the now cemented-into-place Sable toward the kitchen. "Let's go call Christie."

Sable's hands clamped viselike on Melissa's arms. "No, don't you see? Tia never came home last night. She told me she was going to be with Drake. He hasn't seen her. Christie hasn't seen her. None of her friends have. This—" Sable choked on a sob.

"This what?"

Sable dumped the contents of her purse right in the

middle of the courtyard. Wallet, coins, credit cards, tubes of lipstick and various scraps of paper fell onto the cobbles. She grabbed an envelope from the middle of the mess and thrust it at Melissa. Melissa glanced at Tyler over Sable's shoulder. He raised an eyebrow in question. His presence gave her a confidence that surprised her.

"It came this morning. With the newspaper." One could set a watch by the steadiness of Sable's morning routine. Paper and coffee were started precisely at seven and consumed before her private trainer arrived at seven-thirty. Exercised, showered and dressed, she was ready to start her day by nine. "It's a ransom note," Sable wailed. "Someone's taken my baby. You have to release the funds. You have to."

"Did you call the police?" Tyler asked as he returned Sable's belongings to her purse.

Sable gripped Melissa's forearms, digging her nails into the skin. "No! No police. It says no police. I want her back alive."

Kidnappings rarely ended well. But there was no point in quoting statistics. Melissa didn't want to even entertain the possibility of her half sister coming to harm. For all her flightiness, Tia wouldn't hurt a fly on purpose. She'd always been a bit of sunshine in Melissa's drab world.

Melissa shook her head. Through the worry whirring like a bird caught in an attic, she tried to think logically. The Dallas police might be of help; the local law certainly wouldn't. Maybe they should call the FBI. Maybe Sable was right. Maybe paying the ransom was the easiest way to guarantee Tia's safe return. "A million dollars is a lot of money."

Sable's eyes narrowed and hardened. Her gaze murdered. "It's nothing to you. Pocket change. We're talking about Tia's *life!*'' Her voice hitched, then her knees gave out, and Melissa followed her slow-motion melt to the courtyard cobbles. ''She's William's daughter, too. It's her money, too.''

''Of course,'' Melissa said softly. ''I'm willing to release the funds, Sable, but it's going to take a few days to cash in assets. It's Friday—''

''I need it now,'' Sable sobbed. ''Today.''

Melissa brushed away a tear-soaked strand of hair from her stepmother's cheek. ''I probably can't get anything to you until Monday.''

Sable's eyes rounded in desperation as she shook her head. ''No! Don't do this to me, Melissa.''

''Mrs. Carnes,'' Tyler said, as he crouched next to them, ''why don't we go inside? You can tell me exactly what happened while Melissa calls her broker. Before we start panicking, let's see what can be done.''

Sable sniffed. ''I need my baby back.''

For all her faults, one thing was certain about Sable— she loved Tia with all her heart. Melissa understood the depth of Sable's torment. She'd do anything to protect the child that might now be growing inside her.

''We'll do our best to make sure she comes back home safely,'' Tyler said in a rich soothing voice.

Nodding, Sable scuttled to her feet. ''I told her that boy was bad news.''

''Drake?'' Melissa asked as Sable leaned heavily on her.

''I don't like the crowd he hangs out with.'' She swiped at the tears running down her cheeks. ''Such rough characters.''

''You think Drake's friends have something to do with Tia's kidnapping?'' Melissa asked. That certainly would narrow their search. And surely Drake's friends wouldn't harm Tia.

"I don't know. Who else? She's a good girl."

"Of course she is." Melissa and Tyler shared a look over Sable's head. Did whoever was playing this awful game of chess know how much Tia meant to her? Was Tia's kidnapping just another way to get to her? Or was it an unrelated event?

"Sable, was there a chess piece with the note?" Melissa asked as she guided her stepmother through the kitchen door.

"Chess piece? No, why?"

Not related. That was a relief. "It's not important."

While Tyler settled Sable on the couch in the sitting room of Melissa's tower—displacing a not-too-happy Selma—Melissa reached her broker and made arrangements for the transfer of the ransom money and its delivery to the castle.

Sable was crying a river of tears while Tyler gently attempted to extract information from her.

Tyler's patient manner with the woman he thought was out to hurt her zinged Melissa's heart with tenderness. In such a short time, this man had managed to invade all of her: heart, body and soul. There were layers to him that would take a lifetime to unearth. And suddenly she wanted that lifetime with a fervor that made her heart contract. These past few weeks had shown her how short life could be, how precious. This new crisis brought the lesson home with urgency. She could not go on living this half-life.

Once Tia was home, she would talk to Tyler. She would tell him about the baby they might have created. She would bare her heart to him, her hopes and dreams. Shuddering with icy premonition, she stepped into the den.

After everything she'd done to him, would this misrepresentation of her fertility make him turn away from her? She noted the irony of the situation. He might leave her not because of her ugly face, but because of her ugly lie.

"Saturday, Sable." Melissa sat on the arm of the couch and reached out to touch her distraught stepmother. "I can get you the money tomorrow."

And for the first time in twenty-two years, her stepmother hugged her.

HE WAITED until the deep of the night to place the call. He wanted to catch her off balance, at the peak of anxiety. Night had a way of exaggerating everything. The phone barely had a chance to ring once before the tremulous "Hello?" warbled over the line. He smiled.

"I have your daughter. Do you want her back?" Technically a lie, but he could get hold of her should the situation warrant it.

"Yes, yes! Oh, God, yes!"

"Then listen, because I'll only say this once." He said his piece, then waited.

"Don't make me do this."

She was whining. Why did they always have to whine?

"The choice is yours."

The silence was long, but not nearly as long as it should have been. "When?"

"How soon do you want your daughter back?"

She gulped, and his smile broadened.

"What about the ransom?" she asked.

The math was simple. He'd known the answer all along. For her daughter, she would do anything.

"Make sure you get that first. It would be a shame to kill for nothing."

SATURDAY MORNING the reverend and his followers were deep into Bible recitations when the fax machine spit out Freddy's background report on Drake West.

After Sable had left last night, Tyler had faxed a copy of the ransom note to Freddy and asked him to make discreet inquiries. Freddy was not too happy about the fact Tia had not only spotted, but ditched, the man he'd had tailing her. Because Tia's kidnapping was possibly another maneuver to weaken Melissa, he and Freddy had decided the best course of action was to avoid involving the law for now and pay the ransom.

"Drake's family is wealthy," Tyler said, as he passed the top sheet to Melissa. The scent of roses, wafting through the open window, reminded him of the petal softness of her skin, and his finger lingered on her hand for a moment. How could he possibly want her again so soon? "But Drake's been cut off."

Just like a flower seeking the sun, she leaned into his touch before taking the page from him. "How long?"

"Since he quit school one semester before graduation." He handed Melissa the rest of the report and stuck his hands into his jeans pockets to keep himself from reaching for her. That would only anchor the bond between them, and he needed to find a way to cut it without breaking her heart. "Must have been tough to have the silver spoon yanked out of his mouth like that."

She looked up at him from her curled position on the corner of the couch. Heat colored her cheeks as she became aware of his admiring stare. Her hand started to rake hair over the left half of her face. When she realized what she was doing, she hooked the hair behind her ear and smiled at him. A punch to the gut would have hurt less than that show of trust. "You don't think he'd set this up just to get a hand on her money, do you?"

"Anything's possible," he said, trying to order his thoughts.

"But wouldn't marrying her be easier and more lucrative?"

"Not if he's not sure of your intent toward your sister."

"What's a million dollars when there's billions where that came from?"

Tyler pointed at the financial section of Freddy's report. "Looks like he might need funds right now, judging from his bank balance."

She shook her head, sending blue ribbons of sunlight rippling through the soft waves of her dark hair. "So he'd have her kidnapped? That doesn't make any sense, either."

"It does if the debt is an illegal one. He has no official record, but it looks like he got himself in a financial bind last year."

"What happened?"

"From what Freddy can figure out, it looks as if our boy likes to play the ponies. Someone came to the rescue."

"His parents?"

"Doesn't say. Maybe he's on his own this time. Gambling isn't a fever that disappears overnight."

She stabbed the report with a finger and looked at him with a determined look that had panic twisting his gut. "I want you to go there."

"Where?"

"His house. It's not far from here. It's out near Trinity Meadows. You need to go there and search it."

He shook his head. "Not a good idea."

"Why not?"

"For one, I don't like the smell of this." Any of it.

Why strike now? It smacked of coincidence, and Tyler had never believed in coincidence.

"There are no chess pieces involved," Melissa said, stretching her long legs in front of her. He stared at the curve of the arch of her foot, thought of planting a kiss there and wondered when he'd developed a foot fetish.

"It's not related," she said. "And if Drake is responsible for Tia's kidnapping, then he's sure to have left some clue behind. Maybe she's even there at his place." She ran a hand through her long hair, causing his fingers to twitch with need. "At least if Drake is the one who's holding her, we know he won't hurt her."

We know no such thing. Greed had a way of clouding judgment. He didn't like the annoying itch between his shoulder blades. It always announced bad news. "I can't leave you."

She cocked her head and lasered her gaze on his. Temper crackled in the deep green of her eyes. "Why not?"

The reverend's disciples were growing more restless by the day. Who knew when they'd try to breach the moat and do more than preach at Melissa? And there was still their unknown chess player to contend with. What if his plan was to leave Melissa without anything or anyone to protect her before he made his final strike? What better way to leave her vulnerable than to take away her support network? Grace was still in a coma at the hospital. Deanna was out of town. Even her favorite horse was away. And with the kidnapping, someone was conveniently keeping Tia and Sable from filling the gap. Not that they would have, anyway, but it certainly took care of the possibility. "I don't want to leave you alone."

She dismissed him with a wave. "I've been alone all of my life."

He bent down, resting both his hands on the couch's arm and met her gaze. "But not like this."

Not with danger all around her and with them no closer to finding the source than they were two weeks ago. He reached for her and pulled her tightly against him. His mind was full of her. He wanted to hold her so much that sometimes it hurt. The words he wanted to give her were nothing more than a jumble in his mind. He wanted to tell her his involvement with her was more than just a promise to Freddy. Why had he thought he could leave her? In the past few weeks she'd touched a part of him he thought had died with Lindsey. He could almost imagine living, loving—happiness—again. With her. And it scared him.

A slow smile, full of feminine awareness, graced her lips. She leaned in and kissed him. It was warm and gentle and solemn. It was a pledge and a bond. It was whole-hearted trust. And it nearly undid him.

"Sable will be here any minute now," Melissa said, eyes shining. "And the broker's due soon with the money. I won't be alone." She gave his chest a little shove. "Go."

"Stay right here," he insisted.

"Where would I go?"

"You're still under house arrest," he reminded her. The last thing he wanted was to have her put in jail again for violating the arrangement Freddy had worked so hard to gain her. "You can't leave."

Smiling, she kissed him again. "Go."

DRAKE'S ROOM, not far from the racetrack, reflected a lifetime of growth, Tyler mused. And fom the bronzed baby shoes on the pressed-board dresser to the tarnished football trophies on the plywood shelves hammered into the wall with iron brackets to the betting tickets littered everywhere, it was apparent that Drake liked to hang on to things.

In typical bachelor style, clothes were strewn all over the floor, and the full-size bed was unmade. The odor of sweat and sex arose from a pile of dirty laundry by the bed. Above the cluttered desk hung a corkboard covered with pictures.

Drake as a baby being held by his beaming mother. Seeing the resemblance to J.R. Randall in the woman's face cemented his belief that this kidnapping was no co-incidence.

Several pictures of Drake holding a sleek Thoroughbred horse in the winner's circle. Flymaster owned by J.R. Randall. J.R.'s Mastermind owned by J.R. Randall. Black Witch owned by J.R. Randall.

Drake with his arms around a ragged band of spoiled brats who'd been handed too much too easily and didn't know what to make of themselves. Rebellion was stamped on their faces. Tyler pocketed that picture. Maybe Freddy could come up with names.

There was another photo of Drake with Tia, who was looking at him in wide-eyed adoration. If Drake was in-volved with Tia's kidnapping, Tyler would break every bone in his body.

On the desk Tyler found a recorder attached to the phone. Why would Drake feel the need to tape his tele-phone conversations? Tyler hit the rewind button. What he heard chilled him to the bone.

"Mom'll worry."

"She's too busy to take notice of you. Come on, Tia. It's only for a few days."

"Okay, then. When will you be by?"

"I have to go pick up a few things. We don't want to

be found until we're ready to be found.'' He laughed. *''Why don't you meet me there?''* Drake followed with directions.

''I'll have to take the long way around. I think Mom's having me followed. But I'll be there.''

Was Tia in on her own kidnapping? Was this her way of squeezing more money out of her sister? Seeing as how Tia was going through it like water and given her greedy nature, Tyler wouldn't put it past her. Didn't she realize how her selfishness was hurting Melissa?

Tyler swore. ''The little bitch.''

TYLER FOUND TIA sprawled by the lake's edge at the Randall fishing camp, and it took all he had not to strangle her on the spot. ''Didn't anyone tell you sun was bad for your skin?''

''I have sunscreen on. SPF 15.''

She didn't seem the least bit embarrassed about being caught in a lie. She lay totally relaxed on the chaise, her tiny fuchsia-and-orange bikini leaving little to the imagination.

''What are you doing here?'' she asked, peering at him over her sunglasses. ''I thought you and Mel were joined at the hip.''

''Do you have any idea of the grief you've caused your mother and sister?''

''Grief? What are you talking about?''

''The fake kidnapping.''

''What kidnapping?'' She picked up the bottle of water at her side and took a long swallow. Cool as a cucumber, this girl.

''The one you and Drake engineered.''

Capping the bottle, she narrowed her gaze at him. ''You know, I thought I liked you, but now I've decided that your cheese has slipped off your cracker.'' She swung her legs over the side of the chaise, wriggled her feet into high-heeled sandals and picked up the color-coordinated wrap puddled at her feet. ''If you're going to throw a fit, then I'm going back inside.''

As she rose, he snaked out a hand and closed his fingers hard on her shoulder. He kept his voice low and enunciated every syllable. ''What are you doing here?''

She whirled toward him, gave an impatient huff and tapped one foot. ''What does it look like I'm doing? Drake's uncle let him borrow his cabin for the weekend and we're making full use of it.''

A sick feeling washed over him. She didn't know. Drake was using her, and she had no idea. ''Where's Drake?''

''Out.'' She lifted her chin defiantly, protecting her scoundrel lover.

He tightened his grip and brought his nose close to hers. ''Out where?''

She batted at his hand, dropping her wrap. ''Ouch, you're hurting me.''

''You're going to be hurting a whole lot more if you don't answer my question,'' he said through gritted teeth. ''Where's Drake?''

''He had an errand to run and said he'd be back by noon.''

Tyler pushed the fuchsia-and-orange wrap at her. ''Put this on. You're coming with me.''

''I am not,'' she said, letting the wrap fall to her feet.

''Your mother thinks you've been kidnapped. Your sister is putting together one million dollars in cash to save your sorry skin. And your lover set it all up.'' He picked up the wrap and shoved it at her once more. ''You're getting dressed and you're coming with me. Now. Neither of them deserves what you've put them through."

"You're wrong. Drake would never do this." Tia pulled on the sheer dress over her head and adjusted it over her slim frame. "Why would he pretend to kidnap me? What does it gain him?"

"Money."

She sneered. "Well, there you go. Drake doesn't need money. His family has pots of it."

"His family does. But he owes nearly a million dollars."

"You're crazy."

"Who pays for your dates?"

She frowned. "What does that have to do with anything?"

"Two to one he's conveniently forgotten his wallet on most of them."

While she blinked at him, Tyler grabbed her hand and jerked her toward the gate he'd sneaked through earlier, then ordered her to enter the code. Instinct screamed at him. He shouldn't have left Melissa alone.

He barely gave Tia time to climb into the Jeep before he set off. Tires squealing, he peeled onto the road and sped toward the castle. "If anything happens to your sister while I've been out looking for you, I'm holding you personally responsible."

Worse, he could never forgive himself.

With one hand, he reached for his cell phone and dialed Melissa's number.

He got no answer.

Chapter Thirteen

The phone rang. Sable lunged for it, but Melissa stopped her. "Let me get the recorder going first." Tyler, anticipating a follow-up to the ransom demand, had left his microcassette recorder behind. She pushed the record button. "Put the phone on speaker first."

Sable's fingers shook as she followed Melissa's instructions. "Hello?"

"Do you have the money?" The voice over the phone warbled with electronic distortion.

Sable's eyes darted to the leather case at the foot of the computer table and the twenty-two pounds of bills stacked in it. "Yes. I want to speak with Tia."

"Farmers' Market in Weatherford. Be there at noon. Alone. I'll know if you're not. Buy a quart basket of cherry tomatoes from the woman in the Indian-blanket-print shirt with the brown cowboy hat. Leave the money—which you'll have in a shopping bag—beside her booth."

Like a rubbernecker at a car wreck, Melissa leaned toward the phone. He was picking the busiest time of the day in a location likely to be crowded. He could just melt into the sea of people. Catching him under those conditions wouldn't be easy. She needed to find Tyler.

Sable strangled the edge of the computer table with

both hands. "Tia. I need to speak with Tia. I need to know she's all right."

"As you leave the market," the kidnapper continued, "you'll see a booth selling pots of herbs. I'll leave Tia's location in a newspaper there."

Before Sable could say anything more, the line went dead. "No!" She punched buttons, trying desperately to reconnect with the kidnapper and managed to get only a dial tone. "No!"

"Sable?" Melissa touched her stepmother's arm. "It's okay. We'll get her back. Take a deep breath."

Sable whirled on her, hands fluttering like caged bats. "I need a shopping bag. A big one." She started searching the room, throwing around papers, paintings and anything that got in her way.

Melissa caught Sable's arm just as she was starting to attack the drawing table. "There're some in the kitchen. Let's go down. Okay?"

Sable nodded, then grabbed the case filled with money and held it tightly to her chest as they made their way down to the kitchen.

From a closetlike room off the kitchen, Melissa withdrew a large white plastic bag with handles that Grace used to gather peaches in the orchard. Sadness murmured through her at the thought of Grace. The floor nurse had said there was no change in Grace's condition today. Maybe the reverend and his crew were starting to have an effect on her, because Melissa sent up a little prayer for her friend's recovery. She shook her head. *It's the hymns,* she thought. They reminded her of Sunday mornings and her mother. Victoria Carnes had had a beautiful voice.

After they'd transferred the contents of the case into the bag, Sable insisted on stowing it in her car. Melissa followed her outside. Sunlight drove a spike of pain through her left eye. The breeze carried the boom of the reverend's bull-horned voice into the courtyard as he described the horrors of hell awaiting her. "...you must cleanse your-a soul before the darkness of-a hell descends on-a you..."

"I'm going to call Tyler and let him know about the rendezvous point."

"No!" Sable slammed the trunk shut. The reverend's voice hiked up an octave as if he wanted his message heard over the noise.

"...power lies in-a the renouncement of the forces of-a evil..."

"You can't go there alone," Melissa said.

Sable shoved both her hands through her hair as if she was going to pull it out. Untidy wisps now spiked out of her careful chignon. "Nothing can go wrong. I'm following his instructions to the letter. He said alone. I'm going alone."

"But, Sable—"

"No buts." Sable opened the driver's door and reached inside. When she straightened, she held a red crocodile handbag at her hip and a silver handgun pointed at Melissa's chest. "I'm sorry, Melissa. I don't want to do this, but I don't have a choice."

Gasping, Melissa instinctively put up her hands and stepped back. Sable looked desperate enough that Melissa didn't want to give her any reason to press the trigger. "Okay, okay. I won't call Tyler. We'll do it your way. Put away the gun."

"No, you don't understand." Her forehead crimped and she gave a sad shake of her head. She waved the gun around, making Melissa feel like a giant bull's-eye. "You're part of the deal."

"You're right. I don't understand." In spite of the sun's heat, a chill shuddered through her.

As Sable advanced, Melissa retreated. The reverend's voice kept cadence with their pace.

"I have to take care of what's mine," Sable said.

"Of course. And you'll get Tia back safely." Melissa forced brightness into her voice and tried to contain the panic building inside her. Glancing around, she sought a way to escape. In the middle of the courtyard, she made a perfect target. The gazebo, the stables, even the kitchen were too far. Sable could get off a couple of shots before Melissa could reach any cover. Because of the reverend and his flock, both the portcullis and the postern doors were bolted.

"Don't even think about making a run. I will shoot."

The determination in Sable's eyes said that she would. "I want you to walk nice and slowly to the southwest tower."

"There's nothing there." Except a dry well that served no purpose other than to preserve authenticity. In its European incarnation, it had supplied the household with water. Now it created a very real hazard for her.

"I know." She waved the gun. Afraid Sable would inadvertently loose a bullet, Melissa saw no alternative except to obey. The sun's brightness made her eyes tear and blurred her surroundings. Sharp rocks, hard doors, thorny bushes all smudged into a watercolor softness. She blinked madly, but all that did was increase the burn and stream of tears.

"Sable, please…"

The reverend's voice dropped into a sudden silence. Melissa filled her lungs with air and opened her mouth to scream. The plea for help died before it was born when Sable's hand steadied and her aim became too sure. The flock took over where the reverend left off. Their voices rose into a rendition of "Walk in the Light."

"Open the door."

Maybe that was her chance. If she played things right, she could knock Sable down with the door and escape. "It's not safe in there."

"I know. Open the door."

Swallowing hard, Melissa pulled on the door. Fear frazzled her thoughts. *Think, Melissa, think.* She couldn't just meekly let Sable walk her to her death. "It's stuck."

"Try harder."

"You won't shoot. Not with people who can hear you just outside the castle walls and testify against you."

"One shot is all I need. They're making so much racket out there, they won't hear one little backfire."

"You'll be the first suspect once they find me. The reverend and his people will remember you were the last person here before I disappeared."

"My dear, they'll think their prayers worked and they banished the evil witch. Open the door."

The rotten wood finally gave way and the rusty hinges creaked as Melissa pulled the handle.

"In you go."

After the harsh sunshine out in the courtyard, the darkness in the tower blinded her. Melissa wiped her eyes with the sleeve of her shirt. "Trust in the Promise" rose on the breeze and echoed against the tower's cool empty interior. "Keep going."

Melissa carefully slid one foot behind the other, keeping Sable's silhouette against the outside sun in front of her. "Keep going."

Her heel bumped against the lip of the dry well in the center of the tower.

"Keep going."

Melissa held her ground. "You don't want to do this, Sable. Tia will come home. There's no need to get yourself in trouble like this."

Sable advanced, her silhouette growing larger with each step.

"Sable—"

Her stepmother swung the red handbag, and the swiftness and the savageness of the blow to Melissa's chest stole her breath and made her stumble backward. She tripped over the lip and fell into the well.

"'Rolling downward, through the midnight,'" sang the faithful.

Forehead, elbows, knees, hips and shoulder scraped against the rough stones, ripping cloth and skin like tissue paper. Instinctively Melissa protected her head. After what seemed an eternity, she landed hard on her left side on a pile of rubble. Pain exploded in a thousand sparks as she gasped for breath. The panic of her own labored gasps rang and repeated until it filled her.

Click. A beam from a flashlight shone down at her. Memories came pouring back. She was eight. It was dark. Pain was eating her alive. *Mama! Mama!* Then a beam of light. An angel. Hands reaching down for her, prying her out of the car. A gentle voice, cooing, *Shh, hush now.* Wind all around, feeding the gnawing pain. Cool grass under her. A woman with long brown hair. She stared at something. Melissa craned her neck. A twisted black lump against gray concrete. A moan inside. A small cry for help. *Mama! Mama's in the car.* The panic in her voice wormed inside her, twisting, tightening, gorging on the pain. But the woman simply stared at the mangled shell. *Shh, shh, hush. I'm sorry, baby, but I have to protect what's mine.*

Silence so deep, so hard, it deafened. A hiss. A crack.

An explosion of color—white flashes, orange flames, black smoke. The heat. The smell of burning flesh. The smell of death.

The child of long ago screamed at the horror. The woman of now had to hold in the pain. *Play dead, play dead. If she thinks you're dead, she won't shoot.*

Sable. She'd been the woman who'd pulled her out of the car. She'd let her mother die. Sable could have saved her mother and she'd let her die.

"I didn't have a choice then," Sable sobbed. "I don't have a choice now. I have to protect what's mine."

Anger, raw and blistering, had Melissa wanting to scramble up the wall to strangle her stepmother. But she lay absolutely still. *Don't breathe. Don't move. Stay alive. You've done it before. You can do it again.*

"Tia comes first. She has to."

The beam of light winked out. Dust and stone fragments came tumbling down as Sable covered the opening with boards. Still Melissa didn't budge.

"Savior be my light through the hours in darkness shrouded," intoned the faithful.

Finally a door slammed shut. A lock clanked into place. A car engine started and faded away.

Melissa screamed for help, but over the congregation's voices, no one could hear her call.

"THEY'RE GONE," Tyler said after he'd searched the tower, kitchen and stables for Melissa. The reverend and his noisy flock were a powerful distraction, but Tyler focused on the task at hand. He rewound the tape in the recorder by the phone and listened to the kidnapper's demands. Sable's car was gone. The fact Melissa had gone with her chapped his hide.

Damn and blast the woman. Couldn't she follow simple

instructions? What would happen if the local police caught her during the exchange? Couldn't she see she'd be thrown in jail for violating her house arrest? Worse, what if Drake saw her trailing Sable and panicked?

Glancing at his watch, he saw he still had time to make the rendezvous. He snatched a scrap of paper from the mess all over the floor and scribbled down Freddy's phone number.

"I want you to call this number and play this tape to the man who answers. His name is Freddy Gold."

Tia took the paper and examined the number. "Melissa's uncle."

He nodded. "Tell him to get a copy of the ransom note and of this tape to the police."

"But Drake—"

"If he's lucky the police will get to him before I do."

Tia's lower lip pursed in a pout. "He's—"

"A rat who used your good nature. And now your mother and your sister are in danger. Do you understand?"

Closing her eyes, Tia nodded. "I'll call."

"Good girl." Tyler gave her arms a squeeze, then bolted for the door. "Stay here. Don't go anywhere until we get back."

SHE WASN'T GOING to die now that she was finally starting to live. She wouldn't give Sable the satisfaction of pulling the rug out from under her world twice in a lifetime.

Reaching for another hold along the wall of the well, Melissa lost her balance and fell back into the pit.

Nothing stirred the hot dank air. It clung to her like an unwanted second skin, causing rivulets of sweat to stream down her back and between her breasts. The smell of dust and age filled her nostrils and seemed to clog her airway.

She wiped her hands along the seams of her jeans and reached up once more. She made it almost halfway to the top before her fingers cramped and missed a hold. Her ankle twisted beneath her as she landed again on the rubble. She howled as much in anger as in pain.

"When I get you, you're going to pay for this, Sable. You're going to pay for Mama, too." Spurred on by her thoughts of vengeance, she got up, dusted her hands on her jeans and went back to the task of freeing herself.

Glancing up, she could see nothing but black. It was as if the darkness were wrapping itself around her—just as it had on that night so long ago. "Don't cry," she told herself. "It's not going to get you anywhere."

Just as tears had gotten her nowhere when she was eight. They hadn't brought her mother back. They hadn't made her father love her. They hadn't taken away the pain. Drawing, peopling her paintings with her monsters, had been the only way to cage the fears, the only way to even dare to think of tomorrow. Action, not tears. The strategy had worked then, and it would work now. Thoughts of payback pushed her on.

How long ago had Sable left? How long before Tyler arrived?

Changing tactics, Melissa chunked stones up against the boards covering the opening and hoped the clunking sound would attract someone's attention now that the reverend and his followers seemed to have taken a breather.

"Help!" she yelled between throws. Tyler would return soon. He would hear her. He would get her out. All she had to do was let him know where to look. She hung on to that thought and launched another missile. "Tyler, help!"

Her throat soon became raw. Her voice was hoarse. Her

arms could barely manage enough momentum to throw. "Help!"

A board moved. Melissa stilled, held her breath.

"Melissa?"

"Tia? What are you doing here?"

"I could ask you the same thing."

"Is Sable here? Tyler?"

"As far as I know Sable's in Weatherford. Tyler went after her. How did you end up down there?"

"Long story. There's rope in the tack room. Get me out of here." *Please. Now. Fast.*

"Hang on. I'll be right back."

When she returned, Tia set the lantern from the tack room on the lip of the well, then lowered a rope. Melissa tied a butterfly hold around her waist, something she'd seen often on the adventure television shows she liked to watch, and prepared to climb. Melissa exchanged few words with Tia while she clambered up the wall. Once she spilled over the well's lip, she fell into Tia's arms.

"Let's get out of here," Melissa said between gasps as she sought to regain her breath.

They hurried out into the sunshine and, blinking madly, Melissa collapsed on a patch of grass. Selma wrapped herself around Melissa's ankles and meowed.

Tia reached for the cat and stroked her. "She's the reason I found you. She was scratching at the door and meowing like crazy. Then I heard you. Oh, Melissa..."

Selma settled on Melissa's lap and purred. Hanging on to the cat with one arm and her sister with the other, Melissa asked, "What are you doing here? We've been so worried about you. The note. The kidnapping. The ransom—"

"I didn't know." Tia launched into an explanation of her stolen weekend with Drake and Tyler's shattering of her illusion. "I can't believe Drake would do something like that to me. I thought he loved me. I thought he wanted this romantic weekend away so he could ask me to marry him."

Tia was crying now, her head against Melissa's shoulder. "I'm sorry, Tia. I know how hard you fell for him."

Tia pushed away from Melissa's hug and swiped at her cheeks. "Here I am crying like a baby over a stupid guy and you're all cut and bruised. How did you end up in that hole?"

She couldn't add to Tia's misery by telling her sister that Sable had tried to kill her. Still cradling Selma, Melissa rose shakily to her feet. "Later. Let's go in. I want to get changed."

Tia nodded and wrapped an arm around Melissa's waist as if her sister was an invalid. Tia was a sweet girl and deserved better than someone like Drake, Melissa thought. What kind of man bartered the love of a woman to pay for a gambling debt?

Something clicked in Melissa's mind and she swayed with the horror of it. "I have to call Tyler."

Chapter Fourteen

East of Courthouse Square, the Farmers' Market teemed with people who milled from stall to stall in no apparent hurry. The scent of fresh produce tangled with that of dust and sweat. Laughter and a medley of voices rode the breeze in waves. Going against the flow, Tyler searched for the woman in the Indian-print shirt selling tomatoes. He spotted Sable first. Her red designer skirt, cream silk blouse and high heels stood out like a beacon in the jumble of shorts, T-shirts and sneakers. So did the snarl on her face in a sea of smiles and good humor.

He feigned interest in cantaloupes while he kept Sable in view as she put down the plastic shopping bag and paid for her basket of cherry tomatoes. Scanning the faces, he searched for Melissa, but didn't see her. With her fear of being out in public, she'd probably stayed in the car. A curl of relief whistled out. At least she'd had that much good sense. He'd need all his alertness for Drake. He'd feel better if she was safe at home, but in a way, it was good to know that she could break her self-imposed confinement for the sister she loved. The sacrifice gave him hope.

Sable's gaze flitted through the crowd. Frowning, she

headed for the herb booth at the opposite end of the row, throwing the tomatoes in the first trash bin she saw.

Hiding behind sunglasses, Tyler kept watch on the shopping bag she clutched. Soon a young, affable-looking man struck up a conversation with the tomato seller. With his sports sandals, cargo shorts, T-shirt and sunglasses, he looked like just another city boy on an outing in the country, but Tyler recognized him from his pictures as Drake. As Drake left, he picked up both his small backpack and the bag Sable had left behind.

Tyler dropped the melon on the table and quickly fell into step with Drake. Clamping a hand on the young man's shoulder, Tyler said, "Hey, Drake, long time no see. How about you and me mosey on down to the parking lot and catch up on old times?"

"Get lost, creep." Drake tried to dislodge his hold, but Tyler held on.

"Now is that any way to talk to someone who has your health in mind? You wouldn't want to attract the attention of that bicycle cop, now would you? It'd be kind of hard to explain what you're doing with a million dollars in your bag."

Drake jerked a look at Tyler and blanched. "It's all in the details, Drake. And judging from your losing streak at the track, I'd say you're not too good when it comes to details."

"What do you want?"

"For starters, the shopping bag." Tyler kept his expression genial and lowered his voice so only Drake could hear. "Then I'd really like to rearrange the features on your face. A man who uses a woman the way you did deserves a good pounding. But for now I'll settle for some answers." He sent Drake a closed-mouth grin. "Mind you, if I don't like what I hear, we can always go back to the pounding.''

Drake swerved, trying to loosen Tyler's hold, and got his head rapped against the camper top of the truck they were passing for his trouble. His sunglasses slipped from his face and dangled from a cord around his neck.

''Let's start from the beginning,'' Tyler said, leading Drake deeper into the rows of cars in the lot. ''I'm having a hard time putting all the pieces together.''

Drake snorted. ''Like that's news.''

At his Jeep Tyler shoved Drake into the passenger seat and threw the shopping bag in the back. Drake tried to launch himself across the seat and exit on the driver's side, but Tyler pinned him with a knee in the small of the back and an arm at the neck. ''Start talking.''

''I have nothing to say.''

''Okay, you want to do it this way. Do you play chess?''

''What?''

Tyler heard genuine puzzlement in his voice. ''It's a simple enough question, Drake. Do you play chess?''

''Nah. It's a sissy game.''

''Yeah, you seem more like a tennis-and-croquet type of guy.''

Swearing, Drake tried to buck Tyler off.

''Why are you trying to scare Melissa?''

Before Drake could answer, a set of fingernails raked Tyler's back. ''Let him go, you idiot. You're going to ruin everything.''

Sable clawed at him like a mad cat. ''There was nothing in the paper.'' She beat him with it for good measure. ''If you hurt him, I'll never get Tia back.''

While Tyler attempted to dislodge Sable from his back, Drake got loose and sprinted away. Tyler pushed Sable aside and set off after him. Sable's voice followed them. "Let him go! I want my daughter back!"

"She's safe, Sable," Tyler shouted as he ran. "Go call the cops."

"No! Tia!"

Drake was rounding the end of the parking lot, heading back toward Courthouse Square and its beehive of people. As he looked back, he tripped over a rise in the terrain, falling hard on his knee.

Tyler caught up to him. Drake held on to his bleeding and swelling knee, whimpering like a two-year-old.

"Deal," a panting Drake said. "Let's make a deal."

Tyler crouched next to Drake. "Only deal I want is the truth. Why the chess game with Melissa if all you wanted was the money to pay off your gambling debt?"

"No choice." Grimacing, Drake took a bandanna from his pocket and dabbed at his bleeding knee.

"There's always a choice."

Drake shook his head. "To get the money, I had to get Melissa off her land. You just couldn't keep your nose out of where it didn't belong. Because of you, she wasn't budging. The goons were on my back, so I had to move to plan B."

"Kidnapping Tia."

Drake nodded, frowning at his knee.

"She loved you, you know. How could you do that to her?"

"She wanted to settle down."

"You didn't."

Drake swore as he hugged his knee to his chest. "Do I look like I'm old enough to settle down with a high-maintenance wife and a pack of rug rats?"

No, he was still stuck in the selfish stage. "Marrying her would have given you access to the Carnes fortune."

"Only if Melissa chose to share. And the bitch keeps tight purse strings. I couldn't wait that long on a horse I wasn't sure would show."

"Seems to me you have a habit of betting on horses with long odds. This one could have fed your habit for years. Your venture into kidnapping turned the goose with the golden egg against you."

"What good is the goose if I'm wearing cement boots in the Trinity River?" Drake removed the blood-soaked bandanna from his knee. The blood had stopped flowing, but the puffy skin around his knee was already purpling.

Time to get some answers, then let the cops take care of him. "Who are you working for?"

Drake licked his lips, but didn't answer.

"It's your choice," Tyler said, gripping Drake by the arm and pulling him up. "You can talk to me or to the cops. Either way it's going to come out."

"Deal?" Drake hissed in a breath. "I give you the name and you let me go." He hesitated. "And I get the shopping bag back."

Tyler silently sneered. The rat was cornered, and greed was still his number-one priority. "Spill."

"Shake first."

"Talk and you get the money."

"Swear."

"On my honor."

Drake hobbled on one leg as Tyler dragged him farther from the crowd. "Randall promised to cover my debt if I helped him get Melissa off her land."

"Why?"

"How should I know? Slow down, would ya!"

Tyler tightened his grip and pressed on. "You just up and tried to scare a woman out of her home for no reason." Then Tyler remembered the survey of Melissa's land that Randall had kindly paid for. Oil? Had Randall faked the results? Had Randall wanted Melissa off her land in order to steal the oil under the castle? With his business crumbling, he needed a source of income to keep it afloat.

"There was a reason," Drake said. "A million of them."

"Why would you rat on Randall and cut off your meal ticket?"

"If it means staying out of jail…" Drake shrugged. "A guy's gotta do what he's gotta do."

So much for loyalty among thieves.

As they neared the Jeep, Sable stopped her nervous pacing when she recognized them. With a cry of anguish, she ran toward them. She grabbed Drake's T-shirt with both hands and shook him. "Where's my baby? Where's Tia?"

Tyler pried her hands off Drake's shirt and pushed her away. "One thing at a time, Sable."

She danced around him, trying to get her hands on Drake. "But he—"

Tyler twisted Drake's arms back and, using his belt, fashioned handcuffs. "I want you to go back to your car. I want you and Melissa to drive back to the castle. Is that understood?"

Hands on hips, steam practically coming out of her ears, Sable paced around Tyler as he pressed Drake into the passenger seat. "But he—"

Tyler straightened. "Did you call the cops?"

Sable shook her head and waved a hand at Drake. "No, he has Tia. He—"

"Hey, you promised no cops," Drake whined.

"No, I promised you'd get the money."

Drake swore. Tyler was about to shut the door. Drake

stuck his foot out to stop the momentum. "Wait!" The expression of his face was one of desperation. He licked his lips, then met Tyler's gaze. "I know who's responsible for your wife's death."

Tyler froze. His pulse roared in his ears. Everything in him wanted to rip this man apart for the answer to the question that had tortured him for more than a year. The feeling he'd had all along that this was somehow linked to Lindsey congealed into certainty. "Spill."

His voice was so low, so cold, Drake's eyes widened with fear. He snaked his tied hands toward Tyler. "Untie me first."

Tyler gripped Drake's throat and slowly squeezed. "Spill."

Sitting with his wrists bound, Drake tried to break Tyler's hold, but only managed to tighten the choke. Sweat poured down his face. "Randall," he choked out. "Randall."

"All I've got is the word of a worm trying to squirm out of a bad situation."

"I've got proof."

Tyler drew in a long breath of air, but none of it seemed to fill his lungs. "Where?"

Drake gasped. "Safe. Taped conversations."

He shoved Drake back in his seat. Drake coughed and hacked.

"You and me are going to take a little ride," Tyler said.

"What about Tia?" Sable asked, her tone surprisingly meek. "There was nothing in the paper. I need to know where she is."

"Take Melissa back to the castle," Tyler said as he locked the Jeep door and slammed it shut. "Tia's there."

"At the castle?"

He nodded. Sable's eyes bugged out in surprise. "How? When?"

"Take Melissa home." She'd be safe there. And when he made peace with the last part of the puzzle of Lindsey's death, they would have to talk.

Nodding, Sable trotted off toward the other end of the lot.

Tyler rounded the front of the Jeep and got in the driver's seat. Without giving Sable another thought, he fired up the engine. "First stop your safe, then you'd better pray Randall's home."

MELISSA SNARLED as Tyler's cell number connected her once more to his voice mail. She jabbed the off button. "He's not answering."

"It's probably good news," Tia said from the couch in Melissa's den. She stroked a purring Selma. "They found Drake and they're down at the police station sorting everything out. You'll see. He'll be here any minute now."

"He would have called." But the tension of something wrong clung to her with its icy teeth and wouldn't let go. Drake had been deep in debt last year when Tyler's story was killed, and magically his debt was erased. He owed again this year and he'd kidnapped Tia to raise the money he needed. She didn't like the coincidence. She paced the length of the room and punched in Tyler's number once more.

A car honked outside, startling Tia and cutting short Selma's purring. Both women rushed to the window in time to see the portcullis raise and the reverend and his faithful shake their placards at the black Lincoln Town Car. "Sable."

They tromped down the stairs and met the car in the courtyard. Tia flung herself at her mother. Sable clasped her daughter to her and wept with such heartfelt relief that Melissa found the edge of her hatred cracking.

Holding Tia, Sable met Melissa's gaze and fear flitted through her eyes. "I'm sorry," she said. Her painted nails curled around the child she loved, the child she was willing to kill for. "I'm so sorry."

"Mom?" Tia asked as she leaned out of her mother's crushing embrace. "What's wrong? What happened to Drake? Where's Tyler?"

Gaze still glued to Melissa's, Sable swallowed hard. "I'm glad you're—"

"Save it, Sable." Tia didn't need to know of her mother's betrayal. Drake's duplicity was enough to handle in one day.

"I didn't want to. I didn't have a choice."

For Tia's sake, Melissa bit back the anger she wanted to let fly at Sable. "Where's Tyler?"

Stroking Tia's hair, Sable shrugged. "Probably at the Randall estate."

"What do you mean, probably?" The tension straining Melissa's shoulders snaked down her spine.

"He wasn't exactly in a sharing mood," Sable said, using the car door as a shield. "He ordered me here and left with Drake. I'm assuming, given that Drake said Randall killed his wife, that they're headed for a showdown with James Randall."

Tyler had been right all along. James Randall, her friend, her mentor, was behind all this. Melissa closed her eyes and took a long breath. This was not good. The child's cry echoed in the recesses of her mind, filling her with a burning sense of helplessness. Tyler was going to face his wife's killer in the killer's own territory. The odds weren't good. She couldn't lose him. But she couldn't deal with this alone. She needed help.

There was only one person who knew as many details of this story as they did.

Swiveling on her heel, Melissa headed for the kitchen. She reached for the phone above Grace's desk, drew back, then with a huff picked up the receiver and dialed the number she knew by heart but had never used. While the phone rang, she swallowed hard. At the sound of the voice, her hand shook and she almost slammed down the receiver. Pain, so much pain between them. And she was responsible for half of it.

"Uncle Freddy," she said, cursing the croak in her voice.

"Melissa." The voice held both elation and apology.

For the first time in twenty years, guilt nudged at her conscience. Her sweaty hand tightened on the receiver. She swallowed the tight knot in her throat. "I need your help."

"Anything."

She closed her eyes at the eagerness of his voice. Why had she rebuffed all his efforts to get close to her? Stubborn pride. She couldn't let it get in the way again. "I can't reach Tyler, and I think he's in trouble."

"Where is he?"

Tears burned her eyes at the concern in his voice. "The Randall estate. He has Tia's kidnapper with him. And, Freddy…?"

"What?"

How could she have so misjudged James Randall? How could she have missed his ruthless streak? How could she have loved this man more than her own father, this man who would kill another man's wife to hold on to a business secret? "According to Sable, Drake said that Randall was responsible for the death of Tyler's wife."

She felt a pulse of understanding zing along the line.

Tyler had lost so much that day. Would it cloud his judgment?

"You hang on," Freddy said. Urgency spiked the calmness he tried to inject into his voice. "I'll get him help."

"How long?" She had both hands on the receiver now and wished she could crawl through the line and be at Freddy's side doing something, anything.

"As fast as I can."

She hung up, but couldn't shake her feeling of doom. What little color remained of her world was bled out. She looked around the kitchen—at the gray stone, the black hearth, the smoke-streaked ceiling—and knew that nothing would ever be the same. The world she'd created for herself was a lie.

And if James Randall had killed Lindsey just to keep Tyler from a story, he wouldn't hesitate to rid himself of Tyler now. Explaining the situation to the authorities would take time—even for Freddy. By the time anyone responded, Tyler could be dead.

She'd watched helplessly as the mother she'd loved was consumed by flames to protect aspirations. She couldn't simply stand by while the man she loved was taken from her to conceal greed.

Despite her sprained ankle, she flew out the kitchen door and across the courtyard.

"Melissa, wait!" Tia cried, running after her.

"I can't. Tyler needs help."

"Let the police handle it."

"They won't get there in time."

She felt the brush of Tia's hand, but kept going.

Finally Tia snagged the sleeve of her T-shirt and pulled her to a halt. "You're hurt. I'll go."

Melissa turned and gave her sister a quick hug.

"You're sweet, but I know the estate. I can get in without being seen."

"God, Melissa," Tia said, hanging on to her sister. "I've already almost lost you once today. Let the cops handle this."

"I'm not planning on getting hurt. You go make sure Sable doesn't leave. I need to talk to her."

Melissa spun to leave, but Tia caught her arm again. "She did this to you, didn't she? My mother pushed you into that well." Tia's eyes brimmed with tears. "Why?"

"It doesn't matter." Melissa entered the coolness of the stable and reached for a bridle in the tack room.

"It does too matter. You could have died. What if I hadn't found you?"

With quick efficient moves, Melissa bridled Breeze. "Tyler would have found me."

"How can you be so calm? She tried to kill you!"

Melissa led Breeze out onto the concrete aisle and touched her sister's cheek. "She did it for love, Tia."

Tears streamed from Tia's eyes. "I don't want the kind of love that would kill."

"Oh, Tia," Melissa said, giving her sister a fierce hug. "If I were in her shoes, I'd have done the same thing. For my baby, I'd do anything."

"No, you would have found a way around death. You always do. Look at all you've done, at the life you've created. I've never seen anyone as strong as you."

A smile wavered on Melissa's lips. How could she hate Sable when she'd given her the only sunshine in her life? "I love you, Tia."

She let go of her sister, grabbed the shotgun from the tack room and pocketed extra shells. "I have to go."

"What can I do?" Tia wrapped her arms around herself as if to keep warm.

Melissa glanced toward the faithful gathered at the end of the driveway. "Pray."

While the reverend preached at the front gate, she slipped out the postern door. Leading Breeze against the castle wall until they reached the far side, she mentally mapped a route through her neighbors' land to the Randall estate. Once she reached the ridge of woods circling the castle, she vaulted on and urged Breeze into the maze. To the rhythm of galloping hooves, she muttered a little prayer of her own. "Keep him safe. Keep him safe. Keep him safe."

Chapter Fifteen

Listening to the tapes in Drake's messy room had broken Tyler's heart, then hardened his determination. Randall would pay for what he'd done. Randall's greed had already cost him one woman he loved. Tyler couldn't let him destroy Melissa just to preserve his shaky house of cards.

With all the tapes on their way to Freddy by courier, along with a note, and the cops notified, Tyler had Drake gain entrance to the estate, then marched the young man into the house. A uniformed maid attempted to stop them, but Tyler pressed Drake deeper into the cavernous house.

Arms windmilling, the maid threatened to call the police. That fit right in with Tyler's plan. The cops had been a tad skeptical about his claims. Now they would have to respond.

Tyler wasn't sure what he was going to do once he came face-to-face with Randall, only that he wanted to look the man in the eye and have him confess his sins. For Lindsey who had so loved the pursuit of truth, he wanted more than justice—he wanted the truth.

Through the French doors of the library that opened onto a patio with an Olympic-size pool, he could see

Randall swimming laps. Without hesitating, Tyler prodded Drake outside.

A wedge of dark clouds homed in on the blue of the sky. Wind whipped the trees into a dervish dance of leaves and limbs and crowded the light garden chairs together at one end of the pool. A paper napkin, held down by silverware, flapped, creeping the knife and fork closer to the edge of the glass table. The plastic dome covering the china plate took flight and landed on the manicured bushes bordering the patio.

If the sight of two men looming above him in the pool gave Randall any pause, he didn't show it. He finished the return trip of his lap and calmly exited the pool.

Standing there, white hair slicked against his head, mustache dripping, slack chest muscles gleaming wetly, Randall didn't look like much of an adversary. But rats came in all shapes and sizes—and their deceptive appearance didn't make the diseases they carried any less deadly.

Randall slipped the goggles from his head and dropped them by the side of the pool. "I wasn't expecting any company."

Tyler thrust Drake, whose wrists were tied behind his back, into a garden chair. Still counting on earning his freedom, Drake didn't move a muscle.

"Melissa loved you like a father," Tyler said. He reached for a towel on a cabana bench and threw it at Randall. "How could you hurt her like that?"

"You can blame yourself for any pain that's come her way." Randall patted himself dry. "I only have her best interests at heart."

"Thornwylde is the only place that gives her peace. You were going to take it from her for the oil buried in the ground."

Randall reached for the robe on the chaise and slipped it on. "Thornwylde is a prison for her."

"So you were going to help her by stealing what belongs to her?" Hatred swelled in a nauseating wave, throttling his objectivity. "You have a talent for that. Can you really justify theft, murder, that easily?"

Randall pressed the intercom button on the small wrought-iron table by the chaise, then turned back to his guests. "If you'll excuse me, I have business to tend to. The maid will see you to the door."

As Randall turned to leave, Tyler grabbed his elbow. Randall fell clumsily into a garden chair, making it rock from side to side on the pool apron.

"We're not through."

The maid arrived at the French doors. Wringing her hands, she said, "Mr. Randall?"

"Sofia, fetch Ray."

"And call the police," Tyler added.

Eyes darting from man to man, Sofia backed into the library, then hurried away.

From his back pocket, Tyler plucked the spare microcassette recorder he always kept in the car and pressed the play button.

"Tail Collins and make sure he doesn't talk," Randall's voice on the scratchy second-generation tape said. *"I want the story killed now."*

"I didn't sign on for that kind of business," Drake's voice whined. *"Scoping out a castle is one thing, but this—"*

"If you'd gotten things right the first time around, it wouldn't've come down to this. If you like, I can always give your bookie's flunkies your new address."

"I don't see why I need a gun."

"Power speaks louder than words. The gun gives you

power. It's not registered and no one can trace it back to you.''

"What if I hit him by mistake?"

"Then make sure the shot is fatal and no one catches you in the act."

Randall spared Drake a deadly glance before focusing on Tyler. "That doesn't prove anything."

"My wife was murdered the night I went to meet Lester Collins. He'd told me about your creative accounting and the companies you used to hide that creativity. Your financial statements were nothing more than smoke and mirrors. You were cooking the books. My story was going to expose your losses and show that your profits were nothing more than hot air. It would have brought your company to its knees. And you couldn't let that happen."

"If you want to blame anyone, blame your friend here. He's the one who pulled the trigger."

"It was an accident," Drake said, shaking his head. "I wasn't trying to hit anyone."

"How much of your own stock do you own?" Tyler asked, ignoring Drake.

A muscle tightened Randall's jaw. Pushing his hands against the chair arms, he started to rise. Tyler shoved him back down.

"I'll bet my last dollar you collared your position and dumped your stock. Let the little guy eat your mistakes."

Heavy footsteps sounded on the rock footpath. "Ray," Randall said without looking at the arrival, "escort this gentleman to the door." He reached out a hand toward the recorder. "I'll take that."

Tyler tossed Randall the tape. "It's a copy. The original is safe. If anything happens to me, your business practices will come out on the front page of every newspaper—where everyone will see the deep rot. The Securities and

Exchange Commission will have a field day going through your books.''

Randall rose to his feet. "Words are cheap, Mr. Blackwell.''

"You didn't think so when you sent your errand boy to play with the gun that killed my wife.''

Randall's mustache twitched. "You've been a thorn in my side for too long. Ray—''

"Look what I found squeezing through the back gate,'' Ray said as he rounded the corner.

At the sight of Melissa held captive against Ray's chest, hunting knife poised against her neck, Tyler froze.

Randall turned to face the new arrivals. A smile quirked his lips. The odds had shifted in his favor and he knew it. "Ah, Melissa. Normally I'd be glad to see you out and about, but you didn't pick a good time to do so.''

But Melissa wasn't looking at Randall. Her murderous gaze cut right into Drake. "You! What are you doing here? Didn't you cause enough damage the first time?''

"Don't look at me," Drake said, sinking deeper into the chair and jerking his chin toward Randall. "It was his idea.''

Her eyebrows pleated. "James?''

"He wanted me to have a look around," Drake continued in his defense. "Without an article you'd have been suspicious, so I had to write it.''

Article? Tyler wondered. What article? And what did Drake have to do with it?

"The choice of words were his," Randall said. "I wanted to promote your art.''

"Promote my art by having him turn me into a wicked witch? What are you having Brent Westfield write this time? How I get my inspiration from the devil?'' She gasped. "You're the one behind the rumors turning Fallen Moon into another Salem."

Brent Westfield? "This is Drake West, Melissa," Tyler said. "Tia's kidnapper."

Her face turned ashen as she looked from Drake to Tyler and back. "Last summer he pretended he was a reporter named Brent Westfield and wrote a cruel article about me."

Tyler had read the blistering article during his research. There truly was nothing sacred for this man. Drake didn't deserve the energy it would take to punch his lights out. The pretty boy wouldn't much enjoy jail, and Tyler would make sure he'd be there a long time.

"I needed money," Drake said. "He told me if I got you to give me a tour of the castle, he'd pay my debt."

"Tia?" Melissa asked. "Was she just another toy for you to use?"

Drake looked sheepish. "What can I say? I've had a streak of bad luck lately."

Her eyes narrowed as her gaze skewered Randall. "Was it your idea for him to use my sister?"

"Marriage to her would have been profitable and gotten him off my hands."

"Why are you doing this?" she asked, shaking her head.

"It isn't personal, Melissa," James said. "You have something I need."

"Not personal!" She fought Ray's hold, but couldn't free herself. "Was it all a lie?"

Her eyes looked so hurt that a knife of pure agony twisted in Tyler's gut. Freddy's quest to help Melissa had crushed everything and everyone she believed in. What did she have left? Had the truth gained her anything?

Ray held the knife pressed against Melissa's neck. A

glance at Drake told Tyler he'd get no help from that quarter. Paralyzed with fear, Drake would not budge an inch unless it was to save his own skin, and inaction was the prudent course at the moment. There was nothing Tyler could do to protect Melissa without putting her in graver danger. Through the heavy feeling of impotence, his brain worked feverishly to find a solution.

"Was what all a lie?" Randall asked.

"The friendship, the mentorship..."

"No, my dear," Randall said gently. "I've simply tried to give you your freedom. You and your art belong out here where there's life, not locked away in that dead monument of the past."

"If you'd asked," Melissa said, eyes bright with unshed tears, "I'd have given you what you wanted."

He shook his head and allowed himself a small smile. "You would have thought me a foolish old man."

"You were my friend. Oil is business, and I understand business."

Her head drooped sideways, causing the knife to pinch the skin and draw blood. Tyler had to fist his hands against premature action as adrenaline gushed through him.

He tried to catch her attention without telegraphing his intentions to the muscle-bound goon who held her. *Help is on the way. Hang on.*

"Oil is the least of it," Randall said as he pulled the tape from the cassette.

"Then what?"

Randall gave a one-note laugh and a shake of his head. When his gaze met Melissa's, it burned with fervor. The tape in his hand snapped in his grasp. The brown ribbon undulated like a maddened eel in the gusting wind. "Gold."

"There is no gold." Then her eyes widened as understanding dawned. "But Thorne's alchemy is just a legend. It isn't real."

Alchemy. He'd been right. The article on the mason had sparked Randall's interest in Thorne's recipe.

"That's what I thought, too," Randall said. "Deanna never did find anything in the castle that remotely dealt with alchemy. Neither did Drake. But I knew—"

"Deanna?" The blow seemed to hit Melissa right in the solar plexus, bending her forward.

Tyler felt the blow of betrayal as if it were his own. Yet another piece of her life was slashed to bits. A drop of blood splattered on Ray's boot. Tyler wanted to tear the man limb from limb. "Enough!"

Ray jerked her up. Tyler tensed to hurl himself at Ray and free Melissa from his cruel grasp. Ray slid the blade of his knife into the tender skin, widening the cut on her neck.

Straightening, Melissa caught Tyler's gaze. A new urgency covered the skin of betrayal, and her eyes darted all about as if looking for a safe place to run.

Calm down, calm down, Tyler silently urged. *Look at me.* He had to get her out of here and back to the safety of her castle. He should have let Freddy handle this. But he'd just had to satisfy his own guilty conscience. He'd just had to have someone else accept the blame for Lindsey's death. He hadn't done this for Lindsey; he'd done it for himself. And once again his selfish purpose had put the woman he loved in jeopardy.

If he could signal her to become dead weight, she'd pull Ray off balance and give Tyler an even chance to free her. When her gaze rested on him, he focused on her, let her see his love for her in his eyes. Once the fear vanished, he made a tiny downward motion. She acknowledged it with a blink.

"Then the mason found those markings." Randall lifted his shoulders. "I always knew they existed. Your father's success didn't come through normal channels. He'd found Thorne's secret and used it magnificently all those years. And then he hid it right there in plain sight."

"Daddy wheeled and dealed." Her voice was icicle sharp. "His own cunning brought him his success."

But even as Tyler felt proud of her strength, he silently willed her to keep quiet. The situation was explosive and he didn't want it to escalate.

"No," Randall said, "he wasn't smart enough to use his own ideas to grow a business."

"That's why he used his skill to promote other people's ideas."

Randall gave her an avuncular smile. "He had to have something more."

"It's called guts, James. Daddy worked hard for every penny he made. He took risks, and they paid off."

Tyler edged closer, trying to position himself nearer Melissa. But Ray anchored her more tightly to his body and pointed the tip of the blade right into the hollow of her throat. A line of blood ran down the too-white skin of Melissa's neck. Anger pulsed through him, twitching muscles desperate to act. Gritting his teeth, he reined in his flaring temper. To help Melissa, he had to remain detached. If he gave in to emotion, he risked losing her.

"You were always naive," Randall said. "Living alone like that, it's really no surprise. If your father had had any guts, you wouldn't be a recluse today." He signaled to Ray. "Take them to the lake cabin and hold them there for now."

Tyler met Melissa's glance over Randall's head. Now,

while attentions were divided, was the time to act. He gave a tiny nod and saw the small flicker of fear in Melissa's eyes quickly replaced with determination.

In one swift movement she sank like a corpse, pulling Ray down. To keep his hold on her, Ray had to drop the knife and lean forward. Tyler sprinted toward them and grabbed the knife skittering along the concrete. Melissa's dead weight crashed through Ray's weakened hold. She rolled out of her captor's way as he fell onto his face. Using both feet, she shoved Ray's unbalanced body into the pool. He landed with a splash that spilled water over the edge and soaked Melissa.

Putting himself between Melissa and the resurfacing goon, Tyler held the knife defensively.

Fat raindrops started to fall, plopping on the concrete and pinging on the wrought-iron table. From the front of the house, car doors slammed. A voice barked out orders.

Randall tried to sneak into the house. Drake, hands still tied, tackled him, pinning him down with his body. "Oh, no, old man. If I'm going down, I'm taking you with me."

As the police spilled onto the patio, Melissa looked from the man in the pool to Randall, and finally at Tyler. "It's over."

"Yeah," Tyler said. Still holding the knife on Ray, Tyler reached down and took Melissa's hand. She rose to her feet, and he pressed her against him. The adrenaline coursing through his blood finally started to ebb. The police would take time to sort through this mess. He'd almost lost her, but Melissa was safe. That was all that counted. "It's over. They can't hurt you anymore."

MELISSA RETRIEVED Breeze from where she'd tied her to the fence. The mare seemed pleased to see her, and Melissa fussed over her, checking to make sure she'd suffered no harm during her prolonged wait.

Tyler found her discarded shotgun nearby. How Ray had managed to catch her unawares, Melissa still wasn't sure. All she knew was that one minute she'd been trying to sneak through the back gate, and the next Ray had his beefy arm wrapped around her chest and a knife at her throat.

"I wish you'd let me send someone for the horse," Tyler said, stroking the mare's neck.

"She needs to be home where she belongs." They'd all had more than enough excitement for one day. Breeze deserved to relax at pasture, and Melissa wanted a long hot bath—among other things.

Tyler played with a strand of her hair. The loving look in his eyes took her breath away. "So do you."

"I know how to compromise," she said, smiling.

His eyebrows rose in exaggerated surprise. "You do?"

When it suited her purposes, and Tyler suited them just fine. "I'll ride along the road, and you can follow in your Jeep."

"I'll take it. I'm not ready to let you out of my sight anytime soon."

"Yeah?" The warmth trickling down to her stomach felt good.

He kissed her and she melted. "Yeah."

He took Breeze's reins and led the mare across the manicured lawn to the front of the estate. Melissa fell into step beside him, took the shotgun from him and slipped her hand into his.

"We need to talk," he said.

"But not now." She needed a little quiet time before she faced more disruption. Her lie, Dee's betrayal, Sable's treachery. She'd have to deal with all of them. But right now she was simply grateful to be alive, to have Tyler by her side and to have the mystery of the chess player solved. For the first time since her mother had died, she could actually imagine an almost normal life. One with Tyler. One so close to her fantasy it frightened her a bit. They had a lifetime to work things out. Right now she just wanted to savor the moment. "I want to get home."

THE NEXT FEW DAYS were the happiest of Melissa's life. Even outside events like the explosion of the Randall Industries scandal all over the media or the reverend's continued quest to save her soul couldn't dim her optimism.

Tyler was by her side, and life was finally all she'd ever hoped for. Her days reverted to the natural rhythm of day and night. Daylight was spent venturing farther and farther from the confining walls of the castle, nighttime in sensual explorations with Tyler. Even her painting took on a new brilliance that seemed transcendent. Gone were the monsters camouflaged in the landscape.

She saw the worried look in Deanna's eyes, the disapproval, but ignored both. Dee had tried to justify her actions as bribery on her father's part. Melissa understood, but she wasn't ready yet to forgive the breach of trust. That would take time. In an ironic twist, Tia's spurning of her mother was worse than any punishment Melissa could have meted out. Now the woman Sable had revolved her life around, had been willing to kill for, wasn't talking to her, and the breach was sucking the life from Sable.

Melissa ignored, too, the continuing rumors of witchcraft. They would die soon enough now that Randall's machinations were exposed.

June thirteenth, her birthday, dawned bright and she didn't want to miss a minute of it. She let Tyler sleep in.

After checking on Grace's condition—it was still unchanged—and seeing to the horses, Melissa rushed to Tyler's room. There was no point in his having to keep going there to change since he was practically living in her quarters. She'd move his belongings to let him know that she wanted him in her life—permanently. In a few days her period was due and she'd know if she was pregnant. There was no sense bringing up the probability of a baby unless there was a reason.

She hummed as she stuffed Tyler's clothes into his duffel bag, stopping to sniff the male scent of him on the sweatshirt he'd tossed on the bed. She jammed the half-empty toiletry bag into the front compartment. She shuffled the papers on his bedside table—an article he was writing, it appeared—into a neat pile. As she was about to slip them into the side pocket of the duffel bag, the title caught her attention. "Seduction of the Beast."

Her heart stopped, then galloped hard against her ribs. Hands shaking, she sat on the edge of the bed and began to read. A soft keening ripped from her as the words he'd written filleted her, slicing her heart to tiny pieces, hemorrhaging raw emotions.

In black and white, her scars were laid bare. Every twist and turn of the ugly landscape of her face, arms and legs was charted like a roadmap. He'd missed no flaw, no discoloration, no intimate detail.

With a roar, she let her pain, her anger, fly and tore the pages of the article to shreds.

All she'd ever wanted was to belong. To fit in. To be loved. She'd thought her dream had finally come true with Tyler. She'd thought her scars were invisible to him. Hadn't he told her he loved her? Hadn't he showed her he loved every inch of her? Hadn't their shared love implied a future?

But all he saw was the witch.

The pretty words, the gentle caresses, the blind love-making had all been lies. Happy endings didn't happen. His story proved that. He'd wanted her to drop her mask so he could expose her flaws for all the world to see.

Just as Brent Westfield had. Just as James Randall had.

And she'd let him. She'd gladly shed her defenses and bared her soul to him. She'd fallen in love with him. Not careful inch by careful inch, but all the way—hard and fast.

Swallowing the insult, she strode to her tower, duffel bag in hand. She'd learned to take care of herself a long time ago. This was merely another speed bump. She'd get over it. She always did.

By the time Tyler emerged from the shower, she had wrapped her rage in a frozen shell and could feel nothing.

Smiling as he toweled his dark hair, he came toward her. She knew every contour of that lean body, craved it with every atom of her being. She knew the texture of every muscle, the feel of his skin, the tender places where one touch could undo him. She knew the meaning of that smokey look in his eyes and felt its fiery impact low in her belly. He bent to kiss her. And the betrayal cut through her knife-sharp. A small wounded sound escaped her as she slapped him.

Frowning, he jerked back. "What the—"

"Get out." Her palm stung from the blow. The imprint of her hand throbbed a violent red against the pale gold of his cheek. She would not let the confusion in his eyes soften her resolve. He'd used her. Knowing the power of his words could destroy her, he'd nevertheless wielded them against her. She couldn't let him know how deeply he'd wounded her.

The towel taut between his hands, he stood stock-still. "What's wrong?"

"Get out."

He dropped one end of the towel and reached a hand toward her. She whirled out of his grasp. "Melissa, talk to me."

She grabbed a handful of paper shreds from her pocket and threw them at him. "How could you?"

His face grew sharp with tension. "You read it?"

He seemed to be waiting for some sort of reaction, approval even, almost as if he feared the impact of *her* words. Well, he should, after what he'd written, displaying her like some sideshow freak. Her voice spat out the venom poisoning her mind. "I read it."

"I see." His eyes hardened to flint as he reached for his clothes and dressed. "You don't feel the same way?"

"How could I?"

A muscle flinched in his jaw. "I love you, Melissa."

Love? Tearing her apart in public—that was love? "You have a strange way of showing it."

"What more do you want from me? I gave you all I had."

"I trusted you." The words came out raw.

He shook his head. "Not enough."

She launched his duffel bag at him, then pointed at the door. Her leashed fury, desperate to escape, had her hand trembling so much that she fisted it and drew it tight to her side. "Get out."

When he didn't move, she spun on her heel and left.

She didn't care that the sun blazed hot. She didn't care that her skin wasn't protected. She grabbed the rainbow-colored rope from the tack room and headed toward the pasture.

Once astride Eclipse's back, she rode until her muscles

ached and her will could no longer contain her sorrow. Falling forward on the horse's mane, wrapping her arms around his neck, she let her tears cleanse her shattered soul.

TYLER DROVE AWAY feeling as if a part of him had died. The emptiness, the aching hole inside him, was greater than when Lindsey had died. He heard the whiskey demon whisper in his ear, felt it tickle his throat. He white-knuckled the steering wheel and concentrated hard on the road.

The events of the past few weeks had shown him that he'd looked for the truth in the wrong place. After a restless night of soul-searching, he'd finally understood that he'd committed the greatest lie of all. He'd lied to himself. He'd chased the scoop. He'd chased the glory. He'd chased the limelight. And in doing so, he'd prostituted the very ideals that had brought him to journalism.

It was that need for success that had killed Lindsey, he realized. He would forever have to bear that mark on his soul, but he couldn't change the outcome. Lindsey was dead. To give her life meaning, he had to let her go and move on. Moving on meant facing the ugliness inside him so he could find his own truth.

So he'd bared his soul in that article, exposed the beast inside him for Melissa, for the world, to see. It was his gift to her, and she'd thrown it in his face.

In the rearview mirror, he glanced at the gray stone walls, at the crumbling towers and down at the moat filled with dark green water. It was her home. Her protective shell. Her world. What right did he have to ask her to change the only constant in her life? He hit the steering wheel with a force that sent pain shooting through his wrist.

Truth shone its own light. He couldn't force her to look at something she didn't want to see any more than he could go back and live another lie.

RAY HAD EASILY MADE bail. After all, it was the big fish everyone wanted, not what they considered pond scum. He'd waited patiently. He'd sent the pictures. He'd sent the college paper and the clippings. Generously he'd allowed Blackwell more than a week to pull the story together. Something of this magnitude was entitled to front cover coverage. Something this big deserved a speedy exposure.

When the next issue of *Texas Gold* hit the stands, he was the first one to buy a copy.

The reporter had failed him.

Ray had thought Blackwell understood. Manipulated out of a story last year when his wife was killed, Blackwell should want to leave no stone unturned to advertise the truth for all to see. Ray had counted on that deep-seated need for redress. Instead of reporting the fall from grace, Blackwell had let others steal his exclusive—and in the process the most important nugget was missed.

None of this story would be possible without his father's invention. William wouldn't have bought his first job with the idea he'd stolen from Royal Lundy. Randall's company wouldn't have had the instrument that had bolstered the rest of his inept attempts to dominate the field.

Crumpling the issue in his hands, Ray strode to his truck. He would have what was his. No one would cheat him out of his due.

Power. There was nothing to beat sheer power. He had it. He'd use it.

J'adoube. I adjust.

The board was down to three pieces. No one could stop him from queening his pawn and winning the game.

Chapter Sixteen

Melissa stared at the stick in her hand. Positive.

She was pregnant.

She should be happy. Ecstatic. On top of the world. She was going to have a baby. She was going to be a mother. She was going to have responsibility for a child's life. Love. Her hand covered the front of her jeans and rubbed small circles. Alone. Without Grace, who was still comatose. Without Deanna, who would surely disapprove. Without the baby's father, who found her beast-ugly.

This baby was a dream come true, and yet the dream was tarnished by the terrible black hole Tyler's departure had caused. Instead of the flush of pleasure, the cold rime of dread filled her.

A soft knock rapped against the bathroom door, and Dee cleared her throat before she spoke. "Melissa? Is everything all right?"

Everything should be right, but everything was wrong.

"Come out, Mel. Please."

Melissa stuffed the stick into the remnants of the kit and tossed both into the wastebasket. She strode past Dee, out of her bedroom and into her studio. Pencil to paper, she made lines without care to their purpose.

"Are you all right?" Dee asked, leaning against the door frame.

"I'm just fine." Melissa bent to her task. The last thing she needed was a dose of Dee's sympathy. "If you don't mind, I'm busy right now."

"So," Dee said, "that's how it's going to be?"

"How what is going to be?" The pencil bit deeply into the paper, making a groove.

"I'm sick and tired of your moping around. That's all you've done since you threw Tyler out. You're acting like a spoiled brat, and I've had just about enough of it."

Melissa gritted her teeth. "This is my home and I'll act any way I want."

"Oh, that's rich." Dee snorted. "You're going to have a baby and you're acting like one. Who's going to raise you both?"

Melissa's eyebrows shot up.

"Don't look so surprised," Dee said. "You asked me to buy you the kit. You didn't think I'd leave you alone to bear the news, did you?"

Melissa wanted to cry. She always wanted to cry these days. "Get out."

"That's right. Throw away the last friend you have."

Melissa's pencil stilled. She shot Dee a stabbing look. She wanted to hurt someone as much as she was hurting. "Friend? A friend doesn't betray you."

Dee's voice softened, and that grated on Melissa's nerves more than Dee's on-target criticism. "I didn't see the harm in pretending to look for his damned alchemy book if it meant I could keep my position here."

"You didn't need his permission to work."

Dee tipped her head to her shoulder and shook it. "I'd just lost my mother. I didn't want to lose my father, too."

"You had me. Didn't that mean anything?"

Dee came toward her. The caring in her eyes hurt. How could she trust Dee—anyone—ever again?

"It did," Dee said softly. "That's why I didn't mention the search." She took the pad from Melissa's hands and stared at the scribbles. "If I'd found anything, I would have shown you first."

Would she have? The uncertainty made Melissa feel as if there was no one at the other end of the seesaw and she was in for a hard fall. "I need to be alone now."

Silently Melissa strolled to the window and stared at the pastoral scene below—horses grazing, ducks floating on the moat, trees ringing the edge of her world. She'd seen the same scene day after day for decades, and yet nothing seemed familiar. All she'd believed in, all she'd thought solid, seemed no firmer than the wisps of fog at the edge of the woods.

"The last thing you need right now is to be alone," Dee said. Melissa swallowed hard, but didn't respond.

Her beautiful castle had given her freedom in a world that kept her prisoner. With its white gazebo, its rose garden and its fragrant herb borders, her refuge had seemed bright and happy. Her home had stirred with life—the songs of birds, the purrs of cats and the whinnies of horses. The views from her tower studio had spurred her imagination and allowed her to create pieces that were therapeutic and had become art that collectors described as powerful and unique.

Now the gray stone walls melded with the steel of the sky, closing off the world. An oppressive silence filled the courtyard, squeezing the life from her soul. The barren windows taunted her with her loneliness. Her once-fluid imagination had run dry, leaving her not even her work to help her heal.

What had once symbolized freedom had become a

strangling prison—all because she'd allowed her body to feel, her mind to care, her heart to love. She didn't know if she had the courage to learn to live again.

"You have a baby to think of," Dee said gently as if she could read her mind.

A baby. Emotion surged through her. She turned and found Dee's open arms ready to enfold her. "Oh, Dee, what am I going to do?"

"First," Dee said, tightening her hug, "you're going to take care of yourself. That means you have to eat. Let's go have some breakfast."

Melissa rested her forehead against Dee's shoulder. "I love him."

"I know."

She leaned out of Dee's embrace, grabbed Dee's upper arms and looked into her friend's eyes. "I can't live here anymore. This isn't what I want for my baby. I want play groups and PTA. I want field trips and friends. I want…" She choked on the tears spilling much too easily now that she had a fragile thread of hope to hang on to.

Smiling, Dee wrapped an arm around Melissa's waist and led her down the stairs. "We'll work it all out."

IN THE WEEKS since he'd left Thornwylde, Tyler had managed to start rebuilding his career and make peace with his guilt over Lindsey's death. In tribute to her life, he would continue to search for truth—and this time, he'd leave ego at the door.

He started with the piece on Melissa. His values would be a matter of public record—even if his confession meant nothing to her.

With careful steps he was working on a probing exposé on the seedy side of the well-respected James Richmond Randall. With the corruption all over the news, people were coming out of the woodwork ready to talk. He tried to focus his energy on his work. But his thoughts kept returning to Melissa.

He missed her, missed her sharp tongue, the artful observations of her art, her passion. He missed talking with her, being with her. But more than that, he missed the way he felt around her—content. The missing was a constant ache, like a bruise that wouldn't heal. She'd never asked from him more than she'd given. And it wasn't until he found himself alone that he realized how much she'd become a part of him.

Climbing the steps to his apartment, he dreaded the silence that awaited him. He wanted to hear her laughter, to see her smile, to taste her warm mouth…to know someone was waiting for him.

When he entered, it wasn't the static of loneliness that met him, but rather the turbulent energy of evil. It skimmed the nape of his neck like an icy finger, making his hair stand on end.

In the middle of the kitchen table lay a decapitated king.

Beside the mutilated piece sprawled a note that read:

To win, one must be willing to sacrifice.
Checkmate.

Melissa.

He bolted out to the Jeep and raced toward Fallen Moon. Reaching for his cell phone, he prayed he would get to her in time.

COMMON PEOPLE lived by routine. That made them easy prey. The woman didn't disappoint him. A duffer just like her father. As the sun kissed the horizon, she mounted the stallion and rode toward him. Ray receded into the shadows of the trees and waited.

Randall was getting his comeuppance—his company was falling apart in front of the world. All that remained was exacting repayment from William.

Steady hoofbeats approached, as horse and rider confidently made their way through the maze. Ray smiled, tasting the sweet flavor of retribution.

Her fiery end would be his triumph.

As she exited the maze and passed him, he nudged Black Witch's sides with his spurs.

Endgame.

NOW THAT SHE HAD a plan, a bit of warmth was slowly returning to Melissa's dead heart. She would donate the castle to the town of Fallen Moon. It would become a park for folks to enjoy, rather than a place of dark secrets to fear. Dee had already helped her find a small ranch where she could move her horses and raise her child.

She would have to tell Tyler about the baby, of course. There was no getting around that. She'd reassure him that her ugliness wouldn't taint his child. After all, when she was young, people often told her she favored her mother in looks, and the mother Melissa remembered was beautiful.

At the edge of the maze Eclipse hesitated, ears swiveling as if to catch a sound. Melissa realized then that she'd let her mind wander and had paid the horse beneath her no attention.

She patted his neck. "It's all right, boy. I'm back now. Let's ride."

But instead of going forward into a canter, the horse sidestepped, turning his head toward the mouth of the maze. His skin rippled beneath her legs, and his shiver of fear echoed inside her. She peered into the shadows, but saw nothing out of place.

The night seemed to pause. No wind rustled through the trees. No cicadas rasped. No bats swooped. Even the mosquitoes ceased their high-pitched hum.

She heard it then, the steady breathing like a hungry dragon deep in the shadows. In the next instant branches cracked like dry skeleton bones, firing the night with malefic reports. And a black mass stormed toward her with tornado speed.

No going back the way she'd come.

Taking charge, she didn't ask, she ordered, and Eclipse responded. He sprang forward, galloping up and over the hill and into the field. She knew this terrain better than she knew herself and led Eclipse on a serpentine path that would take her to Fallen Moon.

She galloped across the Andersons' field. She jumped the fence onto the Grangers' land. Cows looked up and followed her race across their pasture. She plunged into the woods that bordered the north end of town.

Still the creature pursuing her kept on her heels.

Like crooked fingers, branches snagged her hair, scratched at her clothes and tore at her flesh. Eclipse's feet thundered on the ground. His lungs funneled great gulps of air. His body crashed through the undergrowth.

Still she could hear the pounding of the beast behind them, chugging locomotive-loud closer and closer and closer.

A thin line of lights appeared like fairy lanterns through the trees and against the bleeding sky. Melissa aimed for them. The smell of exhaust and burgers on the grill and lawn fertilizer announced civilization. She broke free of the trees and instead of snaking to the sheriff's office, she shot straight for the diner. Even this mad horseman wouldn't dare hurt her in the middle of a busy restaurant. A soccer field separated her from safety.

She heard the whistle first—a sharp slicing of air right above her head. Something dropped like a snake from a tree, squirming as it latched onto her arms and chest. Then it stiffened and yanked her back.

Eclipse faltered at her sudden swing of balance and then came to a dead halt. The tension around her body coiled harder, catapulting her backward.

She landed hard. The crack of bone resounded in her skull. Pain shot down her arm and across her shoulder. Her breath was choked off. Her head rang. The rope grew tauter. And as her body was dragged over the uneven ground, something sharp seemed to pierce right through her. Pain like acid burned right through her belly.

My baby. Oh, God, no. Not my baby.

Rolling sideways, she fought to find purchase and was yanked down again for her trouble.

My baby, my baby.

She had to save her baby.

Clawing at the knot on the rope, she tried to free herself. A laugh cackled above her. "Sorry, sugar, this here's the end of the rope."

"Why are you doing this?" she rasped, squirming to get a look at her attacker.

"Someone's gotta pay." The man moved a few feet from the horse, which was blowing hard. Clucking at the horse, he dragged Melissa back into the shadows of the woods. Frantically she dug her heels into the soft ground and seized handfuls of grass to stay her unwanted ride. But one arm hung uselessly at her side. The heels of her boots slipped like fish in water on the dew-covered weeds. Her one-handed grip wasn't strong enough to stop a frightened horse or a determined madman, both of whom were just out of her reach.

"Pay for what?" Her stomach rolled and she fought the greasy swell of nausea.

"For what was stolen."

"Stolen?" The town's lights blinked out as the woods closed in around them.

"Your father used my father's idea to buy Jimmy Randall's interest."

Panic rippled in hot curls and lodged in her chest. "I— I don't know you."

"But they knew each other. They were in an engineering class together, and your father stole my father's final project."

Her toes, her fingers, scratched for leverage and found none. "You're wrong."

"He never gave my father the credit that was his. Do you know what happened to my father?"

A rock bruised her tailbone, and she gasped. She grabbed a sapling trunk and held on, but the horse's pull snapped her grasp.

"He died a broken and penniless man. He never got over the betrayal. I have to make things right. I have to get what rightfully belongs to us."

The man was insane. He was going to kill her. Delay. She had to delay until she could think. "Tell me about it. About the project."

"The pump he designed made it possible to extract oil from the ground faster at less cost. Guess who owns the patent?"

"I don't know." Her voice was a high-pitched squeal.

"Randall Industries. They've been collectin' royalties from that design for thirty-six years."

"I'm not…" Her mind couldn't grasp the needed thoughts out of the panic soaking her brain.

"That's where your father got his start. With my father's idea." They reached a clearing, and he stopped dragging her. She pitched herself to her hands and knees and lurched up to run. With the sole of his boot, he kicked her down. Landing on her injured side, she howled in pain. He came to stand next to her. Craning her neck, she followed the plain black roper boots up to his face. She could see nothing of his shadow-darkened features, but the weight of his hatred nearly crushed her.

"You're marked by the demon," he said. "Your soul was damned before you were even born."

He raised his hand and brought it down in a swift arc. Something hard cuffed her temple. Stars danced before her eyes. A leaden feeling weighed her down.

Everything went black.

When she came to again, Eclipse's familiar back trembled beneath her. Moaning, she opened her eyes. Her head pounded in a slow piercing rhythm. Her arms were bent behind her, her wrists bound together with rough rope. Her swelling shoulder throbbed in excruciating pain. Her stomach cramped in a twisting inferno.

"Welcome back, sugar. You wouldn't want to miss your own party."

As she jerked her head toward the sound of the voice, the rope around her neck abraded her skin.

"Whoa, there. Take it easy. It's not quite time yet for you to go away."

She followed the dark slinky line to the canopy of an oak that hung over her. A helpless cry was torn from her lips. She was going to die and she'd never even lived. "Please…"

The bitter odor of gasoline filled her nostrils. A quick

scraping sound. Sulfur wafted onto the air. A flame burst and seemed to spring from the tips of his fingers. The flame danced there for a moment, then gyrated downward with his hand.

"Nothing like a good old-fashioned witch hunt to bring a community together."

The flame hesitated, then leaped. It raced in an arc, first one way, then the other. Soon he stood on one side of a circle of fire and she on the other. His face in the wavering light mutated into the monsters camouflaged in her paintings. Smoke caressed her skin. Heat lapped at her, kissing the scars on her cheek and neck. Old terror and new terror fused, paralyzing her.

"When the fireworks start, you'll have an audience," he said, shrinking back into the night. "No one should have to die alone. Not even a witch."

Fire crept inward toward the tails of rockets poised at the sky. Her heart pounded. She couldn't breathe. She couldn't think. Her body quivered like a flag slapped by a storm. Eclipse pranced beneath her, tightening the rope around her neck.

She let out a scream that echoed around her like a nightmare.

Chapter Seventeen

Knowing her habits, Tyler followed the probable path of Melissa's ride, hoping he'd get to her before Ray.

Ahead a circle of flames flared against the night sky, illuminating the macabre scene next to the playground. An old oak, canopy spread, guarded the area. From one of its sturdy branches hung a rope. It wound around a body, propped on a horse. Against the stark light, the stallion's eyes seemed to glow red, his nostrils to breathe fire, his snapping feet to melt. The horse's nervous jitter jostled the body on his back. If he spooked...

A spear of pure terror gored through Tyler.

Melissa.

No more than the length of a soccer field separated him from the horror, but the distance seemed infinite.

Tyler shook away the image of Lindsey's limp body in his arms, of the red blood staining the bodice of her white dress. He cranked the Jeep off the road and sped across the field to the picnic pavilions dotting the playground area. The Jeep skidded when he failed to slow down to cross an access road. He drove as close to the fire as he dared, afraid to speed through the flames for fear of frightening Eclipse.

At the sandbox he slammed on the brakes with the sick

certainty that he was too late. Her body was so still. Leaving the engine running, he snagged the knife from the glove compartment and bolted out of the Jeep and dashed toward the fire.

A godawful cry ripped through the night, tearing at him like the hounds of hell shredding carrion.

The jackhammer of his heart redoubled. She was alive. "Melissa, hang on!"

Flames crackled and hissed. Heat throbbed, repulsing him in breath-stealing waves. A hole. He had to find a hole.

"Melissa! Talk to me, Melissa."

A murmur reached him, its soft, calming tone out of place alongside the raging inferno. She was trying to keep Eclipse quiet.

"That's it," he said. "Keep him calm. Keep him quiet. I'm coming for you, Melissa. Hang on."

Tyler drew his T-shirt over his head and wrapped it around his nose and mouth.

"Tyler! Behind you!"

Melissa's warning hit him at the same time as the blow. It came out of nowhere, smacking him on the back of the head, forcing him to his knees. A brilliant light played in front of his eyes, then blinked out like dead fireflies.

"To your left!" Melissa yelled.

Rolling, Tyler put his arms up defensively and caught the next strike on the elbow. Prickly splinters raced up his arm like a march of frenzied ants. Blindly Tyler swung the knife, heard the rip of material, felt the warm wetness of blood.

Springing to his feet, Tyler swayed dizzily. He shook his head to clear it and charged at the shadow stumbling backward. Lurching like a drunk, he rushed his attacker. His knife connected with the body, taking them both down.

The man cried out. Hands scored at Tyler. He twisted to one side, out of their reach. For the first time Tyler saw the man's face and recognized him as Ray, the goon who'd held Melissa at knifepoint.

Growling like a crazed bear, Ray frantically grabbed the knife buried in his gut and pulled on it. The blade slipped free and fell to the ground. Springing to his feet, Tyler grabbed the bloody knife, then crouched in a defensive posture. Ray staggered to his feet. Blood covered his hands and seeped through his splayed fingers. He plugged the gushing hole with the other hand.

Then bellowing like a dying bull, he charged Tyler.

MELISSA SCREAMED. She couldn't stop. Eclipse grew more frantic beneath her. The rope at her neck chaffed, tightened. The tongues of flame sucked up more of Ray's fuel, stealing closer and closer, their roar almost deafening. Any second now the rocket's tails would catch and she wouldn't be able to hold Eclipse still in the booming thunder of the fireworks.

Tyler and Ray tumbled into the darkness. The grunts and groans of their scuffle added a grim counterpoint to her own helpless cries.

He was gone. She couldn't see him. *Tyler, Tyler, Tyler.* Just like her mother, he was a prisoner in the darkness. Trussed in Sable's arms as a child, on Eclipse's back now, she couldn't reach them. All she could do was cover the sound of their dying with her own anguish. *Mama!* "Tyler!"

Suddenly Eclipse's hindquarters dipped down. He surged forward, leaping over the flames. Her scream froze, stolen by pure terror as she felt herself fall and the rope choke her.

The expected neck-breaking jerk never came. Instead, hands closed around her, holding her tight. "I've got you. I've got you."

Tyler.

Shaking uncontrollably, Melissa melted against him. Her silent scream turned to racking sobs. She cried as he cut her down from the tree. She cried as he freed her hands and her knees buckled. She cried as he lifted her into his arms, then murmured calming words in her ear while they ran through fire.

Pain rolled through her in acute waves—throat, shoulder, stomach—curling her into a fetal position. Rockets winged skyward, whistling before exploding in a shower of color. Eclipse took off toward home safe.

"You're hurt," Tyler said as he gently placed her into the Jeep. "You're bleeding."

"The baby," she cried, and a new wave of fear swamped her. The nightmare kept pressing on. She'd lost her mother. She'd lost Tyler. She was losing her baby, their baby. "The baby, Tyler, our baby."

"Hang on, sweetheart. I'll get you to a hospital."

But it was too late; she could feel her baby leaving, her soul dying.

SHE WAS A CORPSE in a world that had become dead.

News rolled off her like rain on a window. Ray was dead. Randall was facing bankruptcy and jail. Sable couldn't apologize enough for her part in all this mess. None of it mattered.

Even dreams no longer offered Melissa a refuge from the pain. In those black folds she relived her baby's death time and again, and the anguish of it never abated. Even Tyler's forgiveness of her lie didn't matter.

Ray had done what he'd set out to accomplish. He'd stolen what she'd most desired.

The baby had been her last hope for happiness. She'd clung to that dream like the last leaf on an autumn branch, daring the wind to sweep it away. Then suddenly it was taken from her in a single breath.

She was hopelessly empty and always would be. Her spirit snapped like a twig on the edge of winter.

There was no reason left to live.

"I'M NOT SUPPOSED to just marry, Melissa," Tia said as she plumped Melissa's pillow. "I'm supposed to marry rich."

Tia flopped on the side of the bed, setting off a wave of pain that rippled from head to toe. Melissa clung to the sheet with her free hand and cushioned her stabilized shoulder against the pillow. The last thing she wanted was a ray of Tia sunshine. Her sister's bubbly efforts to draw her out only deepened her anguish.

"Well, where was love in all of that?" Tia asked. "I wanted it all—love and money."

"Sometimes you have to make choices." And it seemed to Melissa that she'd made all the wrong ones. For twenty years, she'd made nothing but mistakes.

"Yes, well, I learned that, didn't I?" Tia reached for the brush on the bedside table and ran it through a lock of Melissa's hair. "On the surface Drake was everything I wanted and everything Mother wanted. I hate her for what she did to you—for what she did to me. But you know what?"

Tia paused. Naturally she expected an answer. "No, what?" Melissa asked with effort.

"I'm glad Drake happened. I learned something about myself because of him." Fussing like a hyperactive nurse,

Tia rounded the bed and brushed the hair on Melissa's other side.

Melissa curbed the urge to swat at her sister's well-meaning fussing. "And what would that be?"

"That I have more to offer than money."

"I've been telling you that for years."

"Yes, well, now I can see it." She paused, brush in midair. "I met someone yesterday."

Melissa's effort at a laugh sounded like a seal bark. "Another true love?"

"Even better—a purpose."

Melissa looked at Tia for the first time since she'd entered the hospital room. There was a glow in her sister's cheeks, a brightness in her eyes that hadn't been there before. "A purpose?"

"I'm going to stay with you after you get out of here, then I'm going back to school. I'm going to make something of my life."

"Good for you." Melissa glanced at the clock, wishing for the end of visiting hours.

"When I went to Christie's—you know, the image consultant—house to pay her, she was talking to a friend and her friend, was showing her pictures."

"Mm." Melissa was fast losing interest. Tia's world of beauty was still a galaxy from hers.

"I want you to meet her."

The only person she wanted to see was Tyler, but the doctor wouldn't let her out of bed for another day. Tia had told her he was in the hospital and brought her daily reports on his condition. Burned on both arms. She knew that pain. "I'm not up to visitors—"

"Gina—that's Christie's friend—she's an aesthetic rehabilitation specialist. You should see what she did with this woman. She'd lost her eyebrows and eyelashes and her skin was all blotched from a house fire. The woman was black so the discoloration showed even more than it does on your skin. Gina used this special makeup, and I couldn't believe the difference. Not perfect, mind you, but enough to shift attention from this woman feeling as if she was being defined by her scarred face to being defined for who she is. It was a miracle, Mel, a real miracle. And I want to make miracles like that happen.''

Tia finished plaiting Melissa's hair into a single braid and tied a lawn-green ribbon at the end. Then she sat on the bed hip to hip with Melissa and took her hand. If the squeeze was too hard, it wasn't malicious. The fervor in Tia's eyes almost made Melissa believe in miracles.

"I don't want any other little girl to go through what you've gone through, Mel. It makes sense when you think about it. What do I know? Beauty. All my life I've been trained to look beautiful. Now I'll be able to give that gift to those who really need it.''

The ice around Melissa's heart softened. "Oh, Tia…''

"And when you're ready,'' Tia added softly, "I'll take you to Gina.''

Melissa's lips trembled. She didn't have the heart to tell Tia that she might never be ready. With Tyler and the baby gone, she had no reason to care.

"I'M SO SORRY for your loss,'' Freddy said. He stood at the door of her hospital room, looking both confident and scared. She'd seen his picture on the editorial page of his magazine, but of course, that was posed to make him look like a serious businessman. Tonight the soft contours of his face reminded her of her mother, and the heart she'd thought too bruised to feel contracted.

After a long while, she nodded, accepting his condolences.

"May I come in?"

She shrugged, not quite knowing how to breach the wide gulf between them.

"I…" he started, then cleared his throat. "I owe you more than an apology."

She turned her head away, staring at the dull blue sky through the window. She'd been so stubborn, so hard. She'd closed so many things, so many people out of her life. "No, you tried, and I didn't give you a chance."

He fidgeted with the magazine in his hands. "I brought you something."

She waved vaguely at the chair already piled with magazines and books Tia had provided.

As he walked toward her, he thumbed through the pages. He folded the magazine over and placed it in Melissa's hands. "Read this."

Noticing Tyler's byline, Melissa let the magazine fall on her lap. "My eye hurts."

"Long ago," Freddy said as he sat in the chair beside the bed, "I told the world I stood for truth, but when it came to you, I turned a blind eye." Gaze on the floor, he shook his head. "I didn't have time for an eight-year-old girl who was in physical and mental pain. The truth is, I didn't have the heart for it. Sable kicked me out and I didn't fight back. I let myself believe that your family would take care of you. I let you down." He put the magazine back in her hand. "I have a son. I understand now how much you needed someone on your side." Frowning, he shook his head. "I can never repay—"

"It was a long time ago," she said.

He pointed at the article. "Read it."

Melissa looked stubbornly through the page until the print grew fuzzy.

"I want to see those eyes moving. Read every word."

He tapped the print with a sausagelike finger. "I'm not leaving until you do."

Melissa closed her eyes, then opened them, refocusing on the print. "Seduction of the Beast."

A great sob tore from her. She lifted her hand to throw the glossy magazine across the room. Freddy stayed her hand.

"Read it," Freddy said. "It's not about you."

Swallowing hard, she let her eyes catch the first word and glide on to the next. Soon she was caught in the poetry of the confession, in the beauty of his prose.

Tears streamed down her face, and the page blurred once more. Tyler had portrayed himself as the beast, not her. The ice in her frozen heart cracked.

"He sees me." He didn't see the witch or the scars. He saw the woman. He saw *her*. She covered her mouth with a hand to stifle another round of tears.

"He does. So much it hurts him."

She turned her teary gaze to Freddy. "I've lost him for nothing."

Freddy closed his fingers around hers. "It's not too late, but the next move is yours."

THEY TOLD HIM he was good to go. He didn't feel good enough or ready to go anywhere. But Freddy would be here in a few minutes and he would need reassurance that Tyler wasn't going to closet himself in his apartment praying to the god of whiskey.

He sensed someone at the door. Plastering a smile on his face, he turned from his task of stuffing his belongings in the duffel bag on his bed and looked up. "Fred—"

He stopped short at the sight of Melissa standing there. Her green dress reflected the color of her eyes and hugged feminine curves that could make him salivate even through the pain of the second-degree burns on his arms. The sling supporting her dislocated shoulder added an awkward, yet endearing touch to her appearance. She had never looked more beautiful.

"Hi," she said. Her smile held a mixture of anticipation and measured reserve.

He tried to respond, but his tongue was too thick and his throat too dry.

"I just came from seeing Grace."

"How is she?" he asked, pulling the zipper tight on the duffel.

Her smile hiked up. "Making demands and bossing everyone around. She'll be her old self in no time."

"That's good news."

"Yes." She pressed her lips tightly together and her eyes became shiny with tears. "I'm sorry about the baby. I'm sorry I lied to you about being fertile. I'm sorry..." She glanced at her tightly clasped hands and frowned. "I didn't deserve to be a mother."

He started to reach for her, then dropped his hand. "Don't say that."

"Why not?" Her head shot up and her eyes blazed in fury. "It's the truth. I lied to you. I made this baby on a falsehood. How could it possibly grow into a strong child in that kind of soil? A child grows out of love, and I made this one based on my own selfish desires."

"It takes two to make a child." He wanted to touch her. He wanted to hold her. He wanted to tell her he still wanted a child with her. But he had to let her find her own way back to him for her to trust in a future together. "What Ray did to you wasn't your fault."

She looked down again, nodding in a way that said her head understood, but her heart still needed time. "I gave the castle away."

That surprised him. "Why? It's your home."

She shook her head. "It's dead and…" She lifted her slinged arm. "I'm a little battered, but I'm still alive. It's time I tried living in the real world."

"Where?"

"I bought a little ranch with enough room for the horses. Dee will help with the horses. Grace will come with me and we'll help each other recover. Tia is also moving in now that she and Sable aren't on speaking terms. She'll stay until she goes back to school in the fall." Melissa paused, shifting her weight from one foot to the other. "It's not too far from the highway." She smiled shakily, her gaze so hopeful it brought a lump to his throat. "I hope that maybe you'll consider giving me another chance."

"Melissa." His heart thumped hard once. She was making a leap of faith, and gladly he was there to catch her. Awkwardly he enfolded her in his arms and inhaled the sweet scent of her. He'd missed her so much. Her sob of relief hitched against his neck.

"I know it won't be easy," she said, speaking quickly as if she was suddenly in a race for time. "I know it's not going to be happily ever after. People are still going to stare. They're still going to point. They're still going to pretend too hard that there's nothing wrong. But I'm ready for that." She cradled the side of his head with her good hand and kissed him urgently. "I'm so sorry for throwing you out without giving you a chance to explain. Your article…it was the most beautiful thing I've ever read."

"I wanted you to know." The words that had flowed so easily on paper now deserted him. "When you threw those pieces at me, I thought you didn't care."

"I love you, Tyler. I've loved you since I found you by my gate. Give me another chance to prove it to you."

"Marry me, and you can prove it every day."

Tear spilled down her cheeks and joy seemed to radiate from her. "Tyler—"

"I love you. Everything about you. I love how we are together." He kissed her and held her close. After a moment he let her go, the blissful melody that stemmed from his soul warming him. The whole world felt right and good. "Let's go home."

She grinned. "Yes, let's go home."

"You know we can't just elope," he said as he slung an arm around her shoulders. "It's going to have to be a big wedding. Nana Leonardo isn't going to stand for anything less."

He laughed at her openmouthed surprise and reached back for the duffel bag on the bed.

"Do you think she'll mind having a witch in the family?" Melissa asked, smiling, and wrapped an arm around his waist.

"She'll love it. She'll love you. How could she not?" He gently squeezed her shoulder. "And my sisters are going to insist on meddling with every plan we make."

"They are?"

"I'm thinking September would make a good compromise. Enough time to let everyone have some input, but not enough for a family feud to break out. What do you think?"

Her smiled dazzled. "Yes, I'll marry you. Any time. Any place."

They leaned against each other as they made their way down the corridor.

"We make quite a pair," she said, laughing. "You with your bandages and me with my sling."

''That we do.'' She rested her head on his shoulder. He brushed a kiss on her hair. They were blessed with a second chance and they wouldn't waste a minute of it. ''We make a perfect pair.''